DR. LEONAR
INSTINCT BAS

MW01067821

THE ONLY ANSWER ™ TO STRESS
ANXIETY & DEPRESSION

THE ROOT CAUSE OF ALL DISEASE

21 PUBLISHERS
READING YOU LOUD AND CLEAR

THE ONLY ANSWER
TO™ STRESS
ANXIETY & DEPRESSION

Copyright © 2010
Church of Inner Healing
Second Updated Edition

ISBN 978-0-9827616-0-1
Cover: Lee Fredrickson
Book Design: Lee Fredrickson

21C PUBLISHERS
READING YOU LOUD AND CLEAR
www.21cpublishers.com

DISCLAIMER

Disclaimer: For over 20 years I have been curing cancer. I have found the one and only remedy, and it is God's/Nature's Cure. You are created to be healthy, happy and successful. You are not supposed to suffer for the financial profit of the pharmaceutical industry or medical profession or the power-and money-hungry American Cancer Society and all of their pawns in politics, the media or "self-help groups."

It is my opinion that the main goal of government agencies like the FTC or FDA (they have to legally be dissolved, and fast!), and other organizations is to protect the profits of the pharmaceutical and medical industry. We have to wake up and take charge of our own health!

They definitely do not have our best interests in mind or they would never have made laws or regulations stating that only a drug can treat, cure, diagnose or prevent any illness or condition—that is in itself absurd. No drug ever cured or prevented any disease—ever! So they knowingly set us up to suffer, pay and ultimately die.

I am telling you that the only one that can prevent or cure any disease is you! (Or God or Nature as based on your personal beliefs.)

I have personally experienced, for over 30 years now, that every illness can be cured, but not every patient can be cured since some people subconsciously want to die or are just not willing to do what it takes to be healthy.

Legal disclaimer: Unfortunately we live in a world of sue-happy idiots and paid destructive groups, corrupt politicians and privately owned media, so I have to legally tell you: This book and its contents do not cure, prevent, diagnose or treat any disease or condition! (Only your own self-healing powers can do that.)

The only purpose for this book is educational, for research and entertainment. If you have, or think you may have, any health condition or disease, see a competent, authorized health practitioner (if you can find one) and do not attempt any of the techniques, ideas, knowledge, suggestions or comments in this book without consulting the health professional of your choice first.

The author, the publisher and everybody involved in the creation, publication and sale of this book do not take responsibly for any outcome or result from the use of the information in this book.

Please be advised that the entire content of this book is solely the opinion of the author. Nearly everybody in the orthodox medical field disagrees with almost everything said in this book, along with the ideas, techniques and systems published herein. I, the author, don't really care! Why? Because I have the results to show, and can reproduce cancer cures anytime I want, if I would be given the legal authority to practice my IBMS™.

In my experience cancer can be cured in 2 weeks to 4 months unless too much damage has already been done by the treatment of "poison, cut and burn" of the orthodox medical profession, or if the patient is not willing or capable to do whatever it takes to experience true heath. In cases where the patient is already far too damaged by the health challenges he or she endures, the techniques may not work–but in my experience that is very rare.

So, it's up to you and your God-given rights; your right of freewill, your right to choose, your right of self-defense, and all the wonderful rights our great constitution has given us to do whatever we choose! But you have to do this at your own risk and responsibly, and accept the consequences of your decision and actions. We do not take any responsibly for anything you decide to do.

Any cure you experience is solely because of you the reader. You are the only one responsible for your own success or failures based on your actions.

FTC, FDA, etc. Disclaimer: My legal team tells me you don't have any jurisdiction outside of Washington DC and that you don't have any order of deferred authority. I don't know if this it true or not and I really don't care because I do not trade in any form or do not sell anything. The entire content of this book has been previously published in different languages and is protected by national trade agreements, etc.

Most of the original copyrights are with NAPS University Verlag GMBH Europe. I am exercising my right as an author and my right of free speech. The entire content of this book is 100% based on my personal experiences and opinions and I do not claim any acceptation of any industry or any part of government or make any claims of facts. All other authors that contributed to this book simply state their own opinions and conclusions based on their experience and are responsible for their own publication within this work. Dr. Leonard Coldwell and/ or the publisher do not take any responsibility for the publications and use of the individual authors information by the reader, or the other authors in this book.

To the clowns out there acting as if they where a legitimate government: I do not consent to you having any kind of jurisdiction over me or my work. I do not give you my consent to contact me directly or indirectly. I do not consent to your courts authority or your corporation regulations or company policies—which have no power over me. I do not consent to your admiralty courts or being contacted or trialed by them. I am a free man living on the land and do not consent to be trialed by admiralty or marital law. I insist on the application of common law and, if there is any lawful reason, I only accept trial by jury of my peers in a common law procedure and by the court of record. So you get it? I do not consent to anything that you the corporation or the ones acting for the corporation imposing to by our rulers or dictators or for that matter a lawful government. To me you are not and keep the Washington DC based corporate employees and their unlawful actions away from me. I will use all lawful means to protect my common law rights. My legal team tells me that every US of America corporation employee acts in his own name and authority and is not protected by any immunization from personal and criminal responsibilities or law suits if they step out of the framework of what their job allows them lawfully to do (That is what my legal team confirmed to me). Whatever I do or say now or in the future, does not mean I give you jurisdiction over me or my matters. I will never give you jurisdiction or consent to anything. You do not have any consent to anything regarding me, I will never give you and further, you do you have any jurisdiction or authority over me or my matters.

No FBI, FTC or FDA etc has any jurisdiction over me as a free citizen of the Republic. The constitution is the supreme law of the land and every law, rule, act etc that is unconstitutional, has no enforceable lawful value. The only jurisdiction are my unalienable rights and the constitution of we the people and the bill of rights. Get it guys? I do not consent to anything regarding you! This is the conclusion of extensive research of my legal team and I trust they are right. UCC1.207

And here it is, in my opinion and experience and with absolute conviction: *The Only Answer to Stress, Anxiety and Depression*

Visit our YouTube channel and hear Dr. Leonard Coldwell talk about *The Only Answer to Stress, Anxiety and Depression* and other subjects.

http://www.youtube.com/user/drleonardcoldwell
and visit www.instinctbasedmedicine.com
www.drleonardcoldwell.com

Follow Dr. Leonard Coldwell
on www.drleonardcoldwell.com

Mama Coldwell, summer 2009, was cured by her own son, Dr. Leonard Coldwell, from liver cancer, liver cirrhosis and hepatitis C in the terminal state over 35 years ago. Today, she is the healthiest and most vital and living proof of Dr. Coldwell's ability to cure cancer!

DEDICATION

I dedicate this book to everyone who is willing to accept the challenges of life and take conscious control so they can determine their own destiny.

To those who are no longer willing to be satisfied with less than what they can reach and possess some day.

I know that you, dear reader, belong to that group of people who want to take action, and that is why you bought this self-help book. You want to mold your life into the adventure it deserves to be. And so, this book is personally dedicated to you!

You are a sublime image of nature's perfection. Use your wonderful potential.

Dedicated to my GIN Brothers and Sisters, and everybody else who is not willing to settle for less than the life of a champion. That will never allow themselves to be satisfied with less than they can have, be or achieve! Winners that will not allow themselves to have less than 100% of the Health, Happiness, Success and Freedom that they deserve.

For more information or even to become a part of the Global Information Network—GIN, go to www. GlobalInformationNetwork.com and become an affiliate for free by using the referral code: Coldwell.

You will have free access to seminars and education on the highest level for all parts of life. Please listen to the Cancun audio presentation; the last two hours and Punta Cana the third hour. These were powerful motivational seminars that I presented to thousands that attended the meeting and you can listen for free.

CONTENTS

WHAT INTERNATIONAL LEADERS ARE
SAYING ABOUT THE AUTHOR

D r. Coldwell's books have always had an immediate and positive impact on my doctors and their patients. They successfully move us to confront the truths behind our challenges, and how to take effective action. They are a must read for all.

—Fred Van Liew, Author "Adrenal Exhaustion & Chronic Fatigue: How To Stop The Nightmare!"

The Only Answer to Cancer and *The Only Answer to Stress, Anxiety and Depression* are two of those rare books which can save your life or someone else's life. Natural Cancer treatment is very dear to my heart since I was diagnosed with terminal cancer in 1994 but, through totally natural means, lost the cancer and gained optimal health through its treatment. You can, too, following the deep wisdom in this book.

The cancer establishment doesn't want you to know that you have safe, effective and inexpensive natural options since cancer is the single most profitable disease ever encountered by mankind. Brave leaders like Dr. Coldwell are dangerous to the industry that depends on your illness and your ignorance: nowhere is that more true than the multi-trillion dollar cancer industry.

Dr. Coldwell is a gifted doctor whose special gifts are curing people and telling the truth about disease—and the industry that wants to keep you as sick as possible as long as possible. His pioneering work has brought him the success and reputation to back up what he says. I believe in his new books, *The Only Answer to Cancer*, and more recently, *The Only Answer to Stress Anxiety and Depression*, because I know that Dr. Coldwell's work has helped huge numbers of patients with cancer and other terminal diseases. I am proud to have Dr. Coldwell as my fellow health freedom fighter.

—Maj. Gen. Albert N. Stubblebine III (US Army, Ret.)
President Natural Solutions Foundation
www.GlobalHealthFreedom.org

"It was an honor to be able to work with Dr. Coldwell for all these years and to witness the daily miracles that seem for Dr. Coldwell just simple "normal." I have seen patients that have been on their deathbed recovering from cancer or patients with no hope. I have known Dr. Coldwell's main miracle his own mother that Dr. Coldwell cured from liver cancer in a terminal state over 3 decades ago, for many years and I have researched all of her files and data and the more I read about how sick she was with her Hepatitis C, liver cirrhoses and terminal liver cancer, and the more I read the more impressive her total healing became to me.

I have seen many patients that Dr. Coldwell cured from cancer and other diseases like Multiple Sclerosis and Lupus and Parkinson's and even muscular dystrophy and many, many more and I am still in constant awe of Dr. Coldwell's talent and results. I am so glad I could study with him personally and to learn his IBMS™ directly from him. When he left Europe, he left a huge hole, a massive empty space, in the world of cancer treatment behind. I am honored and excited about the possibilities that Dr. Coldwell opened up for me as his Master student and that he has the trust in me and my talents, that he picked me as his successor when he retired from his work with patients. "

—Dr. Thomas Hohn MD NMD Licensed IBMS Therapist™
www.goodlifefoundation.com

Research in the USA and Australia reveals the 5 year survival benefit to chemotherapy patients is 2%, that's a single week, for living in hell for 5 years! Orthodox medicine butchers, burns and poisons patient-victims and frequently shortens their lives, meanwhile their life savings are transferred to the medical establishment. Dr. Coldwell is a heroic pioneer who has delivered thousands from this fatal ordeal. This humanitarian's vital book may save you or a loved one from a world of pain. Step "out of the box" and study it carefully for your own sake.

—Dr. Betty Martini, D.Hum, Founder
Mission Possible International
www.mpwhi.com

My son is my hero and the hero of countless other people that he touched with his outstanding greatness. God gave him the special talent and power to heal. I was his secretary when he had his first office when he was just 14 years old and I saw so many miracles happen every single day. I always believed in my son and his abilities to help other people to overcome their life's challenges and when he simply cured them in the shortest amounts of time.

I know what it means to get a death sentence. When the doctor told me that I had liver cancer in the terminal state and only had 2 months to a maximum of 2 years to live, I locked myself in my bedroom and cried for 3 days. It was my own son that gave me the reason and motivation to fight and to live. It was my own son that cured me from a terminal disease with no hope of healing or survival 38 years ago. Now I am 74 years old and in the best shape, health and vitality of my life. I owe this to my wonderful son, Dr. Leonard Coldwell, the greatest healer of our time.

Even if he always says: "It isn't me that has cured my patients, they have cured themselves" I still know and insist that it was him and the powers God gave him that cured me and all the other patients. Without him we would not exist anymore!

Son, you gave us the strength to fight, to hang in and to survive. You gave us your love, trust, honesty, and your knowledge, but most of all your inner strength. In turn, this gave us the strength to believe in ourselves and our future. It was always you that motivated your patients, readers and seminar attendees to get up and fight and to get up and walk and to never, ever accept any other outcome but total health, success and happiness. It was, is and always will be for me: Always YOU!

Your loving Mother,
—Mama Coldwell, summer 2009

Dr. Leonard's books are packed with the most advanced health information to back up the fact that God heals! In over 15 years in the natural health field I've never met anyone who has worked as hard as Dr. Coldwell has, to bring the health message to the masses. I am glad to, because his message is so needed. It is no surprise to hear that stress leads to disease, but what is a surprise is not too many people talk about it on the level Dr. Coldwell addresses it in this book. If you want to lose weight, gain energy and avoid or heal disease, the suggestions in this book will bring you right on track to achieving you goals. This is very informative information in this book and anyone serious about maintaining his or her health should read it. I think it belongs in ever home! Let's face it, stress is the root cause of all disease and dr. Coldwell does an excellent job in destroying the root.

—Paul Nison-Raw Food Chef and Author - www.PaulNison.com

This book has an energy—an energy that can change your life for the better! Dr. Coldwell provides the simplest and most practical steps, complete with exercises, that you can use to eliminate the primary cause of all disease from your life. Stress leads to energy loss which inevitably results in illness. Should you implement the practical steps revealed within this book, you will inevitable suffer from great joy, vitality and a love for all life!

If you want to live a long and healthy life, open this book, follow the guidelines, do the exercises—and you will do so. Not because you get lucky —but because you are now aligning yourself AND living principles that result in optimal health and longevity! Health reveals itself to all those who are ready to live according to the natural laws Dr. C so clearly writes about in *The Only Answer to Stress, Anxiety & Depression.*

—Robert Scott Bell, D.A. Hom.
Homeopathic practitioner and nationally syndicated radio host
also known as "The voice of health freedom and liberty!"

Visit our YouTube channel and hear Dr. Leonard Coldwell talk about the Only Answer to Stress Anxiety and Depression and other subjects.
http://www.youtube.com/user/drleonardcoldwell
and visit www.instinctbasedmedicine.com
www.drleonardcoldwell.com

FOREWORD

Dr. Leonard Coldwell has written this remarkable handbook for health with two voices. Like a singer producing not one beautiful tone but two at the same time, these two voices blend into a harmonious song of health and potential. And the remarkable thing is that every single person who reads—and follows—this beautiful book will be able to sing that way, too. And their words, and the glorious melody of health and empowerment will be theirs, and theirs alone!

The two voices are the voice of the deeply informed, knowledgeable expert in physiology, medicine, neurology, biochemistry, pathology, research and clinical care—of which Dr. Coldwell is—and the homey, chatty, straight-from-the-shoulder Dutch uncle who tells you what is really going on, with compassion, but with no patience for self pity or soppy excuses.

So, in your hands, on the pages of this book, you have a tell-it-like-it-is friend and a scientific integrator who can make the complicated business of the life sciences simple, clear and, most important, comprehensible.

Dr. Coldwell ties all of the relevant sciences into one neat package with your life and shows you how, in simple, concise and well-laid-out steps, how it works and what to do about it.

Stress kills! Of that fact, there is no doubt. However, stress, without the well-developed diseases it causes us to develop is of no financial interest (except as it allows anti-stress drugs to make sales, of course). If stress were to disappear tomorrow, the entire medical industry (which

17

really means pharmaceutical industry) would go up in well-deserved flames, except for the emergency room services and skills.

Without stress to precipitate at least 85% of all diseases and more than 90% of all doctors' visits, the economic cataclysm, matched only by the magnitude of the joy and health—and recovered wealth—of billions of people, would be nearly unthinkable in size. So treating stress has very little money in it, and a great deal of income and economic potential through so many people being so sick for so long.

Some years ago, during my medical practice in New York State, I had a problem. Using NeuroBioFeedback, my husband, Maj. General Albert Stubblebine III (US Army, Ret.) and I were using NeuroBio-Feedback (then called "EEG Biofeedback") to treat a wide variety of difficulties. These were people with diabetes, cancer, heart disease, cataclysmic head injuries and just about everything else you can think of, that had no hope, no cure and no where to go. They came to us because word travels fast when very ill people get cured and suddenly become radiantly well.

The results we were getting were nothing short of fantastic: within a short time, generally using three treatments per week of 30 minutes each, whatever it was that the patient came in with was gone and the patient was not only symptom free, but gloriously, radiantly well. The conventional medical experts could not believe it and—predictably—said we must be quacks, because no one could fix whatever it was that their patient had come to us with. While the logic escapes me on that, the reason that frightened people would behave that way was instantly clear to us. They had no idea whatsoever how we were accomplishing this and, as experts, it made them very nervous, indeed, to have something they could not even describe, let alone reproduce, taking place. Simply put, they had no clue what we were doing that was working.

The problem was, neither did we? We knew the protocols because we had studied with just about everyone teaching any kind of biofeedback and understood the mechanical part quite well. We knew the outcome, because we were able to measure it in laboratory and other objective ways. But what we did not know was why the treatment we were using worked and, more to the point, why about 85% of our patients become radiantly well, but nothing at all happened for the other 15% other than some calming.

In other words, we were delivering miracles, but only at a B+ score. Anyone who knows either General Bert or me will tell you how deeply they understand that B+ is simply not an option.

I do not do statistics because I am a math phobic. Dyslexic to the math, my ability to do the calculations required by statistics is less than zero, although I understand what they do and how they work. We knew that the answer lay within our very precise and detailed data, but we did not know how to get inside it, to find out what the secret was that would allow us to deliver an astonishing 100% miracle rate, an A+++, to every single patient who came through our door.

Fortunately for all of us, we had a dear friend named Professor Michel Bounias, PhD, who was a world renowned toxicologist living in the South of France. Now toxicologists do numbers and statistics. It is their meat and potatoes. So I called Prof. Bounias and told him that I wanted to get him together with my data for about two weeks.

I asked him if he had the time to leave France for that long and come examine our data. He said "Yes!" The project was not two weeks long. We published, over the next 11 years, about 50 papers: 25 on NeuroBioFeedback physiology and neurology and about 25 on the mathematical physics of consciousness, thought, intent, will and their impact on the physical world.

These papers, in their totality, became known as the "Alexandria Papers" after the Alexandria Institute of Integrative Medicine, our medical practice. They attracted the attention of mathematical physicists and Nobel Prize winners. A UNESCO meeting was convened to deal with the staggering implications of the work and Prof. Bounias began winning international honors as a Mathematical Physicist for the new mathematics of consciousness that he developed for these paper.

But we still did not have our on-demand miracle. It was not until the last paper in the series, 11 years after we began to try to answer my simple questions, "How does NeuroBioFeedback work and how can we make it work better?" that we got the answer: the mental images formed in the brain at the conscious and unconscious levels create changes in the receptor states, position, and function of every single cell.

You see, there are huge numbers of proteins sticking through the membranes of every single cell. They change their configuration and therefore their function, on the basis of what is anticipated, not what has occurred. Therefore, every receptor in every cell in the body responds not to what happened, but what was perceived. Health, then, returned, seemingly miraculously, when we taught the patient to teach his/her own brain/body/cell/being to reach for what would create wellness.

In other words, the killing stress of the patient's life and often impending death, which was instructing every receptor in the body to act as if the terrible thing anticipated in the chronic stress state had already, happened. The mental images and the programs they rested in were directing the receptors to bring about the very thing that was so difficult or problematic to the person who had the disease or diagnosis.

But we realized that through the NeuroBioFeedback, different conscious and unconscious mental and emotional images were being constructed and installed. The net result was that we were triggering the body's own capacity to heal itself, based on its total and unique depth of empowered capacity.

We learned from this how to focus differently for the reluctant 15% and our clinical "grade" went from a B+ to and A++; but not an A+++, since there are always patients who do not want to get better or relived of their disease. These people stopped treatment before the treatment was finished, stating clearly that they did not want to live, were not willing to give up their disease (or, sometimes, their disability payment) and, although we saw this as a tragedy, it is up to each and every one of us to decide what becomes of our health, our fate and our bodies so we respected the wishes of the patient.

Ironically, when Professor Bounias, a man who we not only respected intellectually, but loved personally, and referred to as our "French Scientist-in-Law" because we spent so much time together, traveled together to meetings, etc, and regarded as a beloved family member, developed signet cell cancer (a virulent type of stomach cancer), although he came to us for treatment, it was only because he knew he should, not because he wanted to live.

How did we know that? First of all, although he knew the success rate of our work with cancer patients, he waited four months to call us and tell us his diagnosis. During that time he did no treatment, not even through enhancing focuses and stress relief, although he understood very well how powerful that could be. Instead, he waited.

After four months, he called us and told us that he had a rapidly progressing tumor. I immediately arranged for a ticket to be waiting for him at De Gaulle airport in Paris the next morning. He took the plane and arrived at our office.

After getting him settled in his hotel, we began treating him. In the first NeuroBioFeedback session, after his arrival, we were setting goals (as Dr. Coldwell teaches you to do in his book) and asked him to see, hear, feel, smell, taste what it would mean when his health was perfect. He did not do that. Instead, he said, "I have done all I have come here to do. My work on this planet is finished."

No amount of input from us had any impact. His mental/emotional image was that he was finished. Because we loved him, we did not accept that and proceeded to conduct our treatments. Within days after he arrived, he needed emergency surgery because the cancer caused serious internal bleeding. The surgeon came out of the Operating Room and told us that he was so riddled with cancer that there was absolutely nothing to do but make him comfortable and make funeral arrangements.

We did just the opposite and three weeks later, when another surgery was performed to debulk, or reduce the volume of the tumor, I was present in another Operating Room when the surgical oncologist stared down in wonder and said, "There is virtually no tumor here! There is only one tiny patch on the outside of the esophagus! My GOD! What have you been doing?"

Our beloved friend, however, had other plans for himself. As Dr. Coldwell says so beautifully, "I can cure the disease, but I cannot cure every patient." Professor Bounias abruptly terminated all treatment, said goodbye to us for the last time and went home to France to die. The cancer was curable. His determination not to live longer was terminal.

Use Dr. Coldwell's book wisely; use it deeply and use it well. Remember that every page is full of both wisdom and science and even if the process is unfamiliar, or even uncomfortable, the resolution of stress through its mental/emotional/neurological/physical detoxification and replacement with healthy neural connections, which then lead to healthy mental/emotional and physical outcomes is the doorway to health, empowerment, authentic living and stress free accomplishment and joy in a healthy body, mind, heart and spirit. Because, you see, the distinction between them is artificial. There is nothing in the mind that is not represented in the body. There is nothing in the body that is not represented in the mind. And the spoiler, the flat tire of the elegant mind/body/heart/spirit vehicle of consciousness, is stress.

"Eustress," or positive stress, is a mobilizer. No one gets sick or dies from the pumped up energy of joy, accomplishment, delight, dedication and devotion. But pathological stress kills. So teaching you how to turn stress in power, to eustress and accomplishment is a great gift.

Take Dr. Coldwell at his word: stress causes disease. Learn how to reformat stress at the deepest levels and the cause of the disease is out of the way. Then the magnificent, instinct based healing system which you are endowed with can take over, with a little help from its friend: you!

Be well. Be joyous and be free of the destructive impact of killer stress. There really is only one answer to stress. You've got it in your hands. Use it.

Yours in health and freedom,
Rima E. Laibow, MD
Medical Director
Natural Solutions Foundation

www.HealthFreedomUSA.org
www.GlobalHealthFreedom.org

THE COLDWELL PROMISE

Dear Reader,

I promise that if you read and practice this program your life will never be as it was before. You will learn how to take charge of your feelings, your behavior and your energy so you will finally be able to take control over every part of your life.

Your future will no longer be a fearful, unaccountable and uncontrollable occurrence, lacking conscious design, but the logical result of conscious planning.

This book you hold in your hands is a powerful manual that can change every area of your life. It will help you to turn your life and the lives of those around you into an adventure, an experience, a pleasure, and above all it will offer you the opportunity to be free of the influence and manipulation of others.

With the information contained in these pages you will at last have the opportunity to use your unlimited potential every day, so you can make your life continuously more successful, harmonious, content and happy. In short, you now have the opportunity to change your life forever and to shape it into the masterpiece it should be.

Your new friend
—Dr. Leonard Coldwell

THE GREAT CHALLENGE
WE CALL LIFE

IBMS™—Instinct - Based - Medicine® - System™
(All rights reserved)

I have written this book with the latest information pertaining to the science of success, success training and conditioning, and with the information made available in personal motivational conditioning. Stress is simply the response to a threat, real or imagined, and the more we feel our life is threatened (whether it's financially, physically, mentally or a relationship, a job situation, or simply the need for life's recognition from our peers etc.) the better the chance that this stress will either trigger a flight or fight response. Stress is triggered when we feel we cannot fight or run away from a dead-end job or relationship and we feel we are stuck with it. The more we hate our situation or cannot stand it anymore, the more mental and emotional stress we create—feeling of helplessness—causing depression or/and anxiety. Mental and emotional stress is the main cause—86% to 95%—of all illness. Illnesses are usually caused by living in constant fears, worries doubts, lack of self love and self esteem, hopelessness and most of all lack of success in all parts of life. Anxiety is simply the reaction to stress, causing you to feel over-whelmed by life itself or certain parts of life or tasks, goals etc. Depres-sion is nothing less then the knowledge life could be better than it is right now—the feeling of losing, being out of control or simply having no hope! Depression and anxiety is always caused by not doing the right actions and not having a true foundation built on your own individual personality, your individual character traits, your common sense and in-stinct! Living with compromises against yourself on a regular basis is the guarantee for one or all: Stress, Anxiety or Depression. With this book I will help you to create a stress, anxiety and depression proof life! I will give you the education tools and coaching you need to learn how to see and treat life's "problems" and how to see them as "challenges" and I will give you the knowledge and action plans as to how to take on this great opportunity—this great change that we call "LIFE" in a manner that will enable you to always have your individual:

"Only Answer to Stress, Anxiety and Depression"

The Cause of Stress, Anxiety and Depression

Most stress, anxiety and depression is caused by imaginary challenges or by believing falsely that we have no choice or possibility to succeed or win or be healed or be financially independent or create and keep private or professional relationships, and when we can't handle a task or achieve a specific goal—or even have the self-worth to have goals or directions in life. After you have worked with this book, and have completed all the exercises in it, you will understand that successful and healthy, strong people do not have less challenges in life, these people simply have learned to deal with the daily tasks and challenges, more effectively, so that they don't even create stress. Most of the time these people have even learned to enjoy overcoming challenges and difficult tasks in life and to do this on a daily basis. So, if you believe some of these issues we cover in the IBMS™ and this book have nothing to do with Stress, Anxiety or Depression elimination or prevention—you will soon change your mind after you understand that: you can be living your life as a champion—the champion you are suppose to be and you are using your full potential and possibilities and uniqueness on a daily basis—then there is no Stress, anxiety and depression anymore!

I would like to give you some background as to how the program was developed so that you can get a better understanding of the IBMS™ program. This training originated from the core of my scientific work in the study of the bioelectric and neuro-chemical processes in the body.

At that time I started working with self-help and self-healing techniques. I have thoroughly studied every program in existence and have combined them in an easy to understand and quick-to-apply system.

With the knowledge I gained in my research of the conscious application and activation of the self-healing and regenerative ability of the body, I have developed this vital program for self-help. Stimulation of the nervous system by triggering the corresponding neuro-chemical and bioelectrical processes is necessary to foster effective and optimal healing, and are an integral part of my program. This self-help program is easily understood and can be just as easily and quickly applied. It was developed in 1976, when my first book came out and has been constantly improved. The 2010 version that you have now in your hands is the end result of putting all my knowledge and experiences together in a book format that is easy to learn, understand and to use.

After I had combined my research material with my experience, I was offered the opportunity to lead a research program that concerned itself with the prevention and treatment therapy of health problems in mental and physical situations. Again, I had the opportunity to collect new information and experiences which I could integrate into my newly developed form of therapy.

With the knowledge gained from observation, in research, and from practical experience, I have come to the conclusion that lasting success is questionable with therapeutic help from outside. I therefore developed "help toward self-help" into a science and philosophy. IBMS™ , a work-program for personal achievements, perfect health and life-long success in every area of life evolved out of my other self-help systems. It is important to understand that I developed this system by personal research and trial and error. Because I did not take it from someone else or by simply copying someone else's findings and work, it is easy for me to teach you my system! Do not follow a follower, only the originator. (It does not mean that others did not make similar discoveries on their own, but I have not seen anybody else being able to produce a system that works on all levels of life and with nearly 100% of the people who apply the system.)

I came to the realization that every human being has the ability to deal with all of life's challenges and can emerge a winner. We all have the ability and opportunity to be successful in all areas of life we desire.

Assurance of Success

The IBMS™ program I developed is the foundation of this book. Regular practice of the program is important so you can be assured of the greatest success in all areas of life. The information I will share with you will help you to reduce the stress in your life, as well as boost your vitality and health.

I present to you here the IBMS™ technical program; a manual that will help you develop a personal recipe for success based on your own needs, desires, dreams and goals, while taking into account your unique talents, skills and possibilities. You can use the information in this book for yourself and for the people who are important to you.

There is no healing force outside the human body and there is no outside force that could make you happy, successful in every part of life, healthy and free! Therefore, I created the IBMS™, for you to learn about your true uniqueness, your true potential, your true greatness and your unlimited possibilities for life—the life of a true Champion which you surely deserve! In this book you will find all the tools you need to feel strong, alive, invincible and, most of all, to love and respect yourself— that is the foundation for success and the only way you can love others and turn every part of your life into the masterpiece it is suppose to be! You can be, have and achieve everything you dream of!

Every other system, no matter how good it is, has its limits, because it is a "one time" approach. The IBMS™ training concept (a guideline for achieving unlimited personal success) is a program that will help you discover your own great successes throughout your life. One size does not fit all, and this manual will assist you in creating guidelines that correspond with your personal and individual needs and possibilities. You will then use these steps to improve and perfect each area of your life, shaping it into the masterpiece it deserves to be. When you achieve your current goals, you can use the program again and again, creating new and powerful goals for yourself.

This is my gift to you, an opportunity to once and for all lead a life free from pressures of the past, free from guilt and unneeded stress, from unwanted patterns of behavior, energy swings or other negative emotional entanglements. Even though it appears to us to be truly real; stress, anxiety and depression are not

> **An obstacle standing in your way is not a problem; it's a challenge to help you grow!**

real, and are only a result of our own mental and emotional actions or lack thereof. By abusing our body, mind and spiritual powers we create fear, doubts, the feelings of hopelessness and helplessness and therefore we create our own personal experiences of stress, anxiety and/or depression! But with the IBMS™ tools you can use your individual unlimited personal powers to create and achieve the feeling and realities in your own personal life—and the good thing is, no one else can take it away— you are in control of your life in every way and you know you can and will master every task, and overcome every challenge that life presents to you. From now on you can be in control over your actions, emotions and results. There is no reason for fear or self doubt any more, after you apply the knowledge and techniques of the IBMS™.

I have created this program so you can produce excellent and effective results each and every time you use it, but only if you work it. I'm giving you the tools, but you need to put them to use.

At first the information and suggestions may not be what you're used to following in other "self-help" books. My program is indeed different! But, after you've worked through the complete program, you should find that several positive changes have occurred in your way of thinking, feeling and acting. You may even find that you are enjoying more effective results and that your life has improved for the better in many areas.

Since this program is different, you will want to read it several times, as you learn to reprogram yourself and ultimately achieve your dreams and goals. You learn by reading this book and applying the new knowledge simply in your mind first, automatically, without even consciously memorizing or learning. And when you start to do the exercises you will automatically grow dendrites (Brain Cell Connections) that ensure that my system becomes your system, and that you have changed after you are finished reading this book and are applying the exercises to your daily life. That means, when you change, the results of what you produce in your life changes!

Notebook Essential for Reference

Before you start though, you should have a notebook handy so you can write down all of the information I give you, as well as answers to questions I'll be asking. By keeping a record of your thoughts and reactions, it will help you to develop a more perfect you. You'll be able to go over your notes and witness, in your own writing, how you truly think and feel, what is holding you back, and how you are changing over time.

Be sure to keep this notebook for future reference. Months, or years from now, you can read these old notes, and your thoughts at this time, and use them to understand your cycles of development, along with the lows and the difficulties you've faced. You will see how much you've grown, how much you've accomplished, and if you ever find yourself slipping back into the old you, you'll have a solid roadmap of just how far you've come—and you'll never want to go back! But most of all, you have your own manual for how to control your own life and future. Be aware of the fact you cannot save someone that sinks into quicksand by jumping in after that person! You need to have stable ground under your own feet first, and then you can easily help the other person out of his or her misery! The same is true for life: you cannot help someone else to overcome stress, anxiety, depression, lack of self love, or even self hatred, hopelessness, if you have not first developed stable ground under your foundation of who you really are! So, if you want to help your spouse, children or friends, you have to start with your own life, your own foundation first! Your children, spouse and friends deserve the best: parent, spouse or friend you can be!

Answer all questions completely, even though they seem similar to answers you gave before. Also, write down all repetitions, because that is part of the IBMS™ technique procedure. It will not only help you to recognize your current programming, but also to condition the desired mental, emotional and physiological behavior patterns you're seeking. Everything you desire in your life will soon become a natural part of your thinking, feeling and way of acting.

Treat yourself and buy a nice, hardcover journal and write on both sides of the pages. This way you're mentally preparing yourself for something special, and you also won't be tempted to rip out any pages if you need to make your grocery list or write down a phone number.

Your personal success journal can help you many years down the road. By going back over your notes and seeing how you dealt with a similar problem before, you'll be able to eliminate other conflicts easier and more effectively. This success journal can also become a valuable reference aid for your children and others that are important to you.

IBMS™ Defined

To understand it well, I will again give you my definition of IBMS™ (The Instinct Based Medicine® System™.) IBMS™ is a method that will help you achieve your highest personal goals and unlimited success in every area of life, while sustaining the best possible health and vitality.

I have developed and perfected this system with knowledge gained from extensive research, as well as observation and experience gained in my practice with patients. It is a system created for personal motivation, self-healing and self-help for every area of life.

My friend, I offer you this self-help philosophy for your personal and individual use.

THE INSTINCT BASED MEDICINE® SYSTEM™

YOUR INDIVIDUAL MANUAL FOR PERSONAL STRESS FREE LIVING

All illness comes from lack of energy, and the greatest energy drainer is mental and emotional stress, which I believe to be the root cause of all illness. Stress is one of the major elements that can erode energy to such a large and permanent extent that the immune system loses all possibility of functioning at an optimum level. The fact is that 86% of all illness and doctor visits are stress related and then I just learned that the Stanford University concluded after a major study that 95% of all illness is stress related. I am referring to the mental and emotional stress that is caused by continuous and/or long-term compromises against yourself. These vary from person to person, but some examples include living in unbearable relationships and marriages, doing jobs you hate or hating your boss, or experiencing problems with family, all of which lead to you compromising your sense of self. Emotional and mental stress comes from living with feelings of constant fear, doubt, hopelessness, lack of self-esteem, worry, and, most of all, always compromising your inner feelings, instincts, and personal needs. The main component of all these energy drainers is fear. But the Bible tells us over 100 times: Not to fear and to trust in God! Your faith can heal you from fear!

The solution is to start by defining what it is in your life that keeps you from feeling happy. Can you answer the question of why you don't respect yourself enough? Or love yourself? Now identify what needs to change or happen in your life to make you feel good about yourself and your personal environment. What is it that you don't want to do, accept, or take anymore from yourself, your spouse, your children, your boss, or your coworkers? Is there someone in your life that makes you feel badly that needs to go? What are your wildest dreams and goals? Looking at your life, what is it that always takes away your energy, and where do you compromise your personal needs and feelings? Identify everything in your life that keeps you from being your true self, and start working on the development of the true you! This is the first and most important step toward achieving optimum health and happiness. And remember that happiness and hope are the most powerful healers and energy creators in your life. Pay attention to your instincts, listen to your inner voice, and start loving and respecting yourself so that you behave according to your true personality. You need to accept the statistical fact that the medical doctor or medical profession is the number one cause of death in America. That means you cannot rely solely on another person, the MD, with your health and life. What is even worse, is that I believe today that the US Government or better the different agencies of the Government like the FDA and FTC are the leading cause of death in this world because of their manipulations, suppressions, rules and regulations that prevent natural health, natural healing methods, natural cures, healing foods and supplementation and natural healers to do God's work.

If you do not live your life according to your needs, you will get or stay stressed, which will reduce your energy and eventually produce an illness. You are the only one who can change your life and improve your health. So start today by defining, creating, and living your life the way you believe is right and good for you. Create your own self-healing system—This book is my personal one for educational purposes only.

Please read the entire book first before you attempt to apply any changes for your life and health and before you do anything ask a qualified professional for help and support. You can also write to me and or licensed and practicing MD's that I have personally trained in my system (Instinct Based Medicine®—IBMS™). Write to instinctbasedmedicine@gmail.com

What is IBMS™?

IBMS™ is the acronym for Instinct-Based-Medicine® -System™. It is a method by which we can use the abilities and skills of our bodies to send messages to the brain, inducing bio-electrical and neuro-chemical stimuli that correspond with our wishes, feeling and behavior.

The brain is nothing but an enormous bio-computer, which functions in the same manner as a commercial computer-system. Only, the commercial computer is a far cry from the unbelievable diversity and capacity of our brain.

Our brain responds with certain reactions to stimulation over our nerve endings, which is only possible as a result of internal and external communication; our nervous-system controls our behavior with mental and physiological stimulation.

During my years in medical research I came to the conclusion and could prove scientifically that it was possible for every human being to trigger and release helpful, healing and energy enriching neuro-chemical processes in the body, in a very short time.

Every neuro-chemical emotional condition of emotional origin in our organism, can be followed physiologically and can be measured in the circulation of our blood and the cells of our body. We therefore know that we can influence our nervous-systems significantly, and so stimulate the neurophysiology of our health, our enthusiasm, passion, contentment, harmony and love in our bodies and our lives.

The IBMS™ – System I have created is a "Help to help oneself-system," which I have later enlarged into a "Teaching-method for limitless personal success and excellent health." It is nothing but a manual that tells you how to stimulate and program your brain, so that the self-help system will always be available when you need it.

A strong stimulus can, as we learned from the experience by the Russian scientist Ivan Pavlov, activate internal neuro-chemical reactions at a pre-determined time. This led me to the realization that human beings could also install stimuli in the nervous system by activating one of the five senses, which would release a neuro-chemical reaction in our body in return.

It would make it possible for every person to assume control of his energy, health and his emotional and physiological behavior.

While I developed my IBMS™-system for the conditioning of personal success and motivation, I have continually searched for new ways and possibilities to produce quicker and better results for every area of life. The most important recognition was the realization that the only true help was help to help oneself. Based on the information I wrote a concise manual for self-help. It would make it possible for every person to use his talents and skills thereby assuming control of his energy, health and his emotional and physiological behavior.

The IBMS™-system can only work if you are willing to modify the directions according to your own needs, your own imagination, dreams, wishes and goals, so that you can create your own personal success system and turn your life into the masterpiece it is meant to be.

How did IBMS™ develop?

The IBMS™-system was originally, like many other systems a hypothesis, a great dream. The need to overcome helplessness and a wish to take control, were the motivating factors.

The illness of my mother (the final stage of cirrhosis of the liver and terminal liver cancer) combined with the diagnosis of her physician that she had only two more years to live, contributed to my search for ways and opportunities to realize some better positive results for my mother. The fight for her life and my continuous search for alternative and even metaphysical ways made me realize that the solution to every human problem lies in the person himself.

Research at the University of California pointed unambiguously to the fact that the brain can be stimulated to produce a larger amount of interferon in the fight against cancer. Similar scientific results have moved me to keep searching for new and more effective ways to help people in the ability to concentrate on their own healing and regeneration.

From the successes I enjoyed and from the people, who experienced "miraculous healings" similar to my mother's, I received the self-confidence and strength to keep on searching, so that I could use this knowledge in every other area of life.

To bring this information to other people I augmented this system into a manual for self-help in every area of life.

My documentation of the conscious stimulation of bio-electric and neuro-chemical processes in the organism through desired internal and external triggers of the senses attracted attention in the medical profession, which offered me the opportunity for extensive study and research in America. I was then in a position to perfect and broaden this thought process and its application.

How does IBMS™ work?

My system works because you get in tuned with your common sense and instinct again and you will learn how to life your true life your true you the champion in you. You will learn how to define your personal true goals, your individual motivational techniques and to condition the behavioral patterns of a champion. You will learn to see your individual uniqueness and how to unleash the winner in you to become the champion you were born to be. You will develop individual action plans and strategies for total success. Total success means: Optimum happiness, health, success in every part of life, great personal and professional relationships and most of all that you find and live the true YOU.

The IBMS™ is an essential summery of every existing success and result producing system for human success, happiness and health combined with my over 30 years of experience, success and knowledge. I developed this system in a way that it is easy to understand and to apply to everybody's life. The IBMS™ is the action manual to live your true potential and experience life on its highest level.

Because we are aware of only a percentage of our skills, possibilities and strengths, we use them ineffectively and partially; the results we produce are inconsistent and random. Einstein believed we are using 10% of our brain and neurological capability but modern science proofed that we are using only 1 to 2 % of our potential.

Because, with IBMS™, you can take conscious control over your internal and external communication, as well as your visualization and the optimal stimulation of your physiology, you can control your energy and your emotions. This allows you to determine your behavior at any time.

You will learn to control your emotional, mental and physiological behavior. You will be able to determine the results you want to produce in your life. You will know your true goals for every part of your life and you will learn to produce action plans and how to put them into action and your goals into reality.

The true success of this system comes from the fact that you are enabled to uncover and live your true self and the true you. As you have read, in all my books—you have to uncover the root cause of life challenges and success production and use this knowledge to produce success in any part of life that you desire. There is no difference if it is related to health, love, success or happiness. The IBMS™ is the manual to help you find and to live the true champion in all parts of your life. If you are sick, unhappy, unsuccessful – stressed, depressed or experience anxiety then you have not found your true self and you don't live and use your full potential. You may be controlled, brainwashed or manipulated to live a life that is not your life. That would be one possible cause of a life filled with STRESS.

To eliminate and reduce stress, to prevent or stop depression and anxiety, you need to uncover the true root cause of these symptoms of not living your full potential in every part of your life, and you need to eliminate the root cause that lead to these symptoms of an incomplete life. The IBMS™ is your manual to find your individual way for stress reduction and elimination of depression and anxiety. Always remember; your conscious and unconscious decisions and actions caused the stress, anxiety and depression. And only your own decisions and actions can change this. Only then can you be happy, healthy and successful. If you learn to understand that you were born to be a champion and that you deserve that best of the best in every part of your life you will not take anything less from life then "The Best of the Best" —never anything less than what you can be, achieve and have. There is only one way to total happiness: YOUR WAY!

IBMS™ is your personal manual to happiness, health and success.
The IBMS™-system, therefore, offers you the possibility to take complete control of your life. The working of the IBMS™-system is based solely on natural bodily functions, on every person's inborn skills, talents and possibilities.

You have certainly heard or read that I have been able to help patients with chronic illnesses, including cancer, muscular dystrophy, rheumatism, gout, asthma and cirrhosis of the liver.

I have also worked with many athletes, helping them to reach the pinnacle of success in their country and even the world.

Because there are no standard solutions for every human being in the many diverse individual life stages, you must tune the knowledge and intelligence you have gained through your IBMS™-training to your own needs. You alone can change your life according to your own desires. Only a you, can create and maintain a life free of stress, a life that is effective, productive, filled with love, harmony, and success.

The methods I offer you in the IBMS™-system are luckily easily adopted in every area of life. You can modify my directions yourself, so that you can develop your own IBMS™-success–system out of mine with a short period of practice, so that you can determine and influence your own health and success.

IBMS™ is "only" the promotion of a method for an effective way to handle one's personal life. IBMS™ does work only when it is used in correspondence with your own personal desires and needs.

Defined exactly, IBMS™ is a training manual for personal development, for programming success, motivation and health, "a manual for a method" we create for ourselves, so that by using this method we can make the best use of our talents, skills and possibilities in every area of our lives. It teaches us to produce and reproduce this success, hold on to it and use it to build and broaden our potential, continuously.

You are a miracle of nature with limitless possibilities and IBMS™ is the method to realize this masterpiece—a perfect human being. Nature has given you everything to create this success and acquire this quality of life; IBMS™ will help you to recognize and use your full potential!

The IBMS™ is the world's most advanced scientifically grounded self-help training system. This system represents the culmination of 30 years of research, therapy, and experience in the development of self-help applications which are proven to target and eliminate the root causes of mental and emotional stress that can lead to illness.

When you use this system, you will be training your brain from the ground up, and you will discover that what you are experiencing is nothing less than a total rehabilitation of your brain's cognitive functions.

These applications have been scientifically proven to do the following:

- Eliminate the root causes of mental and emotional stress that inevitably lead to illness.

- Facilitate active stress reduction and regeneration of the entire nervous system.

- Enable your body to utilize oxygen, a crucial component for optimizing your health and energy, at its maximum level.

- Boost your determination, self-esteem, confidence, and power to act.

In addition, most people who use **IBMS™** report:

- A sense of calm with more energy and lucidity than before.

- Feeling well-rested and better able to cope with and solve problems.

- Improvement in the ability to sleep at night.

IBMS™ A Truly Unique Approach!

IBMS™ is a manipulation-free self-help system that uses your personality and character traits to assist you in realizing your personal dreams, goals and instincts by giving you total control over your self-conditioning and stress reduction. You will attain a state of deep relaxation during your sessions where your body is totally relaxed physically while your brain is clear and alert. This gives you total control over your sessions and its outcome, enabling you to holistically address the root cause of stress and stress related health problems.

This system is the only known system that can guarantee that there is no manipulation of any kind and that all conditioning is entirely determined by you.

The World Wellness Organization™ reviews other techniques:

Hypnotism is based on manipulation and can make people dependent, schizophrenic, mentally and emotionally weak, and can eventually lead to multiple personality disorder or delusions.

Meditation is usually only good for short term relaxation and can lead to passivity.

Positive thinking can lead to tragedy, failure or can even be life threatening because it is generally followed by inactivity and/or passivity. Positive thinking without positive actions is a guaranty for failure.

NLP is the most dangerous of all techniques as it can suppress emotions and the cause of problems; it can also hide important symptoms with very dangerous consequences. In health conflicts, it can camouflage or suppress the symptoms and root cause of illness and create or increase major health problems.

"The primary cause of illness is lack of energy; the primary cause of lack of energy is stress, mainly mental and emotional stress."
—Dr. Leonard Coldwell

The Deadly Stress Cycles Stress, Energy Loss, Illness

Overweight

Stress causes many people to overeat and gain unwanted pounds causing more stress and leading to more eating and so on. A generally unrecognized fact is that, when you are stressed, your digestive system basically shuts down so you are unable to convert food to energy...and, in the opinion of the author; lack of energy is the primary cause of illness.

Depression

Stress can lead to anxiety, which can lead to depression, which can lead to more anxiety then more depression, and so the cycle continues. It all leads to lack of energy, and lack of energy is the primary cause of illness.

Health

Stress induced health breakdowns lead to increased stress which leads to a weaker immune system, thus resulting in greater and more dangerous health breakdowns. This cycle stems from lack of energy, and lack of energy is the primary cause of illness.

What is stress?

Stress is the body's reaction to a primary stimulus: danger. Danger is perceived by human beings as anything that threatens their mental, emotional, or physical well being. Under stress, people can experience confusion, loss of control, abnormal behavior, and irrational fear. When the body is threatened with danger, it immediately produces stress hormones.

These hormones trigger fight or flight reactions, but since people cannot run or fight in normal life situations, the hormones stay in the body and alter emotional, mental, and physical behavior. This can lead to abnormal actions and reactions such as binge eating, panic attacks, nervous or physical breakdowns, random aches and pain, depression, burnout, even suicidal tendencies.

Are mental, emotional and physical stresses different? YES

Mental stress comes from **creating** or **remembering** disturbing mental images. Examples would be imagining negative outcomes of future events—such as an irrational fear of being fired or humiliated or harmed—or recalling images of threatening situations, domineering parents, abusive caretakers or teachers or spouses, etc.

Emotional stress comes from **experiencing** threats, severe illness, worry, hopelessness, helplessness, anxiety, self-doubt, fear of failure, lack of self-esteem, or living with unfair compromises. Some examples would be suffering in a bad relationship or oppressive work environment, being physically or emotionally abused, undergoing divorce or bankruptcy or death of a family member, or being helpless to aid or comfort a loved one.

Physical stress comes from exceeding normal physical capabilities that lead to physical exhaustion. Examples would be excessive drinking or eating, exhaustive physical exercise, constant extreme pain, sleep deprivation, unruly children, and working under deadlines. Also included are internal toxic and/or acidic reactions, some allergies, as well as nutritional deficiencies.

NOTE: All three stresses can be interdependent and interrelated.

Is one type of stress worse than another?

Continuous, uninterrupted mental and/or emotional stress often goes unrecognized and untreated. This will sap the body's energy reserves and eventually lead to a health breakdown and severe illness. Complete physical exhaustion (stress) will halt the body's ability to continue any activity at a specific point in time, but will seldom cause a health breakdown. Physical stress can be alleviated by proper rest and nutrition and/or reducing workload.

What are some of the symptoms of mental and emotional stress?
The **symptoms** of mental and emotional stress can be divided into two categories: physical symptoms and psychological signs.

Physical Symptoms:
Exhaustion, fatigue, lethargy
Headaches, migraines, vision problems
Heart palpitations, racing pulse, rapid shallow breathing
Muscle tension, aches, spasms
Dehydration
Joint and back pain
Shakiness, tremors, ticks, twitches, paralysis
Nervousness, panic attacks
Heartburn, indigestion, diarrhea, constipation, nausea, dizziness, ulcers,
Dry mouth and throat
Sexual dysfunction, lowered libido
Excessive sweating, clammy hands, cold hands and/or feet, poor circulation
Rashes, hives, itching, eczema, adult acne
Nail biting, fidgeting, hair twirling or pulling
Loss of appetite, bulimia, anorexia
Obesity, overeating
Sleep difficulties, insomnia
Teeth grinding
Asthma, allergies
Increased use of alcohol and/or drugs and medication
High blood pressure, weakened immune system

Psychological Symptoms:
Irritability, impatience, anger, hostility
Anxiety, panic, worrying, denial

Agoraphobia

Moodiness, bipolar tendencies, sadness, feeling upset

Energy swings

Emotionally exhausted, overwhelmed

Involuntarily crying, depression

Helplessness, hopelessness, lack of self-esteem

Neurotic or uncommon behavior, schizophrenia

Paranoia, claustrophobia, ADD, ADHD

Intrusive and/or racing thoughts

Memory loss, lack of concentration, indecision

Lack of motivation

Frequent absences from work, lowered productivity

Feeling overwhelmed

Loss of sense of humor

Why does stress affect our health?

All illness stems from a lack of energy! Emotional and/or mental stress is the greatest energy drainer affecting you. Continuous, uninterrupted emotional and/or mental stress will inevitably lead to an energy breakdown, which in turn will be followed by a health breakdown from a compromised immune system.

What else does stress cause?

Stress can cause dehydration, nutritional deficiencies, lack of oxygen and restful self-healing phases. Stress is also one of the main causes for diseases and symptoms such as:

Cancer, heart disease, ADD/ADHD, Parkinson's, Alzheimer's, sexual dysfunction, bulimia, pre-aging, lowered immune function, rheumatic/arthritic/fibromyalgia, joint and muscle pain, constipation, insomnia, memory loss, suicide, toxemia and acidosis.

Is dealing with stress really that important?

Untreated, constant (chronic) mental and emotional stress can shorten life expectancy, poor quality of life and result in numerous health challenges. Alleviating the stress allows you pursue a happy life on your own terms.

What is the primary physiological effect of stress?
Chronic stress leads to dehydration, one of the primary causes of physical degeneration, atrophy, and death.

Scientifically confirmed symptoms of **dehydration** are:
DNA damage
Lowered immune functions
Inability to absorb foods, vitamins and minerals
Lack of energy supply from digestion
Reduction in efficiency of red blood cells
Some emotional manifestations of **dehydration** include:
Depression
Anxiety
Feelings of inadequacy
Irritability
Dejection
Self-consciousness Cravings (caffeine, alcohol, drugs, etc.)
Agoraphobia
Scientifically recognized physical signs of **dehydration** include:
Fibromyalgia
Asthma
Bronchitis
Allergies
Indigestion/acid reflux
Chronic arthritic pain
High blood pressure
Higher cholesterol

Chronic fatigue syndrome

Angina

Strokes

Ear related symptoms, dizziness, equilibrium problems

Deafness

Visual problems

Cataract

Vitreous detachment

Uveitis

Multiple Sclerosis

Note: The main cause of dehydration (other than not drinking water) is stress!

Some facts to consider:

- Scientists at Cambridge University have evidence that the human life potential can reach 160 years.

- 112 million people take stress related medication.

- 250 million prescriptions for tranquilizers are filled annually.

- 25 million Americans suffer from high blood pressure.

- 15 million people have social anxieties.

- 14 million are alcoholics.

- 5 million people are depressed.

- 3 million people suffer from panic attacks.

- 1 million people have heart attacks each year.

- Muscles are a primary target for stress manifesting in cramping, spasms, back and jaw pain, and tremors.

- Stress can play a significant role in circulatory and heart disease, sudden cardio death and strokes.

- Stress can increase blood pressure, raise cholesterol levels and speed up blood clotting.

- Stress causes more heart disease than smoking.

- Heart disease kills more people than any other disease.

- The Harvard School for Public Health published that 65% of all cancer can be prevented by diet.

- The American Cancer Society published that at least one third of all cancer could be prevented by diet.

- Studies have shown a 66% decrease in cancer among women with a higher oxygen level.

- Mainstream medicine agrees that your body can only heal while asleep. Experts worldwide agree that a positive attitude contributes to a major part of health and wellness.

- Today 86% of all illness and physician visits are stress related.

A scientific review of the IBMS™

Every IBMS™ session provides stress reduction. However, it is important to note that while you are in a state of deep physical relaxation and total mental clarity, it is also possible to effectively and quickly condition your brain to achieve specific objectives like building self esteem, improving your golf game, conquering test anxiety, overcoming trauma, etc. Every IBMS™ session can provide an immediate benefit to everybody because with the body's enhanced ability to fully relax, it is supplied with an abundance of energy, oxygen, nutrition and optimum blood flow.

Fundamentally, the system works because the brain needs a comprehensive blueprint and the proper software to direct the nervous system to achieve a desired goal. Normally, this blueprint develops over years of trial and error decision making combined with constant repetition, which is the foundation for dendrite formation (software) that directs your mental activities. Using golf as an example, the sport requires years of practice, on-course play, the selection of proper clubs, the development of an ability to relax, focus, align, breathe, and swing in order to play well.

All of these are components of the blueprint to pull off the perfect game. By practicing you build the dendrites (software) to execute the swing and play the game. IBMS™ assists you in achieving your goal faster while bypassing all the years it would normally take because you can quickly condition your brain to perform the desired swing and play your best game while listening to IBMS™ program. Results will vary with each person.

Remember, IBMS™ program utilizes a combination of brain states and generic "I" based audio commands to effectively program the mind and nervous system so that the result you want is permanently installed as software in the brain. It is important to understand that you must be in a specific brain state at a specific time in order to achieve the proper programming. You must be in the beta state (14-30 hertz) to clearly define your objective. You then must shift to the alpha state (7-13 hertz) to be able to create a blueprint for action. Immediately thereafter you must return to the beta state (14-30 hertz) to commit to the blueprint. Then you must transfer to the theta state (3-6 hertz) so that the brain can begin building the new dendrites and install this new software throughout the nervous system.

Note: The brain has no sense of the concept of time.
With this process, you are able to produce results that might normally require years to produce. IBMS™ was created to function within the natural mechanism of the nervous system which is why the sessions are so effective. It simply allows natural neurological mechanisms to function faster and more efficiently.

Note: You can only achieve objectives that are intrinsically beneficial and derived from your personal goals and desires.

If you instinctively believe that your objective is right for you then you will achieve it. While IBMS™ facilitates your ability to achieve your objective faster and more efficiently, please be aware that any stress reduction or conditioning system that is not based on your instincts will not be permanent and can actually cause negative effects. For instance, hypnotists use the alpha state to manipulate and control human behavior and can direct you to behave in a manner contrary to your natural instincts for a limited time (witness the ridiculous antics of hypnotized subjects on stage), but once you return from the alpha state, there is no further programming. This is because you cannot build dendrites in the alpha state; therefore, there is no software to initiate further action. This is why hypnotic suggestion has to be constantly repeated. It is, in fact, brainwashing. The person being hypnotized is required to give control of their mind to the brainwasher. We believe this can be harmful, and can even cause multiple personality disorders in some subjects. It surely creates a dependency in the subject and has the potential to lead to bipolar disorder and, in extreme cases, to paranoia and/or schizophrenia.

Follow Dr. Leonard Coldwell
on www.drleonardcoldwell.com

THE FOUNDATION TO ELIMINATE STRESS IN EVERY AREA OF YOUR LIFE

You picked up this book because you wanted something positive to help further your life. You expected that with the help of this book, and the accompanying exercises, you could reduce your daily stress and have a happier and more successful life—a life full of enthusiasm, vitality and strength—a life that corresponds with your true potential.

While all of this is possible, you must be willing to do all that is necessary to accomplish these goals. I can help you by offering guidance and giving you the needed instructions, but that's all I can do. *I can't live your life for you, or make necessary changes for you.*

To get the best possible use from this book, you have to realize your human existence and become fully aware of yourself as an individual. You will then be able to make decisions and choose the right path that will take you along the road of success.

Refuse to let self-doubt, hesitation or procrastination stand in the way of your happiness. Start today by making your life a little brighter, more beautiful and successful. No matter who you are or where you are at in life, "You were born to be successful, born to be a champion!"

Destiny

The first lesson on your road to success is to recognize that there is no such thing as an irrevocable destiny. Nothing is pre-planned before your birth. Nothing is written in stone.

You are not a victim, but a creator of the circumstances in which you live. This saying is very true: "Everyone is the author of his own happiness!"

Life is neither fair nor unfair—life just is as we understand it and accept it. Our lives take shape according to how we act and react to any given situation.

For instance, a hailstorm destroys the cornfield of a rich farmer in the same way as it destroys the field of a poor farmer. The one who does not give up, but sees every disaster as a challenge, and who rolls up his sleeves and acts, will be successful. I call that person a winner, because he or she does not give up, but works and fights and finally wins.

Right now, I want you to realize that you were born to be a winner. A winner is, in my opinion, not someone who defeats somebody else, but a winner is someone who conquers themselves, who can subdue their inner beast, their own doubts and fears. A winner is someone who overcomes the adversities "fate" throws at them, who can repeatedly motivate themselves to act and who is willing not to give up, no matter the demands life makes.

You are born to be a winner. In fact, you came into this world as a winner. You are the result of your father's strongest sperm. You survived the dangers of pregnancy and birth. You developed from an infant and became an adult. Think about it, you have already won several unbelievable victories in your life that you've probably never noticed or paid much attention to. Be aware that you are as nature intended you to be, and that you are perfect the way you are. And you will only get better.

Every person is the master of their destiny!

Letting Go Of The Past

An unwillingness to let go of the past is, for many people, one of their main problems. They have been programmed and conditioned by the problems of their youth that have been ingrained in their subconscious permanently. However, I want to familiarize you with an important principle of the IBMS™ training:

"The past does not determine your future! And: " Stop whining and complaining and having self pity parties with yourself, let the past go: GET OVER IT AND MOVE ON!

This statement is only true if you are no longer willing to give the past power over your behavior and your future. As long as you look back with self-pity, complaining how unfair and hard life is, how badly fate has treated you, how difficult your start in life was, then all your energy will be completely focused on the negative. Your thinking will be focused on talking, worrying and being frustrated, instead of on solutions, strategies and actions.

As long as you look back you will not be able to change anything in your life, because all your energy and strength is turned backward. No matter how much you would like to, you cannot change your past.

Also, the so-called "working through and conquering the past" is completely absurd, and often even detrimental. I could show you several examples of people who have received years of unsuccessful therapy, and were released from their fears, phobias, depressions, etc. with only one IBMS™ conditioning session, without even suffering from side effects or setbacks.

My IBMS™ will help you to destroy the neuro-associations you have had programmed in your mind since childhood, and destroy the age-old belief that your past determines your future.

People often believe that because they failed somewhere in the past, they must also fail in the future. They believe that because they have two or three failed relationships behind them that in the future they will fail again. They believe that because they have lost control over their thinking, behavior and feelings in certain situations in the past that this will happen again in the future.

This is not true! People *can* be in control of their feelings and behavior in every stage of their life, if they are determined to do so. Life demands flexibility, a willingness to act, and the perseverance to be in control, so that we can achieve the success we desire.

Say, for instance, that you've gotten up at seven in the morning for the last ten years. It doesn't mean you have to get up at the same time for the next ten years. Instead, you can decide here and now to get up a quarter till or a quarter after seven, or whenever you feel like getting up. You don't have to talk to a psychoanalyst to make the change, nor do you have to process or assimilate the change. All you have to do is to make a clear decision, and change the necessary activity.

This may sound over simplified, but it isn't. Every change in our human existence demands a lucid and effective decision.

Because the past does not determine the future, you have to become at ease with this thought process. You set the goals, giving your life direction, which fulfill or squash your dreams. You are the one that decides to act or be passive. You are the one who decides to focus on solutions or to look back mournfully in self-pity, looking for excuses.

Because you are only accountable to yourself, you can stop looking for excuses in past failures and negative results. You no longer need to fool yourself as long as you recognize the truth in your subconscious.

I would like to demonstrate this with a brief exercise. Pretend you are on a boat, floating on the sea of life. You keep looking backwards, looking where you came from, but by doing so you will not be able to influence the direction of the boat. You won't see ahead and you won't be able to recognize and avoid obstacles. You will capsize quickly.

It will be the same if you are too entangled in the here and now, and you only see the bottom of the boat. You may eventually see the troubles ahead, but it will be too late to react. You will be able to recognize problems and goals, prepare yourself and react as needed, only when you focus and look ahead. People, who look forward and give their life direction with clear goals, will be able to influence their life in the way they desire.

Later in this book you will find exercises to help you let go of the past and obliterate the neuro-associations regarding your past.

Living without Guilt

You came into this world with a strong and unbelievable need for further development, for growth, and for the use and expansion of your human skills and talents. Therefore, you not only have the right, but also the duty, to shape your life the way you see fit so that it agrees with your own needs, wishes and dreams. Don't let anybody take it away from you!

Many people don't believe they have the right to do everything necessary to be happy, content, healthy and successful in all areas of their life. Victimhood had been drummed into them since early childhood.

Ignorant religious teachings often cause a lot of misunderstanding within people. The waiting rooms of psychoanalysts and psychiatrists are filled with people who suffer from guilty feelings caused by the preaching of others.

It makes absolutely no sense to live in humility with imaginary feelings of guilt—such an existence is not natural. Everyone has the right to regularly do those things that give them joy and allow them to be joyful.

You deserve to be the best of the best! Go and get it!

Value Concepts

We are not just stimulated and propelled by our great goals; our value concepts are also responsible for the way we act and for the intensity of our behavior. We can only recognize ourselves, and our struggle in the fulfillment of our desires, when we know our values and the values of those around us.

The greater the possibilities of finding satisfactory value concepts in our work, the more motivated we will be to do our work as effectively and as well as we can. It is therefore absolutely necessary that we have a clear picture of our values and also consider what the values are of our colleagues, friends and family. Knowing this makes it easier to conquer our problems and, importantly, reduce our stress.

It is easier to understand another human being when you know where their values lie. We are all different. Some may prefer praise, while, for others, money is more important.

Exercise:

1. "What is most important in my life in the area of _____?" (for instance, love, career, health, friendships, money, etc.). Write down at least ten things that are important to you in every area, while you keep in mind your own values and those of other people.

There Are No Mistakes

The fear of failure prevents most people from acting at all. This leads to tension and rigidity which continuously stimulates stress in the nervous system, causing the release of stress hormones, and eventually leading to catastrophic behavior.

Once we become aware that every good experience in our life is the result of a previous bad experience, we understand that a poor result is only a necessary step in a process that takes us to the next level, ultimately leading us to our goal.

The many failures that an inventor experiences while working in a lab will bring him or her progressively closer, if they continue to search, to find newer combination and possibilities. These many so-called failures are responsible for new products and greater accomplishments.

Success is nothing more than taking action, learning from the results, changing your procedure and repeating this until the goal has been reached. There's rarely a person who can produce the perfect final product they want with the first try.

I'll say it one more time: "There are no mistakes, there are only results." Every result is the way we wish it to be, or not the way we want it to be. And if the results are not the way we want them to be, then we must keep trying until we produce the results we do want.

Thomas Edison produced several thousand failures in his search for an electric light bulb. Before finding success, someone asked if he was finally willing to admit defeat after so many failures. His answer: "I have not failed. I have just found 10,000 ways that won't work."

To the question, whether he was willing to give up finding a light bulb after searching for two years, he answered: "Why give up, I will soon find the answer, because I am running out of possibilities to fail." Edison had 25,000 unsuccessful approaches to create a battery.

If we keep a concrete goal in front of us, so that we keep moving consciously in the right direction, we will produce result at the end of our road. If we keep adjusting our attitude and say, "I will realize the goal for which I am aiming, and I will absolutely not give up before I reach my goal," the thought of failure will no longer play a part in your life.

Personal Decisions

Every change in our human existence starts with a decision. But hardly anyone is quite aware what the concept of a decision really entails. A decision means that we decide to move in one certain direction, exclusive of all others.

It is therefore the decision that changes one's life, because a real decision calls for immediate action. If you decide to make a change in your life, an action will necessarily follow. The most important decision you have to make is the decision: To never be satisfied with anything less than the best. With anything less than the best you can achieve and, most of all, that you will never ever again accept less from life than you can be or have! Now make the decision to be the champion you are designed to be!

This shows how our life is changed by our behavior. Right now you must take responsibility and make the decision to never allow others to influence your behavior again. Instead of remaining a victim, by taking responsibility for your decisions and actions, you will now be in control. If you don' take control of your life, others will always do it for you. They will exploit you and use you. They'll use your strength, your money, your energy, your efforts and your ideas. If you do not take control of your life, you will be blown about like a leaf in the wind, without any influence of your own.

If you're unwilling to take charge of your own life, feelings of help-lessness take control, preventing you from acting on a logical and physi-cal basis. You therefore will remain stuck.

Helplessness is the most serious form of failure I can imagine. No-body wants to live with helplessness or dependence. You must learn to accept life-situations as they are, to see a problem not as an obstacle but as a challenge to help you grow and develop. Nobody can take away your emotional and physical investments in yourself. Overcoming obsta-cles makes you stronger and more experienced. Overcoming problems makes you more self-confident and secure.

You will always face new obstacles and problems in life. You must not fall for the superstition that if you avoid one obstacle you will never have to face another. Life is filled with difficulties. As soon as you start accepting life's challenges, you will learn that every problem and every obstacle you overcome will make you stronger; you will amaze others and they will respect you. Success means nothing else than the fact that you stand up one more time than life throws you down. "Winners Never Quit—and Quitters Never Win."

Successful people do not have fewer problems; they have simply learned to deal with them effectively.

I want you to decide right now that you will no longer see your life as an accumulation of random incidents, or to let your life be deter-mined or controlled by other people. Take control of your life starting today so that you will be the one who determines your future.

The Danger of Compromise

Every compromise you make in life leads to tension, lower self-esteem, energy depletion, possible illness, and always adds to emotional and physical stress. A compromise is a decision you make but would prefer not to make in the manner it is presented. Making a compromise means that you will do something that you would prefer to avoid, but for some reason you are compelled or feel forced to do. A compromise is something you are willing to do, while you know you could have done it better, bigger, or more effectively, but are somehow willing to do less anyway.

In a compromise you are working with limitations and restrictions. You give a signal to your subconscious telling it that it's okay to give less than 100%. A compromise is something you do not really want but accept anyway. It's something you would really rather not do, if you could make a more intelligent decision since it doesn't really correspond with your wishes, needs and skills.

It's your life, refuse to compromise!

In this program you will see that I cannot change your life for you, that I cannot solve your problems and that I do not have solutions to solve your conflicts. The only person who can have that much influence on your life is you. My goal is to motivate you to act and take positive steps with my program. I will try, with all my knowledge and ability, to help you put together a program so you can reach the goals you have set for yourself.

More than anything, I want to make you aware that you are greater and stronger than any problem or obstacle that life puts in your way. As a human being, you naturally possess an abundance of strength and energy. The power to act consciously, and the ability to be flexible, is what sets us apart from the animal kingdom.

I have developed my IBMS™ (Instinct Based Medicine® System™) to make people aware that they don't need help from others to help themselves. They can overcome their own problems and transform their life into the dream they deserve.

As long as people believe they cannot cope with their immediate life situation, they will unavoidably develop an inferiority complex, a feeling of worthlessness—and that is exactly what I want to prevent. You should forever banish the thought that you need medicine or the help of others to turn your life into a wonderful adventure.

The most important thing you can say to yourself every single day when you wake up is: "I can and I will do it!"

No matter what the current path in your life is, no matter what obstacles and hurdles life hands to you, you can succeed. After putting this program into action, you will soon be able to find solutions and realize your dreams. You just need to be goal oriented and act intelligently.

Finally, we must stop looking for excuses for our failures, stop whining about what is unfair or moaning about what is just not right or bad in our lives. We must learn that life is neither fair nor unfair, life just is. Develop a new belief system immediately: *"I can succeed in everything I undertake!"* In modern psychology we say: If someone says that they can or can't do something, they are always right, because their behavior is determined by their belief and attitude.

The Importance of Setting Clear Goals

The main cause of developing stress symptoms is the inability to give ourselves the time to clearly define what we really dream and desire, what it is that gives meaning to our lives. While most people carry a goal in their minds and start doing things to fulfill it, after awhile they forget what they were doing and why they were doing it. They get sidetracked by obstacles and diversions. They have lost the picture, they no longer act, just react, because life no longer has clear direction, there are no minor fulfillments, no further developments, no concrete goals.

Human beings only feel good about themselves when they grow and mature emotionally. In my understanding, the real purpose of life is personal growth and development. You will feel happy and content when you see that you have grown as a human being, that you have matured and have increased your talents and strengthened your abilities and possibilities. When life is stagnant you feel utter discontent.

How can you be proud of your development, and how can you produce success in your life, if you have no clear direction, and you don't even know whether you have overcome an obstacle or have moved a single step ahead?

Without goals you are like a soccer ball being kicked around, landing somewhere at random. It's the goals that give life direction. Goals help us decide to change our behavior and make it possible to do so. When you have a goal firmly in place, you will notice if you start moving in a different direction than you planned and will easily be able to redirect your course.

Many people set out on the stream of life in a boat without a motor. They let the river take its course and follow its current. Some day they will be startled by a raging noise and realize they are drifting toward an enormous waterfall. They will try to row for all they're worth, but it will be too late. They will soon face emotional, financial and physical destruction, or perhaps the loss of a partnership, simply because they never set a course, and now it is too late to take positive action.

Also, if you keep looking backwards your boat will hit every obstacle in its way because you will not notice them in time and your boat will capsize. People who keep looking backward at their past will suffer the same fate, because, even though they are aware of the obstacles, they will be unable to react in time for the reason that their mind was elsewhere.

Only those people who look ahead can decide clearly which path to take, which direction to follow, how to react and make course corrections. These people will reach their final destination.

Goals help us look far ahead and give our life direction. They make it possible to check whether we should stay the path or drift away from our objective. In that way we can produce success on a daily basis and observe whether we're moving in the right direction and we will ultimately realize our dreams. Our goals help us when we deviate from our path and take the wrong road since they can guide us back in the right direction enabling us to consistently move forward.

With a clear plan for the future we have a map of the territory so we will feel at ease, rather than feeling lost in an area where we don't know the landscape.

Our self-esteem and self-confidence will improve by defining and realizing clear goals and by constant modification and focused action. In a crisis situation you will be calmer and react with more composure than before, because you learned that you can cope and produce the results you desire in every situation.

Let this be your new belief-system: *I am in charge of my life! I will shape and determine my future and my fate!*

With this new belief-system many of your fears, worries and apprehension will disappear because you will no longer feel at the mercy of your life and fate. You will have learned that no matter what situation you may face in life, you know how to react, and you can focus on a goal that leads you in the right direction, even though circumstances and restrictions may sidetrack you or obstacles may turn things topsy-turvy.

Through the clarity of your goal you can view your problems as assignments, difficulties as opportunities, and use them to grow and strengthen your self-esteem and self-image. You will have a whole new focus on life. The quality of your life will improve considerably. You will enjoy solving your problems and overcoming difficulties. All of this will lead you to personal success. You will now be able to smile about the challenge that used to fill you with so much fear and frustration. You can now take full control of your life.

I would like to mention that you don't need a calm personality to conquer your stress. What you need is the ability to take your fate in your own hands, at any time, so that every day you are reaching a little closer to the realization of your wishes and dreams.

Don't believe that you must tackle and conquer all your goals at once. That thought alone causes stress and tension!

If you change your life just one percent every day; in one hundred days that will make one hundred percent. In other words, if you have a hundred unfinished jobs lying on your desk and you tackle two or three each day, you will soon finish all of the things you know you had to do. In this way you have little triumphs each day and you see that your work diminishes as your success increases.

The first step is usually the most difficult, but after you start looking for a solution, the job is often finished much faster than you first expected.

How to Condition a New Pattern of Behavior

If you condition yourself to take charge and program yourself to act every day toward your goals, whether the activities are large or small, you will fill each day of your life with small triumphs. You will come closer to your dreams and you will no longer be passive or influenced negatively by circumstances, other people, or your own past.

Our manners and all of our actions are dependent on learned behavior. Everything we do on a regular basis conditions and programs us. This guarantees that we will act in the future exactly as we have done before. To change this, you must learn to break through old behavior patterns of hesitation, indecision, convenience and passivity, and install a pattern of action.

The human brain functions exactly like a computer, and so the brain is no better than a machine. What we put in our brain is what we get out. Our brain can only play back those programs that have been fed into it through pictures, emotions, and repeated behavior. Again and again we program and input these behavior patterns into our subconscious that lead to automatic actions and reactions in future life situations.

If you've conditioned yourself to simply accept life as it is and merely react, you will do the same in the future because you are not aware of this shortcoming. But, if you reprogram your bio-computer to act and determine your own fate, you will produce your own personal success.

With the IBMS™ program you'll have everything you need to make your life an adventure, an experience, and a success. This system will give you the happiness, harmony, peace and health that you have only previously dreamed about.

When I created the IBMS™ I wanted it to be clear, easy to use and consistently produce outstanding results. However, I would like to point out one more time that you are the only person in this world who can give you the peace and success you desire. Nobody can take away your problems, nobody can remove your worries and fears, and nobody can get rid of the challenges in your life.

Your life will become your own the moment you recognize that you are the only person in the world who can have a positive influence on your life.

IBMS™ —Your Manual for Success

The IBMS™ program is your complete personal success system. Now

I want to get into the details of the program, information, examples, and offer you encouragement so you can develop your own individual recipe for success.

This system isn't new; it's actually the oldest system in the world. It is a manual for the most perfect mechanism nature has created: the human being. When your mind and body act in positive unison, you can fulfill your wishes, needs and dreams, and create a beautiful life filled with success, health and happiness. My IBMS™ program is therefore nothing more than a manual so that your body and mind can use the limitless possibilities nature has given you more effectively and significantly to ultimately reach every one of your goals.

When you work through this book you will probably find yourself saying, "Oh yes, I know that. It's actually so simple I can't believe I haven't been doing this all along!" I hope you will soon understand your own greatness, recognize your needs and realize you can live out every one of your dreams—and you're the only person in the world who can make it happen.

I ask you to take conscious charge of your life, of your thinking, your behavior and your feelings so you can finally determine your own fate. Become the person you already are deep inside. Bring that person within you out into the real world.

Case Study of Healing with IBMS™
Finger Amputation Is No Longer Needed

My mother received a frantic phone call from her friend, Linda. The doctors told Linda that her finger needed to be amputated. My mother advised her to visit the IBMS™ center and get a second opinion. This woman had fallen down the basement steps, crushing the joints in her pinky finger. She waited six days before consulting a doctor. Apparently, the delay made the damage irreparable. Linda's finger was dark blue, extremely swollen and hurt so severely that painkillers could not help.

Two doctors, independently of each other, had advised Linda to have her finger amputated. She came to see me with little hope, but with great motivation to keep her finger.

I led Linda into a mental state where she found herself strong and confident. She visualized her finger returning to its normal size and color, with the joints tightening and healing. This mental vision was associated with feelings of self-confidence and was strengthened by her overwhelming desire to recover. Linda trained and programmed herself intensely and repeated the exercises several times throughout the day.

Surprisingly, Linda called my mother later to say that she was pain free. Her finger was regaining its normal color and shape. Today, Linda's finger is fully functional.

STRESS:
THE ROOT CAUSE OF
ALL DISEASES

The main tool I used in my clinics and healing centers in Europe was oxygen therapy. I found this to be the cheapest, fastest and safest way to produce health on all levels!

Oxygen is the most abundant element and the most crucial element in the human body and for life itself. For over 150 years oxygen therapy—or, in this case, Hydrogen Peroxide Therapy—has been used in Germany, Russia, Italy, Austria, and today in Mexico with huge success. It's now curing nearly every viral and microbial infection, even cancer, Multiple Sclerosis, Parkinson's and other deadly diseases.

The only reason why Americans have probably never heard of this fast and safe cure for cancer symptoms is the economic aspects. Basically, the power of the pharmaceutical industry because it costs about 2 cents a day to cure cancer with $H2O2$ (Hydrogen Peroxide). Compare that to the millions and millions of dollars they make through chemotherapy, radiation, and other drugs.

Of course there are the usual scare tactics from the pharmaceutical industry telling people Oxygen Therapy should not be used because of the dangers of oxidation. What many people do not know is that human cells are all surrounded by an enzyme coating which makes the cells resistant to oxidation. Viruses and bacteria and other disease-causing microorganisms do not have this enzyme coating and are therefore oxidized on contact with the application of hydrogen peroxide or ozone. If administered right it is, in my experience, the safest and fastest way to cure cancer, AIDS, flu and all kinds of infections and diseases that are caused by infection.

Note: Please do not administer Hydrogen Peroxide before you have done your own research and have read the entire article and information on my website www.InstinctBasedMedicine.com. I believe, based on my use of oxygen therapy in different forms for over 15 years in my IBMS™ (Instinct Based Medicine Centers™) that nothing is safer or more effective than bio-oxidative therapy if it is applied in the right form.

Prof. Dr. Manfred von Ardenne kept all the former Russian leaders alive and healthy for decades just with his Multi-Step Oxygen Therapy! After the fall of the Soviet Union when their leaders no longer had access to the Oxygen Therapy they literally died like flies in a very short amount of time.

In my IBMS™ we used 35% food grade hydrogen peroxide diluted in 6 to 8 ounces of distilled water or aloe juice 3 times a day on an empty stomach—this is important or you may experience vomiting. We started with 3 drops 3 times a day (always diluted in 8 ounces of distilled water) and added one drop each day until we reached 25 drops 3 times per day for 35 days. We then started to cut down to 2 times a day and then once a day, while slowly getting down to 8 drops a day. As maintenance we used 8 drops of food grade 35% hydrogen peroxide in 8 ounces of distilled water three times day. It is highly toxic and can be even deadly if it is not diluted. It will even burn your skin. Never ever drink it undiluted!

In my centers we have seen massive cancer tumors shrinking within 14 days, and that without any side effects. The success rate was nearly 100% and the hydrogen peroxide therapy gave hope to even terminal and late-stage cancer patients that were often just left to die by the medical profession.

As a reminder, oxygen or ozone therapy usually gets rid of all cancer symptoms quickly but it does not cure the cancer, it just eliminates the cancer symptoms, tumors and cancerous cells. Cancer is a systemic, mental and emotional disease and can only be cured if the root cause is eliminated. You have to find out what caused the mutation or tumor development and malignancy to spread in the first place.

Don't be fooled into believing if you find some elements or ways to manipulate your body—even with something like hydrogen peroxide—that you are cured because you are not! You have to uncover and eliminate the root cause of the cancer development or it will always come back, more vicious and stronger and faster than before. You cannot trick nature and pull yourself from the responsibility of eliminating the illness that you caused yourself in the first place.

Anyone who tells you that natural cures are dangerous or if they try to make them illegal or even access to them illegal should be jailed for life because he/she is a murderer in my opinion! Don't you think it should be a crime for the government or groups like the AMA, FTC, FDA, ACS, etc. to let you know that there are safe, effective and proven natural cures for cancer, AIDS, flu and more? And shouldn't they make them available to the general public? Instead, they do their best to keep the information and use of these natural cures out of our reach!

Doesn't this mean that they are indirectly responsible for the death of you or your loved one if cancer is the cause of that death and they know how it could have been cured easily and naturally?

If you don't fight with me, or at least support my fight for Patient Rights and Health Freedom as an Amendment to our Constitution and to stop the Banker owned Presidents and Government, you may not ever have the tools and elements available if you or your family members and friends may need them. Right now there are groups working to make the cures for cancer symptoms like Hydrogen Peroxide Treatments illegal and make the product inaccessible to us.

Stress is the Root Cause of All Diseases

Stress is the one major cause of acidosis. No matter what you eat or drink, if you have chronic stress then you have acidosis. In turn, this is the main, if not the only, physical cause of cancer, infection and illnesses of all kind.

In my opinion, mental and emotional stress is the root cause of all diseases, especially cancer! Stress can debilitate your immune system so profoundly that it no longer has the energy to sustain health. Every serious scientist and doctor recognizes the importance of stress in regards to health. The problem is that they have no idea what to do about it therefore they mention it and forget about it. Or, even worse, they prescribe drugs and numb the patient to a point where he is not able to fully function on a neurological level anymore. That does not help at all! That would be like having a splinter in your finger, but you don't look at or deal with the problem. Instead, you just push the splinter in deeper and take some pain and inflammation medication instead of pulling it out.

While oxygen is crucial for health and healing and prevention (which is why I invented the IBMS™ Session: Breathing Therapy) oxygen can only cure and support the body if the cells are able to receive the oxygen supplied by the blood. But, for the cells to be able to receive the oxygen they have to be open. If the cells are closed, such as from stress, they are unable to receive oxygen. This makes healing impossible and this is the main difference between the patients that get healed and the ones that did not.

As I just mentioned, the only cause for cells being unable to receive oxygen is stress. That is why stress, in my opinion, is the only cause for cancer—unless they radiate you to cancer and to eventual death!

Normally, all cells are under the control of the parasympathetic nervous system which controls the digestion of food, salivary gland secretion, blood flow to different parts of the body, and the absorption of nutrients. It is responsible for the proper function of the organs. While functioning under the parasympathetic nervous system, all cells are open, able to absorb oxygen and nutrients, get rid of waste products. They are healthy and dividing, multiplying, metabolizing and performing every task a cell needs to do to be a healthy normal cell.

When the cells are open they can absorb oxygen (you can usually feel it during my IBMS™ Breathing Session) and function properly. The body is easily able to heal itself. But, stress shuts down digestion and all other body functions.

The sympathetic nervous system gets activated by stress—either actual or perceived danger. The attack of a dangerous dog or an angry parent or spouse, are a few examples. Every negative emotion like fear, hatred, anxiety, worry or doubt can stimulate a stress response. Every negative memory or mental picture can cause stress.

Stress causes your autonomic nervous system to go into sympathetic mode and your blood flows away from your gastro-intestinal tract as well as from the skin. Your heart rate increases and your pupils dilate, the blood flows into the muscles and your body goes into high-alert mode. That is when the cells shut down! That is why chronic stress causes cancer—and nearly all other diseases.

If you live under chronic stress the body functions most of the time under the sympathetic instead of parasympathetic mode which causes, dehydration, nutritional deficiencies, lack of oxygen and acidosis—all of the physical causes of cancer and other diseases. That means the body functions primarily in the Fight or Flight mode and that causes many relationships to fail too.

Basically you can say that your state of mind is causing your stress and therefore your health or illness. It should no longer be a mystery as to why and how stress can kill! Stress is deadly, no matter what healing modality you choose. That is the true answer to the question why different people using the same treatment do not necessarily produce the same results.

What I see everywhere is that nearly every health author, every doctor or scientist, mentions the massive impact of stress in relation to health and illness. But instead of using the stress as a healing tool they just skip over offering a solution and instead recommend absurd, useless and often more damaging techniques like Mediation, Yoga, Hypnosis, NLP or other modalities. None of these will permanently reduce or eliminate the chronic stress in your life—I am absolutely sure about that! If you suppress stress it makes it even worse and living in denial can kill you. If stress is numbed by medication you will never be able to heal because you will not be able to address and eliminate the root cause of the life challenges that are causing your illness, unhappiness, lack of success, bad relationships and so on.

> Warning: Sometimes people eliminate the root cause of their stress and the second they feel better and are not afraid of dying anymore or the pain is gone, they go back to the stress caus-ing life situation and the cancer comes back faster, stronger and more aggressive than ever before. I have personally experienced that in most of these cases these patients died very fast after they got back into the cancer-causing life situation.

Remember that stress is not caused by external circumstances. Stress is caused by an individual interpretation of an internal image that causes the activation and takeover of the sympathetic nervous system and therefore the shutdown of the cells. That is what causes our cells to go into the Fight or Flight mode or, better said, into a state of self-protection. It is your individual response to an internal image (cellular memory) that determines your stress response.

My IBMS™ is created to help and teach you to deal with these stimuli in a healthy and positive way and to re-program your stimuli responses and to eliminate or recondition your internal interpretations and reactions. If you work with the IBMS Life Therapy™ (IBMS™ Healing Life Kit™) you will see and feel very fast everything I've been talking about! It is all about creating neurological pathways that you want and not just live with the ones that were created by life or coinci-dence and circumstance.

That is why a true stress reduction and prevention program has to include every form of personal development such as: goal setting, mo-tivation, health education, relationship, success, happiness education, training, and coaching. I am able to make all of this available and work-able to you with my Instinct Based Medicine® System™ (IBMS™). With my program you will experience positive results again and again!

You have to learn not to react to external circumstances; you have to be in control of your actions. However, you cannot be healthy if you don't feel successful in every part of life. That is why you should read my books: "You are born to win" or "The Success Guarantee" and use my IBMS™ audio system: Curing Life™. When you do, you'll get the essence of everything I have learned and taught in over three decades of research, therapy, training and coaching, in one simple to understand and easy to use system.

Stress reduction has to be so holistic that it includes every part of life

That is why I wrote so many bestselling books on different life issues. I wrote the most successful parenting book of all time in Europe, the most sought after book for sales people, books on relationships and every other part of life because all of this has to be included into one single system (IBMS™).

Yes, some people copy from other writers and practitioners and put all of these together and think it should work, but it doesn't. I truly believe that I have created a perfect system and I have many leading authorities backing me up on this. The reason is because I found the cure for cancer as a teenager and my results—not hypothetical statements—prove it. I developed the most successful motivational seminars and most sold book—*You Are Born To Win*—in Europe. The updated version of this book that brought millions of people into my seminars will be available soon in English with the title, *The Only Answer to Successs: You Were Born to be a Champion.*

I also wrote the extremely successful book *The Sales Champion* and gave the most successful sales, management and personal development seminars in Europe. I trained and consulted for nearly all of the largest companies in Europe with unmatched success. I have had over 2.2 million seminar attendees and over 35,000 patients that I got direct feedback from. I have over 7 million readers and millions of listeners to my program and radio shows and have gotten feedback from so many of them.

I have overcome countless diseases myself. I cured my mother and countless other people from cancer and can repeat this result any time! I had my own office at the age of 14 and was paying taxes. That is why I am the best one to develop the only holistic system that really works to "Cure Life"™. My Instinct Based Medicine® system is and will be unmatched in success and results because life prepared me for this task for over 40 years!

I was the very first one who created the statement: "You have to eliminate the root cause of the disease or condition and then the illness and symptoms will disappear on their own." What bothers me most is the countless books and so-called experts saying that a single supplement, diet or subliminal audio program can get rid of the root cause of your disease. It can't! Disease is in your body, mind and spirit. It's in your mental and emotional world because we are simply all beings of energy living with the illusion of a physical body.

The only thing that can make us sick is if we violate God's or Nature's laws, and get out of balance, which then leads to an unhealthy energetic frequency. The absolute only way to "get rid of the root cause" is to cure life itself!

So, if you read anywhere that someone promises that you can get rid of the root cause of your individual health challenge by using supplements, herbs or any isolated technique, you can be sure that the person is not well-educated on the true cause of illnesses.

There is no magic bullet. There is no short cut. You made yourself sick over a long period of time and you are the only one that can fix the problem. And the problem is your entire life, not just one part of it. Except for accidents, all illnesses never come from one single source.

I hope that I can make you understand why I am so excited about this issue because it may harm you further or even kill you if you believe that there is only one single cause and one single solution for your heath challenges. You've been wasting valuable time and money, and hope and effort, all over a lie.

It's like chiropractics, which I believe in and love, but it does not get rid of the root cause of your back pain! You need to get rid of the stress that tenses up your muscles and pulls your vertebrae out of line so that you can heal. It gives you nothing but a short period of less pain but not a final solution. Many chiropractors now use my CD system in their offices to handle this problem for their patients.

I strongly believe that everybody can be cured from anything and that the only way to lifelong health is to create happiness and success, to live as your true self and your true personality, to develop and grow as a human being on a consistent basis, and to take charge and responsibility of your own life, your health and your future.

This is what I give you with my Instinct Based Medicine® System. I'm providing you with the education and the tools, the training and coaching to Cure Life™! This is the only answer to Stress, Anxiety and Depression, the absolute answer to any disease or condition. You have to use all the success producing elements that are available to you, learn all you can, follow various techniques or whatever you choose and use it.

That is how the medical profession misleads and tricks the public, they talk about hypothetical results based on statistics that are fraudulent to begin with and make up what they believe the results could or should be. And they are always wrong! Just look at the results that they are producing. They are losing the battle with every illness, most of all with cancer. Even with all the billions thrown into their research that has made them rich, they have done nothing to find the cure for cancer! With all that money, why are they still using primitive "cures" like radiation and chemotherapy?

That is why I beg you, if you have any doubts or when they start attacking me personally and try to discredit me with lies and defamation campaigns, look at my results: I cured my own mother from liver cancer and have, as concluded in two independent studies, the highest cancer cure rate in the world. And I can prove again and again that every cancer can be cured within 2 to 16 weeks.

So why does the government not give me the legal authority to personally practice my IBMS™ in the US and let me show them that I can help nearly everybody, as long as they have not had "traditional" cancer treatments yet?

Help and support me actively in my fight for a Constitutional amendment to Health Freedom and Patient Rights and all of us will be safer, healthier, happier and have a longer, more fulfilled life.

The Consequences of Stress

Stress leads to:

- Drug and alcohol abuse

- Self destructive behavior

- Toxemia—and diseases and pain

- Constricts muscles

- Is the leading cause for Acidosis—the foundation of poor health and all degenerative diseases

- Bad Relationships

- Physical malfunctions

- Sexual problems

- Lack of oxygen and dehydration

- Shuts down the metabolism and all body and neurological functions in part or as a whole

- Stress is the basis of every disease or disorder. In fact, in physics stress literally means: Pressure from the inside out

- Produces potentially harmful hormones such as cortisol and adrenalin which leads to an often unhealthy reaction to the fight or flight response

- Leads to nutritional deficiencies and obesity. It shuts down the metabolism and digestive system, and is the basis for all degenerative conditions, pain and pre-aging

- It depletes vitamins and hormones in the body

- Harms serotonin and melatonin production and

- Destroys vitamin B6 and zinc—needed for serotonin production

Stress Leads to Mental and Emotional Disorders Like:

- Depression

- Anxiety

- Frustration

- Hopelessness

- Lack of self-confidence, low self-esteem and lack of willpower

The foundation of Health

It has been shown that 86% of all doctor visits and illnesses are related to stress, and even though these "experts" in the health or medical field acknowledge the importance of stress in the cause and development of disease, they don't really have the tools or solutions to approach this root cause of all disease.   (That is, with the exception of externally caused symptoms, illnesses and conditions.) I have the highest cure rate with my patients because I have found the solution; the way to avoid, reduce or prevent unnecessary stress reactions. They (the medical profession, as well as other healthcare practitioners) offer absurd, useless, and often dangerous stress management techniques that are often more harmful than helpful. Since they really have no solution, yet still want to appear as the all-knowing experts, they recommend massages, meditation, Neuro-Linguistic Programming (a system of alternative therapy based which seeks to educate people in self-awareness and effective communication, and to change their patterns of mental and emotional behavior-NLP), hypnotism and other time, and money-wasting techniques. These do not get to the root cause of your illness!

How can a massage help you eliminate the stress caused by a bad marriage or harmful relationship? How can hypnotism help you elimi-nate the stress caused by a job you hate or a boss that drives you crazy? How can sitting around and doing nothing except some meditation or yoga help you eliminate your financial stress? Most of all, how can teaching you to live in denial by using NLP and other manipulating and emotion suppressing techniques help you to resolve the challenges and stresses caused by your children, neighbors or life challenges? Actually these just cause other health challenges since they don't get rid of your problems, they just teach you to cover them up, but they're still there.

Then there is "stress management." Who wants to *manage* stress? Don't you want to eliminate it? This is like trying to manage a bullet from a gun that someone shoots into your brain—you die no matter what. You want to avoid the bullet and learn how to avoid the situation that would get you shot in the first place!

Stress Reduction and Stress Prevention Is the Solution

Since stress—mainly mental and emotional stress—is the main cause of lack of energy, and lack of energy is the only cause of illnesses—especially cancer—it is imperative that you learn how to handle stressful situations and how to avoid and reduce negative stress as much as possible.

Yes, a massage relieves muscle tension and is relaxing, but it does not fix any of your life challenges. A good physical workout may help you to get rid of some aggression and enhance your oxygen and energy levels, but it does nothing to relieve the true stress factors in your life. I could go on and on with this issue, but I believe you get my point by now.

Please let me explain to you why reducing and preventing mental and emotional stress is such an important part of health, happiness and life itself. In my opinion, the only true cause of illness stems from:
- a lack of self-love
- a lack of hope
- a lack of forgiveness to yourself and others
- a lack of self-esteem or self-confidence
- a lack of success
- bad relationships
- living in constant worry, fear, doubt
- and feelings of helplessness or worthlessness

Mental and emotional stress also comes from making constant compromises against yourself. Through compromise you deny yourself from being who you truly are and from living the way you really feel would be right for you. The main cause, if not the only cause, for certain forms of cancer symptoms comes from living in denial and self-hatred, and having no respect for who or what you are—Living in the past and having past experiences and traumas influencing your life? That, my dear friend, is another true cause of stress, lack of energy and all disease. All of these mental and emotional factors we just talked about, cause chronic stress. This is the kind of stress that makes you sick, unhappy, depressed and filled with fear and ultimately will kill you.

So do you still think that a massage, manipulating your behavior through NLP or hypnosis, or doing some yoga and meditation can eliminate these true causes of damaging stress? It's simply a waste of money and time and most of all your life! Living in denial, trying to learn to live with compromises against yourself, selling your dreams and hopes or possibilities to avoid standing up for yourself or to avoid confrontation will simply kill you one day.

If you truly look at where mental and emotional stress really comes from you will easily be able to understand why no other program has been able to offer you a true solution. Until now! Through many years of research and development I have created a system that can show and teach you how to define and eliminate the root cause of the true stressors in your life and how to eliminate this root cause of all disease—even cancer!

Why has no one developed this before? This is easy to explain. I was able to develop a system that would cure my mom from liver cancer in a terminal state when I was still a child and not brainwashed and manipulated by the medical or naturopathic schools. I found the truth about natural health and healing by myself and did not follow another follower—which is what most education is about. I used commonsense, instinct and trial and error to find the natural solution, the truth about life and healing, myself. That is why it works! That is why I was able to develop a repeatable system. And this is why I'm able to teach and coach you to heal yourself from the horrors of life.

Illness is nothing more than being out of balance with nature and out of balance with your true self—what you know and feel you should, do but didn't do. Illness is the logical consequence of denying yourself to be yourself! It is as simple as that. Therefore, health is nothing more than the logical consequence of living up to your true potential and desires and not making compromises against yourself or what you really are or stand for.

Life cannot be split up into separate pieces. To be healthy, get healthy or stay healthy, your life has to be *your* life in the whole meaning of the word. That means you need to be happy, successful and fulfilled in every part of your life. Therefore, the only true stress reduction and prevention is to have a stable foundation of self-love and self-confidence, success and control over your life and emotions, so much so that nothing and nobody can shake you to the core. When you're in this state nothing can chronically stress and damage you because you have learned to deal with every situation in life effectively. You no longer have to deny the facts or run away from life's challenges because you are in control of your life and are able and willing to stand your ground and deal with every challenge that life throws your way. You no longer have to live in fear or doubt! You no longer have to compromise your true self and what you really are and stand for. This is the only true stress reduction and prevention program. That strong sense of self and the total control over your emotional experiences can be achieved by anyone.

So why does my Instinct Based Medicine® System work? Because I found a way to help you be *you* in every area of your life. Vibrant health, success and happiness are the logical consequences of being the best you that you can be and being one with nature, one with your true desires, hopes and dreams. That is the absolute and only way to a long and happy and healthy life—there is no other! Another reason why my system can help you is that there is only one truth, one natural balance, one natural way or system. You can learn this system then apply the knowledge you gain from this program and my other books into your life.

For licensed IBMS™ professionals, workshops and seminars or for education as an IBMS™ Practitioner, Therapist or Coach please go to:
www.InstinctBasedMedicine.com

Case Study of Healing with IBMS™
Healing of Impotence Because of Fear of Failure

Impotence is a serious problem that is rarely discussed. Like the aforementioned case, it is a sexual disturbance that can be quickly and easily resolved.

Jerry, age 52, married a woman who was 12 years younger than him. He experienced tremendous misfortune, personally as well as professionally. Jerry lost his confidence and feared that he could not satisfy his young wife. His mental block caused impotence. After 12 sessions, Jerry set clear goals and used IBMS™ techniques to build his self-confidence. He made new plans for the future and visualized them as being real. These experiences anchored Jerry's new feelings of success. He visualized himself in depressing and frightening situations, yet was able to remain calm and level headed. He also conditioned himself to experience happiness and enthusiasm with a snap of his finger.

Jerry also programmed himself to be loving and passionate with his wife. He was able to generate feelings of confidence, energy and strength in any situation, at any time. Jerry could recall his programming and was able to develop effective goals and solutions. His impotence also disappeared and his relationship with his wife was restored.

HOW TO DEFINE AND ELIMINATE THE SYMPTOMS AND CAUSES OF STRESS

I often speak about stress-reduction. Stress is the greatest robber of energy in our lives, and energy is the basis of success. By learning to control your stress, you will have the energy to realize your dreams.

You are no doubt familiar with the simple scientific explanation for Dis-stress and Eu-stress—stress in the negative and stress in the positive sense—and there are many outstanding books dealing with this topic. I don't want to give you scientific definitions for the concept of stress, or go on and on about this already much discussed subject.

Since you've read this far, you already know that I don't speak of stress in a traditional way, nor do I approach the symptoms of stress in the usual way. Rather, I would like to show you the causes that are responsible for the stress you experience.

A real reduction of stress can only take place if you become aware that it has the capacity to drain your energy, ruin your health, and diminish your quality of life. A stress factor can be any stimulation you recognize, directly or indirectly, as a threat.

Whether you sense something as stress or not, and whether you have a release of stress hormones depends on your internal representation of a situation. It is therefore very important to recognize that stress is usually not generated by physical or actual strain. At least 80% of our dis-stress experiences are self-made, created by our own emotions.

There is a saying that goes, "It is not what happens that determines your life, but it is your reaction to what happens that does." And that is exactly how it is. The way you react to stressful situations will determine the havoc stress hormones cause.

The fight and flight reaction is a natural response to the release of stress hormones. Our early ancestors needed the ability to react in seconds and command the energy to flee or engage in combat to the dangers of their immediate environment.

In my opinion, there are very few extreme situations of real danger. On the other hand, there are far more little things that accumulate so unbearably that they may cause consistent feelings of stress.

In today's world, physical danger plays a lesser roll, but mental danger has become the greatest threat in our lives because our subconscious cannot distinguish between real experiences and emotional fears. It considers every fearful image as a real threat and releases stress hormones even if we simply think fearful thoughts.

Because we cannot just give someone a beating in our civilized world or respond by running away, the released hormones are being absorbed by our body and instead of being broken down, they become a poisonous threat.

Controlling Stress

This completely depends on whether you allow the images you produce in your mind to become dark, gloomy and threatening, or decide to see the future as bright, radiant and cheerful. It depends on you whether you see a situation as a problem and in turn create a stressful dilemma, or whether you see a situation as an opportunity to grow and learn so that you can show who you are and what you can do.

Coping with stress starts by identifying those situations in your life that send negative signals through your nervous system and to your brain. If you have already identified a typical stress situation you're currently facing, you can create new and effective behavior patterns. In this way, you can take control of your life and your physical and emotional reactions any time you need it.

Stress prevention always starts with good preparation and optimal internal communication. Your thought process and the way you approach things determines whether you produce stress hormones or not. The fear harbored by someone facing a difficult task can produce so many stress hormones that they will no longer be able to act effectively.

We all know the sad expression, "My job is killing me." And we know from behavior therapy and preventive medicine that this expression carries out its promise in the true sense of the word.

Our private lives suffer frequently from poor time management, misunderstanding and similar ignorant behavior, causing us to miss the opportunity to create a balance. Meanwhile, we expend too much energy and too much effort in our professional lives.

We shouldn't live to work, but work so we can live. If at all possible our work should be the fulfillment of a hobby or a calling. Still, we need to be aware of the fact that we have only so many years to live and that our life expectancy depends on the amount of energy we have at any given time. It's in our best interest to be as healthy and stress free as possible so that we can enjoy our lives.

We spend about two third of our day on the solving of problems, assignments and challenges, and not even a third on regeneration and positive activities. Our energy should be refueled by a kind word to our partner, a hug, a joint venture, or an enjoyable hobby, so that we feel inclined and have the strength to tackle our job again.

Our private lives are often pushed to the background because of the absurd attitude that we "must work very hard to be successful." It is not until we have become ill or suffer financial difficulties that are we ready to appreciate the value of our spouse again. But we have often caused so much damage with our poor behavior that it is too late.

My work is completely focused on improving the quality of life for people because that is what success ultimately means; the ability to enjoy your life and to enjoy your success *with* others.

When I speak of relationships with partners, I mean team play. When you are lonely you can't be happy, content and healthy. You cannot be successful when you are alone. We don't just need our spouse, our children and family, we also need our friends and colleagues to fill our lives.

It's up to you whether your partnerships are a disaster, a battle, and a competition, or whether you use your partnerships to enrich and enhance your life and that of others. The best protection against stress in relationships is the ability to live in harmony with the world around you.

The fear of failure and the fear of loss are serious stress factors, but worrying about your finances, your health, and about those you love can be a heavy burden and consume a tremendous amount of energy, causing serious damage as the result of the stress.

To banish unnecessary stress factors from your life or keep them to a minimum, you should give your fears a reality check. Once you've done that, ask yourself if you have any influence on the situation you fear.

For example, if you're afraid it will rain the day after tomorrow, when you want to have a birthday party outdoors, it may be a genuine worry, though you could always put up a tent. But, if you give in to the fear of a rainy day and feel powerless, you will produce stress hormones.

We build up many worries and fears in our mind, making them bigger and heavier by repeatedly thinking about them. After something happens, how often have you said to yourself that it wasn't half as bad as you feared?

The ability to control our thoughts and the questions we ask ourselves is fundamental to the way we deal with stress. If you keep asking yourself what could go wrong, or what terrible thing might happen, you will live in constant fear. But if you ask yourself, "What is the best way to deal with a certain situation when I come face to face with it?" your fear and a feeling of being at someone else's mercy disappear.

Fear has never been a method of prevention. In fact, just the opposite is true since fear attracts the negative because we're focusing on what we don't want. It's the reason that a driver on a slippery country road starts skidding when they focus on the only tree that grows there and then runs into it.

Each time a fear pops up, put it through a screening process and see if there's a legitimate reason to be afraid or worried. Ask yourself if you can influence the outcome. Determine how you can best prepare yourself and what you could do if the worst happened. When you have prepared yourself with a potential solution, let go of the fear. Other than being prepared and having a plan, there's nothing you can do.

Everything we build up in our mind strives for a solution, because it transmits a direct message to our nervous system. The main problem of futuristic fears is caused by experiencing it over and over again in your mind, and always with a negative ending. Simply thinking negative thoughts will rob the subconscious of the same amount of energy it would use if the event happened in reality!

How the pictures are formed in your mind, light or dark, close up or far away, threatening or pleasant, depends completely on you. If a negative image pops into your mind, you can change it immediately into a pleasant one by imagining it with the best possible solution in that situation.

If you see yourself as a loser in a certain conflict, you will act like a loser when a situation occurs, and it will leave you with a feeling of helplessness. On the other hand, if you mentally prepare yourself for the desired results, you will feel more in control and your self-confidence will grow.

Of course, it's important to reduce the physical dangers that cause stress; those that are the result of overwork, malnutrition, lack of sleep, not enough time for hobbies, etc. Those are the easiest to correct, so start now.

I want to warn you against the dangers of ignoring and suppressing the stress signals of your body. These signals must be caught and corrected or worked through so that stress can be released and avoided in the future. It should never be repressed, because that would lead to more stress and eventually health problems.

The Many "Little Things"

It's amazing how seemingly little things in our everyday life contribute to the increase or decrease of our stress level.

As you've noticed, I don't speak of stress or deal with it in a traditional way. Rather, I want to show you what experiences cause you to enjoy or suffer in your life. True stress reduction can only take place when you become aware that stress is learned behavior. Stress depends completely on the way you evaluate a situation, on your inner representation and your mental communication.

Don't search for large stress factors or stressful life situations because there are actually very few extremely dangerous or life-threatening situations. Instead, it is the little things that keep piling up and cause lasting damage to our energy levels, our ability to achieve, our quality of life and our health.

Stress: Introduction —Definition

The term "stress" is, in my opinion, one of the most misinterpreted concepts. The word stress has become a fashionable catchphrase covering a multitude of sins. We can hide behind it when we no longer want to finish a project at a certain time, or we can use it as an excuse for failures and mistakes. We can resort to it, and fool ourselves, when we are in a situation we can't handle. The concept of stress is frequently used as an excuse in explanations.

What is stress? Stress is a continuous strain that exceeds the limits of our ability. Because too many projects may demand our attention and concentration at the same time, we can't finish even one task satisfactorily. The brain shuts down as a reaction to a stimulus or overwhelming demand, which could be life-threatening. By shutting down certain areas of the brain, we are forced to regenerate ourselves or be left with only enough energy to concentrate on the most necessary task at hand.

Stress develops when we use our energy ineffectively, when we look at what is behind us, or when we concentrate too strongly on problems instead of solutions. Typical stress symptoms arise from helplessness caused by poor thinking, or when we are in a situation where it becomes almost impossible to act. People who concentrate on a mountain of problems instead of solutions are afraid that they can't cope, and tension is the logical result. Stress is nothing but a shortage of energy, resulting from mental, physical and/or emotional failure.

If we don't have enough energy or lack the opportunity to perform a task as needed, yet we forge ahead with sheer willpower, the troubles from which our brain tried to spare us will soon rise to the surface. We hurt our bodies and may damage our energy conservation to such an extreme that we cannot completely recuperate.

To fight stress successfully or prevent it, we must understand that we create what we call stress. We do this to ourselves. All of those stress symptoms will only surface when we over tax our emotional and physical endurance.

Strain and pressure are not negative or dangerous. They often force us to develop ourselves and remind us of those things that should have been accomplished long ago. Lasting pressure and too great a demand on our resources causes lasting damage to our nervous system, our energy or our body.

You can rub your hand against the sharp edge of a table without any harm, but if you do it for an hour you will probably hurt yourself. If you keep doing it for several hours you may do irreparable damage.

You will find that short-term strains do no recognizable damage. It's stress over long periods that will lead to serious damage. If we stay with the above example, imagine that you rubbed your hand along the edge of the table fifteen times, lifted your hand for a half minute to restore itself, and then did it again, you would conclude that you could keep it up for a whole day or even longer without hurting yourself at all, thanks to a phase of restoration. The same is true with the stress in your life. If you tackle projects, take time out to relax, and then get back to it, you'll have more energy, better focus, and will ultimately complete the task.

We use the catchall word "stress" so frequently, intentionally or not, because it's hard to define and evaluate. The scientific divisions in Eu-stress and Dis-stress, positive and negative stress, don't make sense, in my opinion, because positive stress, like joy and happiness, can lead to a heart-attack just like sadness, fear or anger. When I speak of negative stress or dis-stress in this program, to make things easier I'll exclusively mean dis-stress. And when I speak of the absence of stress, I mean a healthy attitude toward stress. Life is stressful and there's no way to get around it, but how you act and react are key to your overall health.

To work as well as possible with the IBMS™ program, you must recognize the need to develop a new definition for the word stress. You need a clear understanding of what you are facing so that you can lessen the troubles stress causes. The better you understand the problems you must solve, the easier it will be to develop solutions. What is traditionally considered to be stress, is simply an artificially created concept that doesn't really exist.

Assuming Control

Helplessness, fear, depression, poor self-esteem, ruined relationships, etc. are phenomenons which occur when we are not using our natural, emotional and physical assets. Your feelings, energy level and behavior influence everything you will achieve in your life. You must recognize that nobody else can overcome your problems for you. Hard work is the only path between theory and practical application. Life does not change, no matter how much you know or have learned. Only action and the application of this information will determine the direction your life will take.

I have learned that positive thinking is nothing but the prerequisite for positive action. Positive thinking alone will not change your life in a wonderful and mysterious way. Only positive action changes your life. If you don't act, others will. When you don't decide, others will do it for you. When you don't give your life direction, others will direct you.

Your life can be *your* life in the truest sense of the word, but only when you are willing to take responsibility and control, and when you are no longer willing to leave it up to fate. It will only be your life when you are no longer willing to let others decide how you are supposed to feel at a certain time. When you no longer let others influence your behavior and thinking in a negative way, when you stop hiding behind excuses, and when you are totally willing to accept responsibility and control, then your life will truly be your own.

You will be able to reach happiness, success, harmony, peace, wholesome relationships, and all the wonderful things you desire, only when you act for yourself and make clear, concrete decisions, develop concise strategies with goal oriented plans and work in a flexible manner.

We all carry infinite wishes, dreams and needs within us. It's up to you to make it happen.

The First Project

I would like you to think back on a time in the past when you decided on your profession.

Exercise:

Start creating a personal success journal. Write down your thoughts, reasons, wishes and dreams, and the pictures you had in your mind of what your life would be like. Write it down with as much detail as possible, including all positive thoughts, wishes and feelings you had at that time.

Then describe all the obstacles, hurdles and difficulties you had to overcome along the way. Describe all the mental and emotional lows, the demands and the personal crises you have overcome. Even if you aren't exactly where you'd like to be in life, you still had to overcome much adversity to be where you are today. You are a winner and can be even more successful.

Do not allow the opinions of other people influence you!

I'll say it again; do not be discouraged by opinionated, offensive remarks, or by pressure from other persons. Don't let anyone judge you unfairly or diminish the opinion you have of yourself by reacting to gossip. The sad truth is, people are always looking to blame someone for the mistakes they've made in business, politics, and their personal lives. They search for victims who can't defend themselves.

Exercise:

Now write into your personal success journal why you are proud of your ability to help others, why you are proud of your achievements, and why you are proud of your current job. Again, even if the job or life you have right now isn't your dream, you have already succeeded in so many ways.

By paying attention to the positive things you do have and have done in life, you'll be much more able to focus on the positive things for your future and ultimately create the life of your dreams.

A First Impression

Headaches, difficulties with concentration, vision problems, stomach and intestinal ulcers, gallstones, heart and circulatory troubles, even heart attacks and strokes are all typical results of stress.

All those physical and psychosomatic symptoms are the result of continuous emotional and physical demands. Eventually they will take a catastrophic turn if the negative flow of energy and the circumstances that led to those conflicts don't change.

Problems with concentration, depression and fear, as well as tiredness and apathy can also be symptoms of stress. They result, as you have seen before, from a continuous overload and not taking enough time for recuperation.

If you don't remove the causes that lead to the stressful situations then you can't avoid the symptoms. When people are under stress they often turn to "stress reduction" techniques such as meditation or yoga, but these are only temporary solutions and actually suppress their feelings. It's like leaving a splinter in a wound and putting a bandage on it so we can't see it. The splinter is still there and we can't expect the wound to heal.

Meditation and yoga are typical examples of fighting the symptoms. In order to bring your level of stress to a normal and healthy level so that you don't suffer from negative side effects, you must learn to remove the causes. You have to remove the splinter from your soul, your behavior and your body, because the splinter represents your intellectual and physical failure.

In my research and therapy sessions I have often witnessed the disappearance of so-called illnesses and symptoms caused by stress, such as stomach and intestinal ulcers, migraines, and lack of concentration or insomnia, when people learn to cope with their lives. I'm not saying that those people learned to *deal with stress*, which would be absurd. We must not learn to cope with negative symptoms or with illnesses. Instead, we must learn to organize and shape our lives so that we can avoid areas of conflict.

If you're in an area of conflict, you must learn to organize your life. Be sure your internal communication is healthy and solution-oriented, and use this information to eliminate the cause. I want to emphasize it once more: In no way should you allow yourself to think that you can cope with stress, reduce your stress, or to accept stress as a natural part of your life.

You should strive for a healthy, harmonious, happy and energetic existence. You should never reconcile yourself with limitations in your life. As soon as you accept stress, or stress symptoms, as a natural part of being human, you will never produce lasting positive changes in your life. Whatever you achieve in life, and your quality of life in general, depends on you.

The Danger of Self-Deception

One of the greatest obstacles to the removal of stress symptoms is self-deception. It's often meant well and executed with deliberate effort without conscious acknowledgment. Examples of these self-help techniques to break through this evil circle of stress development are yoga, self-hypnosis, meditation, breath therapy and others. This is like putting the horse behind the carriage. The people participating in these self-help modalities are never aware that they will not achieve the desired results.

For example, yoga is a good and effective way to relax, increase energy and build strength, but it does not remove the causes that lead to the symptoms of stress. In this way, only one stress symptom is treated. We are not really aware that we should look into our own emotional situation or physical behavior for the cause of the stomach ulcer, headache, tension, insomnia, etc.

A poor division of our time, too many tasks within a certain time frame, difficulty in making decisions and poor self-esteem are all frequent causes of these symptoms. We should fight and remove the causes, not just the symptoms.

There are even people who learn several methods of relaxation and regeneration at the same time, and practice them diligently without getting the desired results. They give their subconscious the message that they are doing something against unwanted stress symptoms and they inevitably convince themselves that, although they suffer small setbacks, they are doing everything possible to remove the stress symptoms.

The only effective way to produce desired, lasting results, is by deciding to use all of our emotional and physical vitality to work until we have reached them. Once we have achieved this result, we should hang on to our goal and expand on it.

If we do not pay attention to emotional and physical reactions to stress we take the first step in poor conditioning and programming. Everything we do regularly, whether it is good or bad, is fixed in our nervous system, stored by our brain, and conditioned in our mind.

The brain can only play the program that has been installed; your reactions and your emotional and physical behavior. Many times it's poor behavior that we program into our subconscious and then it's conditioned to be continuously repeated. This poor behavior becomes a natural part of our life, the model for our behavior. It bothers us initially, and we wonder whether it needs changing, but after a while it becomes habit. The poor behavior is no longer identified and therefore no longer confronted.

Dissatisfaction, inner unrest, anxiety, tension and all types of pain are common symptoms, cries for help, from our subconscious, yet the signals are ignored and nothing is done to correct them.

Exercise:

1. Write down all your failures and unwanted behavior, whether it is emotional or physical. You must be willing to identify every problem, to really search, recognize and accept areas of conflict. Once recognized, you must make clear decisions to change them and develop plans and strategies to change them into desired behavior that increases your energy.

2. Define those situations in your life in which you act differently from the way you want to behave, the type of behavior that you later regret. You may have screamed at your spouse or children because you were overworked, or you may have been irritated with colleagues or clients in a way that was out of character.

3. Set this book down and do the exercise so you will become aware of those incidents. Think about the situations in which you behaved differently from the way you wanted. Because you are not just what you do, and would of course like to become a positive person so you can create a pleasant life, you must work on your self-confidence, self-esteem and self-respect.

To improve the quality of our life, our behavior must first fit our personality.

Never forget: Stress does not come from the outside. Stress is not a virus, or an illness, or a pitfall; we produce the stress ourselves with faulty emotional and physical behavior. The releasing of stress starts with responsibility, by admitting, "I am not perfect, I behave incorrectly, but I can and will change my behavior!"

In my seminars and workshops I often run into serious obstacles that are standing between people and the solution of their problems. The result is that those people can't reach their full potential because they are not willing to admit they aren't perfect. But who wants to be merely average? I don't, and you probably don't want to either. And because we don't want to become robots or turn into zombies, we must recognize that we are not perfect. So, we have a great task, the striving for excellence, ahead of us.

We must recognize that great opportunities lie within our imperfections. It's on this almost blank canvas of our life that we have the opportunity to fill with the colors and designs we so desire. Great opportunity lies in the knowledge that everyone is in charge of their own life.

Whenever life doesn't go your way and you feel you're a victim of fate, remember that it's just the opposite: Your life is a mirror of your thinking and behavior.

Prevention is Better Than Therapy

We are so concerned with managing our stress today that 87% of all people are frequently suffering from stress symptoms. We are fighting stress or coping with the results of stress. Instead, we should be searching for the causes and change our emotional and physical behavior, that way we can avoid the symptoms of stress.

Nothing is more important than preparing ourselves for the tasks and aggravations of life so that we can properly handle the situations that will or may arise. Stress prevention starts with the recognition that stress is caused by our own behavior.

Whether you experience stress or not depends on the pictures in your head, and on the manner you let them occupy your mind. It depends on the way you think and on how you make use of your breathing, posture, movements, and speech. Every reaction is the result of our internal and external communication.

If you speak in your mind in a tired and weary voice: "I can't do it. It's too hard. I can't take it anymore," or if you say with confidence: "I can do this! I'll work hard and do it as well as I can," it will make a great difference. If you speak in your mind with a clear, strong and goal oriented voice, it will greatly affect your emotional and physical reaction, and your ultimate success.

Your train of thought affects your energy and level of stress significantly. Whether you focus on the many problems and difficulties you must overcome, or worry about the many projects that are still waiting for your attention, your focus will direct your thought processes and ultimately your mood and behavior.

If you focus on solving the problems that are facing you and do not waste time on obstacles, problems and demands, your life will be filled with progress and success. You will be looking forward to the future instead of being afraid.

Successful events are very important in the development of your self-esteem and self-confidence, fostering energy, strength and vitality. With this strength you can produce better, quicker and more effective results.

If you focus on problems, then problems will determine your life, your thinking and your behavior. If you focus on solutions, then solutions and progress will fill your life.

You must learn to take control of your thoughts, and of the images, sounds and feelings you produce in your mind, because those factors determine your behavior. It is the only way to enjoy a life without negative symptoms of stress.

Health and a Stress-Free Living Begin In the Mind

One of the most basic elements of health and harmony is often overlooked. People are inclined to focus on symptoms, on illness and pain, or on emotional and physical limits, because they refuse to concentrate on the causes that are responsible for the damage and illness—the causes resulting from stress.

Every physical or emotional illness is due to a poor belief or value system, negative thinking, and uncontrolled emotional conditions like escalating or uncontrolled fear, depression or misdirected focus.

Your focus will determine your life. If you concentrate on health, you will become healthy. If you focus on illness, you will become sick. If you focus on problems and obstacles instead of on solutions, you will suffer from stress symptoms. You can object and say that poor physical behavior, bad nutrition, faulty breathing and lack of exercise cause illness. That is quite true, because faulty breathing, bad nutrition and lack of exercise are the results of a poor mentality. For example, if you let fear control your life, you will suffer from anxiety and physical tension. This will result in poor circulation and a shortage of oxygen and medical complications. If you focus on problems instead of solutions, you will soon detect a considerable shortage of energy. You will not have enough energy for your emotional and physical need, and this will cause stress.

These and many other basic elements of poor emotional behavior determine the causes of illness and deterioration of your health. If you don't start separating the causes and the symptoms of an illness and fight the symptoms without removing the cause, we don't remove the splinter before we put on a band-aid on the wound. We don't solve the problem and the splinter goes deeper and the situation gets worse.

There are many sensible and natural ways to regain your health and avoid stress, but I believe that you must get to the root to remove a problem from your life. This includes the recognition that you are responsible for your own health. The more we try to avoid this responsibility, the more obvious the symptoms become, forcing us to do something—either we do something or we suffer the consequences.

Practical experience made me recognize that help does not come from outside. The only true help is self-help. The only person who can help a sick person is the patient himself. The only person who can reduce your level of stress is you.

Following good advice such as eating nutritious foods, good breathing and practicing all other basic requirements play an important role, but you need to take responsibility for your health and the quality of your life. You should do everything that's possible and necessary to become healthy and stay healthy; otherwise you will never enjoy perfect health.

The development of my IBMS™ program came from the recognition of his fact. It is a concept that gives every person directions to activate and stimulate their own personal self-healing ability for regeneration and enjoy perfect health all through life.

I now have the luxury to say openly and honestly that my ideas have produced results that nobody can overlook or neglect. I'm convinced that there is a solution for every problem, an answer for every question. We must just become aware and accept our challenges and do everything necessary to realize the results we want.

The power of the mind is absolutely limitless. You must only start believing in yourself so that you can activate and use the strength of your subconscious. In that way you can make your life the masterpiece it deserves to be.

The Hidden Causes of Stress Symptoms

Stress is usually produced in areas where we least suspect it. We are only too willing to believe that stressful situations are burdens, crisis situations, or dilemmas in our everyday work. We tend to overlook that stress symptoms result from loss of energy. We may actually be in a stressful situation, or simply worrying about everything that could go wrong.

Nothing that happens in our life, influences our thinking, feelings, behavior and energy. Instead, we are influenced by our emotional and physical reaction to what happens. Whether we feel at the mercy of a situation, or think we can do something about a situation, both will influence our emotional condition considerably and as a result our energy level and our ability to function.

When we are in a crisis situation, we are more willing to give in. We don't bother to look for a solution when we stare at all the obstacles and problems. Instead, we need to concentrate on our ability to deal with the task before us as soon as possible and as efficiently as possible.

Our overall view, the images we have created in our mind, will determine our feelings and behavior. The mental pictures of a person or situation we carry in our mind determine our feelings and therefore our behavior.

Your behavior will be quite different when you picture yourself as intellectually superior and in control of the situation. The pictures in your head are responsible for the way you behave, because you're continuously "living" it in your mind's eye. You program your brain and nervous system to react exactly as you have already reacted in the past. For instance, you will establish a pattern of fear and failure in your nervous system if you experience over and over again fear and failure in your mind.

As I discussed before, your subconscious can't differentiate between an actual experience and an image you create in your mind. It is also the reason why that when you tell a friend about a joyful experience from your past you are quickly in the same positive emotional state you were in when it happened. Your subconscious experiences the story as if it was really happening and triggers all the reactions in your mind and body that were a part of the original event.

This also happens when you remember a negative, sad, frustrating or depressing memory. You will quickly become as sad, frustrated, or depressed as before. Many people cause themselves unneeded stress and loss of energy because they relive negative experiences and fears over and over again.

The Realization and Acceptance of Facts

Just as long as an alcoholic cannot overcome his or her drinking problem if they don't admit to themselves that they are an alcoholic, so you will not be able to reduce the stress level and eliminate the stress symptoms in your life if you do not recognize and accept them. Denial often stands in our way when we have to deal with conflicts, because it is difficult to admit that our emotional or physical behavior can hurt others as well as us. It is difficult to admit that our life is not perfect and not quite the way we would like it to be.

Human weaknesses and failures are a natural part of life. You must become big enough to accept your weaknesses so you are ready to play your part and can work on your mission in life.

The greatest challenge we face when we want to take control of our life and determine our fate is the willingness to admit and define the source of our errors. Misleading others, self-deceit and the repression and denial of conflicts cost a lot of energy and causes a lot of stress.

Exercise:

I want you to define every situation in your life in which you do not behave as you would like or think is proper. Then write down in your success journal how you really want to behave. Read this often, especially if you're going to face the situation again, so you'll firmly have embedded in your mind the way you would truly like to act and react.

Fear as a Stress Factor

At this point I would like to discuss fear with you and how you can overcome it. I have seen in my work how often fear causes stress. One of the greatest causes of stress is the fear of success. This fear prevents many people from getting ahead. Because of this, they don't even try to become successful and reach their full potential.

People with a fear of success subconsciously connect negative side effects like longer working hours, greater expectations and pressure to perform with success. Success can also lead to the disruption of and loss of relationships with friends or colleagues. Why? Because when our knowledge and success increases, personal growth takes place and people who do not experience the same cycle of maturation may fade into the distance.

Fear of success can have many causes, so you must define the disadvantages you connect with success. Once you become conscious of why you fear success you can begin to overcome them.

Exercise:

1. What are the disadvantages of success?
2. How could your life be negatively affected by success?

The fear of negative developments is far greater than the fear of positive results, but every form of fear is the result of internal communication. They are always a result of learned behavior patterns. Fears emerge when we are afraid of losing something. But when we give our fears a good look, we will find that no more than 1% of them become reality.

We must start by consciously accepting the full responsibility of our inner communication. We must recognize that all automatic processes have been installed by regular repetition and that it is possible to extinguish all the programs we recognize as damaging, and to replace them with new, desirable programs.

If you no longer want your energy levels, your stress levels, your vitality and your ability to work, to depend on seemingly uncontrollable causes, you must follow this program for yourself and your personal success.

We can't make permanent and positive improvements in our lives through other people or other situations. If you do not learn to get along with yourself, you will never learn to produce the permanent results you desire and you will not come close to reaching your true potential in life.

Begin installing new patterns of behavior by doing every exercise in this book to the best of your ability. Make sure that your life reaches a new level of realization so that you improve the quality of your results little-by-little each and every day.

Exercise:

1. Write down every fear you've had in the last few days—small fears, large fears, even fears you had only once, and those that you had repeatedly. How did these fears come about? Did something happen that triggered the fear?

2. Now write down all the fears you regularly think about, but that have not come into being or have not actually changed anything in your life.

When you are finished with your exercise you will recognize that most of those fears proved to be untrue or appeared only as figments of your imagination.

From now on be aware that fear does not prevent anything and does not lead to positive improvements. In fact, it is just the opposite. If you allow those negative images in your mind to play out over and over again, they may lead to self-fulfilling prophecies. If you keep focusing on negative developments or bad endings you program your nervous system for exactly what you do not want to happen.

From now on, concentrate on reality. Do not work with hypothetical, imaginary thoughts or fabricated mental fear. Naturally, you must be prepared for difficult situations in life, so that you can react with evasive actions or solutions when they appear. This means that you must develop a solution oriented, goal directed way of thinking and that you must change behavior patterns in your nervous system, so you can respond in an appropriate manner to certain dangers when a crisis arrives. You must focus on solutions and this will eliminate your fears.

If you focus on solutions and avoid thoughts of fear and negative endings, you increase self-esteem and self-confidence. And, because you have programmed solution oriented behavior in your subconscious, you will behave effectively in any crisis situation.

The Basics

The only way you can avoid stress and cope in a way that will not lead to negative stress symptoms is by using your ability to identify those situations that lead to negative stress. How, why and in which way do you experience those stressful situations? From this information you can develop your personal anti-stress program.

Even in those situations that are the most dangerous or are filled with risks, it should not bring you negative stress, because stress is basically the learned behavior that robs you of energy, strength and the ability to concentrate. You cannot function with a clear head and are unable to use the skills you possess with negative stress in your life.

Learn to see problems as challenges, as opportunities for growth. It will change your dis-stress levels dramatically when you learn to break through those old programs. Instead of your old patterns, imagine yourself as part of a solution, with the ability to make good decisions. The actions of your internal representation and communication determine whether you experience negative stress or not, whether you will be able to turn dis-stress situations into eu-stress situations for yourself and others.

You are the only one who can, through effective and optimal self-communication, turn the most difficult life challenges into motivating eu-stress situations. Whether stress situations are unhealthy and make you sick, or whether they are stimulating and encouraging, depends exclusively on your personal and individual approach to so-called stress situations.

You know already that stressful situations and lasting stress can lead to serious illness or put you at risk of becoming ill. Therefore, you should take stress reduction, avoidance of stress, and overcoming stress as serious as possible.

Only when you have learned to identify typical stress situations and begin to meet them appropriately with mental and physical self-programming and conditioning will you avoid lack of energy and the risks of illness.

I completely disagree with the widespread opinion that stress, especially the stress resulting from work, is caused by our jobs. Only those who dislike their work, don't organize their workday, and are not in charge of themselves, can fall apart from work or literally be killed by their job.

If you give your profession everything you have and do everything possible to have an optimal, harmonious career, and when you turn your job into a calling or a hobby, the statement that work causes stress will make no sense.

Of course, many different factors contribute to our stress, such as the demands of our private life, social duties, financial demands, etc. But it still depends on you. Use what you learn in this book as well as you can and react with problem solving solutions and strategies instead of complaining and staring at a mountain of problems.

If you keep looking back and using empty phrases like, "If I only had done this or that," then you will soon realize that the stress is not caused by certain situations but by the value you put on them. If you focus on the problems, your life will become steadily worse; if you focus on solutions, the quality of your life will steadily improve.

Because people spend the greater part of their lives with their careers, most stress is considered professional stress. But as you already recognize, stress is the result of many small errors in negative mental communication, finally leading to an overload, and causing the so-called symptoms of stress.

The dangerous feeling of being crushed by work leaves a sensation of being at the mercy of our job and of being a prisoner. This seemingly inescapable situation has such a negative effect on self-confidence and self-esteem that the person can no longer solve their problems. Instead of coping with the challenges through goal-oriented action and focus, the person mentally flees, which inevitably leads to a nervous breakdown.

It's not easy to take control over one's life and isn't an overnight quick-fix. You have to keep working on it. But the price is worth the effort. There is nothing more wonderful then to assure yourself now and in the future of a satisfied, healthy and successful life.

I know from practical experience that relationships with our partners as well as with our children can cause serious strains in our lives. Certain personality quirks and habits of our relatives, friends and acquaintances can drive us up the wall, along with our own feelings of being hemmed in by personal duties and pressures.

Without talking to others about what annoys you, don't point fingers at them. We should understand that everyone is entitled to his peculiarities and we have our own as well. We must learn to accept that every person should live the life that they think is right for them, just as we expect that others accept us the way we are.

The only person who can limit you and put you under pressure is you because at a certain point you have the opportunity to decide to do something, not to do something, or to do it differently.

Financial worries are another big fear people face which often leads to loss of energy and strength, making us ill or paralyzing our ability to function. We must decide whether the fear over our finances is rational or not. Are there real problems or are we just dwelling on fears of the future?

Fabricated fears of the future can only be overcome with preparation. There's no way you can solve future problems now, so the only thing you can do is prepare a solution in advance for if and when the problem actually occurs.

Do yourself a favor and stop creating hypothetical problems. These so-called looming disasters only exist in your mind and cannot be solved, simply because they do not exist! Learn to react to stress and crisis situations only when they are acute, or when you are certain that they will become acute.

When we face acute financial worries we can only look for new or better sources of income, get our finances in order and overcome those problems. To whine, complain or worry, without searching for solutions and strategies to overcome our difficulties, will lead to real stress.

You must also learn to deal with uncomfortable social situations. To be afraid and either avoid or fight your way through those situations will cause endless stress. For instance, if you must give a talk and are afraid of speaking in public, train yourself by giving the speech in your mind, or practicing in front of a mirror, several times a day. Pretend you have a real audience and condition your behavior in your subconscious as deliberate, calm and confident. There are many outstanding classes that teach public speaking, and we also offer such goal oriented classes.

Don't dwell on the negative judgment of other people because those hypothetical fears can cause serious dis-stress.

If people in your close social circle cause you stress on a regular basis, tell them what they are doing that bothers you and you will see that those stressful dilemmas can be solved with an open approach.

We all know that anxiety, nervousness, irritability, insomnia, muscle cramps, headaches and dizziness can be symptoms of stress. We also know that this type of stress reaction can have a catastrophic influence on the quality of our health and our ability to function. It's very important to learn what triggers your individual stress, the risks involved and how to prevent them. In other words, ask yourself what the best way is to deal with the problems that cause those symptoms.

Stress is frequently discussed in negative terms because people seldom realize that positive stress can enhance our achievements and promotes our well-being; this is called eu-stress. This achievement-promoting stress can be generated by a positive experience as well as by the prospect of leaving the next day for a wonderful vacation.

Many times, stress can be dissolved through recreation, but if we hang on for dear life it may turn into lasting stress and lead to a mental or physical breakdown. You must learn to catch dis-stress, caused by inner tension, so that it won't damage your nervous system. If you have conditioned yourself to keep pushing without taking time for regeneration, it will become difficult to find your way back to normal behavior.

What we must learn is to provide ourselves with as many eu-stress reactions as possible. The easiest way you can do this is by paying attention to the terrific work you have done, no matter how small the job, and enjoy it with pride. Learn to turn small successes into great occasions of eu-stress, and your energy capacity will respond with abundance.

Eu-stress is very stimulating, is healthy and essential in our lives. Eu-stress determines the degree of our happiness and the intensity of the quality of our lives. Be certain that you take enough time for recreation, get enough oxygen, nutrition and exercise. Never forget that you are working to live and not living to work.

You must learn to stop agonizing because only solution-oriented thinking produces eu-stress, gives positive results, and prevents negative stress reactions. The longer a person focuses on problems instead of solutions, the greater their weaknesses and helplessness become. And, the longer inappropriate reactions or feelings of weakness and inadequacy last, the greater the risk will be that they become the final result. If we do not take enough time for regeneration, excessive dis-stress could lead to a feeling of impotence, and the results might very well be disastrous.

In my work I have often observed that many stomach and intestinal ulcers, digestive problems and troubles with concentration are nothing but the result of lasting dis-stress. While only a physician can make the correct diagnosis, you should nevertheless pay attention to your own physical and emotional reactions to stressful situations. If you plan to do only as much work as you can do in a day and leave twenty-percent of your time for unexpected jobs, you will spare yourself from many dis-stress reactions and will enjoy your work more.

Don't focus on problems of the past that you can no longer do anything about; nor on worries of the future. You know from experience that the future can be much different than the negative one you now predict.

Learn To Understand Yourself Better

Try not to do several jobs at the same time. Instead, focus your attention on the solution of the work at hand. The brain is not able to focus on two things at the same time and you will inevitably cause unnecessary stress as a result of failures.

If you are bothered by the behavior of your colleagues, talk about it and find out the reason. Get to know your co-workers and find out what they think about you. Be willing to accept their constructive criticism.

Get your finances in order to avoid getting into a poor financial strait. If you are already into trouble, develop solutions and strategies to end the conflict.

Exercise:

Take time right now to write down your thoughts, plans and goals. By putting them down on paper you give your subconscious the information and control over what takes place and your feeling of helplessness and dis-stress will disappear. You can be as detailed as you'd like or just write down a basic outline of what you'd like to achieve over the next few days, weeks, months, or even years.

Prepare yourself mentally to accept new and unknown situations and to react calmly with composure. Don't be frightened or angry when something completely strange or new happens unexpectedly. Take the time to think it through and then react with mental clarity and inner composure.

If someone disturbs your peace or concentration while you are working, point it out to them and learn to develop a cooperative way of helping and supporting each other. So that other people may understand you better and to avoid unnecessary conflicts and stressful reactions, you should give the necessary information to the relevant person. In that way you can avoid many unneeded situations of conflict. In other words, talk to the person you need to talk to and avoid talking behind someone's back.

In turn, we must learn and accept that we make mistakes and that criticism of our work can be justified. It is not a personal denial when you accept to at least listen to someone else's information, proposals or opinions and to give their side some thought.

Also, others may not always appreciate your career and life successes, but don't become irritated and let it cause you stress. You must learn to do things for yourself, for your own sake, and for the enrichment and quality of your own life. You must stop leaning on the praise of others.

Pressure caused by time is a huge stress factor and is usually of our own making. You must simply learn to say no to a job that can't be done within a certain time frame. You must learn to delegate and to practice time management.

Problems that develop from contact with other people, superiors, colleagues and friends can also lead to considerable stress. We must therefore start with ourselves. We need to teach ourselves as many excellent communication skills as possible, especially skills that avoid areas of conflict. Once learned, this knowledge and ability remove stress-causing problems forever.

If you feel overworked, remember that you're the one responsible. Only you can require more of yourself than you can do. All you can do is the very best in response to the demands of others and of the world around you. No matter what is required, all you can do is your very best.

It is also important to give yourself sufficient space and time for personal development and for the realization of your wishes, dreams and hobbies. If you give your subconscious enough information with the help of eu-stress situations, it will sense the connection between your health, vitality and strength with your creativity and regulate your supply of energy.

It is just as important that you enjoy your free time so that you can produce eu-stress situations, have some fun and pleasure. Don't use your spare time for the solving of conflicts or other job-related problems.

Observe which work leads to success and brings you closer to your goals, and watch what behavior stands in your way. Only by observing your own results can you learn how you quickly and gradually realize your goals, dreams and wishes.

Don't build castles in the sky and don't ignore dangerous situations. Be prepared. As mentioned before, concentrate only ten-percent of your time and strength on thinking of the problem and ninety-percent on the solution.

If you try to get along with everybody, you become like a leaf in the wind, blowing back and forth and somewhere you will lose control over yourself and your life. Learn to find people in your life with whom you can be yourself and who correspond with your true personality, so you do not have to pretend. Keeping up a fake idealistic image is, in my view, one of the most dangerous stress factors of all. Behaving differently from your personal inclination, just to please others or to get along with them will cause you to lose your own identity.

Never read or do work in bed. Let your time in bed be a time of relaxation and regeneration. Don't worry about problems before falling asleep. So many people lay awake at night going over their troubles, chores they need to do the next day, or worry about things that may or may not happen in the future. Just allow yourself to relax and enjoy your sleep. Even if you do have some problems, they'll be there the following day. You can't do anything about them while in bed, but if you get a night of restful sleep you'll be much more able to tackle your troubles with better focus and more energy.

It can be very useful if you air your frustrations rather than holding them in. You could simply go into the woods and scream at the top of your voice, or even scream into your pillow. Studies show that twice as many men die from stress reactions than women, because women have learned to communicate their stress. They communicate their feelings and release the pressure. Men, on the other hand, have been trained to behave like "men." They are not allowed to cry or show their feelings. They must swallow their irritation and hold in their negative energy—and they're literally being killed in the process.

Although we are never really helpless, the feeling of helplessness causes great problems for many people. In the study of the philosophy of success, we have many examples of people who found a way, even when a situation seemed hopeless. They found a way to change their lives in a positive way and even made a profit. Nobody is really helpless unless they believe they are.

As soon as possible, you should remove those unpleasant situations that inevitably tie up your thinking and concentration so that you can avoid their emotional or physical burden. If you get a feeling that you are not either physically or emotionally at 100%, you must look for the reason and eliminate the cause permanently.

People who try to be perfectionists put themselves under stress because none of us can produce better results than all other people all of the time. When we realize that we can't be the best every time, we learn to do the best job possible with the tools and knowledge available to us at the time.

When you feel that other people are rejecting you, don't react; just realize that not everybody will like you. After all, you don't like everybody either. Everybody has the right to reject or dislike somebody.

I have learned from practical experience that it is important to say no if you want to avoid stress. If you repeatedly do something you would rather not do, just to please others, it will lead to double stress. First, you are annoyed because you are doing something you don't want to do, and secondly, you are angry that you are doing it at all.

Many people feel needlessly guilty when they take a day off from work. This leads frequently to an unbelievable build up of dis-stress. If you feel the need to do absolutely nothing, your subconscious is giving you a signal. It's telling you, "I need some rest." Perhaps your body needs all the energy available to help fight off an illness or a virus, something you yourself are not yet aware off. Many times, your brain may need some interruption from work so it's more able to retain information and focus on tasks.

At the conclusion of this chapter I want to ask you to please stay away from tranquilizers and energy pills. Become aware of the real value of your body, your life, your true personality, your abilities, your capacity for work, and know yourself as a loving, intelligent human being. Decide that you are too important to overexert or even destroy your body unnecessarily. Decide to pay more attention to the signals and messages of your body and mind, listen to your intuition and respond to its needs.

There Is Always a Solution

There is an answer for every question and a solution for every problem. We must just be willing to do the necessary work and have the determination to persevere until we have completely reached and realized our goal.

As mentioned before, one of the worst stress factors plaguing more than 80% of all people regularly is the fear of failing. In the psychology of success we believe there is no such thing as failure, there are only results. You either get what you wanted or you don't. If you have not produced the result you wished, you will learn from the result you achieved. You can then modify your approach, start over and work until you reach the goal you desired.

If you think and act according to this solution-oriented point of view, you will conclude that your life is free of failure. You suffer from failure only when you give up and don't even try to solve a problem or finish a job.

Such needless fears for not finishing a project are usually quite unnecessary and foolish emotional fabrications. Concentrate exclusively on what you want to achieve and look for solutions and strategies that need your attention so that in the end you will reach your goal.

Create in your mind only pictures of success, triumphs and the work it demands.

To react negatively to criticism is usually a sign of poor self-esteem. Every person who respects themselves, and recognizes their own value and ability, welcomes constructive criticism so that they can give it some thought and improve themselves. They know that they can use it to grow, or reject it if it is wrong.

Only people who have lost their self-esteem and self-confidence feel personally insulted, assaulted or hurt and react in the same vein with anger, aggression or by hitting back. Cooperative, solution oriented action, so that everyone can get the best results, often includes constructive criticism.

Envy among colleagues, yes, even hostility, is simply a part of life. To react negatively means that we do exactly what the others expect us to do, and exactly what we should not do. We have to earn envy, pity we get for free. We should really be proud when someone envies us for our achievement, for who we are or what we have.

Make sure that you do not allow yourselves to be envious, because as soon as you begrudge someone something, you send your subconscious the message that success, possessions and outstanding achievement are negative. Your subconscious will be stimulated to keep those so-called negative traits with all their strength away from you. The result will be that you will never achieve, be, or possess what you envy in others.

One of the real stress factors from which you will suffer is daily overload and the impossibility of finishing everything on your schedule. Starting today, you must ask yourself if every appointment and every promise you make is realistic, and do you truly have the time?

Then there is the stress caused by a baseless fear of the future. Only people who do a poor job should fear the future and competition. People who do their very best and do their work as well as they can, using their talents and skills, will not have to suffer from these types of problems. Therefore, if you deliver good work with outstanding results you do not have to fear the future.

When you really practice the goal-setting part of this program you will find that you take charge of your future without any problems and therefore will determine and shape your own fate. When you are in charge of your own fate you can control your life and don't need to fear the future.

A fear of physical or emotional lows is also unreasonable because the IBMS™ technology offers you opportunities, taught in new ways, to help you gain insight and give you energy so you can determine your own emotional condition.

Therefore, do not concentrate on your fears or on things that frighten you, but concentrate only on what you want, on your desires, and on the very best results. Give this some serious thought every time you start doing something.

Poor concentration also leads to an accumulation of stress, unless the difficulty is already due to stress. Set aside regular periods for regeneration, regular breathing exercises, and good nutrition and you'll remove concentration problems in a short time.

Conflicts within your family are unnecessary; you chose your partner, you brought up the children you love, but somewhere along the line you stopped giving them the attention they deserve. You have simply stopped searching for constructive solutions together and you are no longer working on a day-to-day basis to improve your family's quality of life.

Another great stress factor is the fear of loss. It results from focusing on the negative, the things you attract by visualization. With every fear you have you should ask yourself, "Is this fear real? Is this fear justified? What is the worst that can happen? What can I do if the worst happened?"

If you suffer from stress because you are overworked, the problem can be solved easily because it is the one and only exception to confirm the rule of lack of organization. Suffering from a lack of time, or a poor habit, is often learned behavior. I have found that you can save a lot of time with good organization and the delegation of work and responsibility.

If you find time to regenerate and relax every day you will actually save a lot of time in the long run because you will be far more effective and efficient. I advise you to go to bed forty minutes earlier at night, get up forty minutes earlier in the morning and do not dawdle over breakfast. Get up full of energy, eat a healthy breakfast, preferably with fruit or fruit juice.

Lack of spare time and not enough quality of life translates into emotional suicide. Without the enjoyment of success, and without stages of recuperation, your subconscious cannot make some sense out of your work and pursuit, and it will no longer send you enough energy to use for doing your work to the best of your ability. Be sure to give yourself enough time for hobbies, training, friends, family and personal interests. If you run into unexpected interruptions that you cannot change, concentrate on a quick solution, try to overcome the obstacle, and you will encounter neither stress nor fear.

There will always be new irritating and energy-draining moments in life. Perhaps the computer doesn't work, a co-worker is often absent and the majority of work is put on you, an unexpected bill comes in, or some other problem. Make it a habit to be prepared, and refuse to become irritated. Those things are part of everyday life. We should accept them and look for the right solutions. Don't waste your time on frustration, define the problem and look for a solution.

Exercise:

Write down what you plan to do to relax and exercise. Do you plan to do these activities for 3, 5, or even 7 days a week? What activities appeal to you most that will help rejuvenate your mind and body?

The Analysis of Dis-Stress

Crisis situations that occur frequently should be thoroughly analyzed, so that you will get a better understanding and make better preparations. If we are well prepared, we will create fewer stress causing situations.

Exercise:

1. Which situations do you repeatedly experience and consider a threat to your personal and professional goals?
2. Now, write down a single component in your behavior that you have or are determined to changed, so that this situation will no longer cause dis-stress in your future.

What Does Stress Mean To You?

Everyone has a completely different understanding of the term stress and of a typical stress situation. What causes anxiety or even panic in one person may not bother you at all. The basis for these different reactions lies only in the evaluation of the personal representation and communication concerning this situation. Therefore, you must first decide what stress and stressful situations mean to you.

Exercise:

Answer the following questions—

1. What does stress mean to you personally?

2. What typical situations cause you stress?

3. What are your usual reactions to stressful situations?

4. How could you change those reactions in the future?

5. What situations in your life, cause you react differently than you would like? How do you usually behave in the following situations and how would you like to act from now on?

Professionally—

Privately—

Physically—

Financially—

To set clear goals and develop effective strategies, you must first know who you are and what you really want.

Exercise:

1. How would you describe yourself, your personality, your skills, your positive and your negative sides?

2. How would you really like to be?

3. What changes should you make, but have not yet made?

4. How can you make those changes starting today? Repeat those tasks every day, so you'll come closer to reaching your goal!

5. What demands do you make on yourself daily, and what expectations do you have regarding yourself and your abilities?

6. How many of these demands are realistic? Be honest!

7. An essential step to bringing down the stress in your life is the ability to delegate. Write down what you can delegate in the course of your personal and professional life. Who can do it? How?

8. What can you do daily to regenerate your mind, body and spirit?

9. What can you do to get ahead in your professional life?

10. What can you do to improve your personal life?

11. Where would you like to be 5 or 10 years from now in your personal and professional life? How do you think you can get there? What steps or choices can you take that will bring you closer to your goals?

When it comes to you personally…

1. Which are the personality traits you would like to acquire or improve?

2. In what areas are you not using your full potential? Why not?

   How can you change that in the future?

3. Define all the obstacles that are standing between you and your life goals:

What can you do to reach these goals?

What is the best way overcome these obstacles?

DEALING EFFECTIVELY
WITH STRESS

Be frank. Do you suffer from some of the following symptoms: tense muscles in your back or neck, painful shoulders, stomach or intestines, do you feel sick or do you lack concentration? Do you sometimes feel dizzy, weak, tense, or do you have difficulty breathing? Do you feel nervous, restless, aggressive, frustrated, depressed or are your hands moist?

Many of us take those symptoms for granted. We compensate and hardly notice that they decrease in time. But we can take only remedial action with careful stress control, by paying attention to the cause, the reactions and symptoms, which cause the stress.

In a recent study done through IBMS™ in the US and Canada, 387 employees who were suffering from chronic stress symptoms were questioned, in order to find the causes and solutions of stress.

The following are the most common reasons for stress from people working in professional positions:

1. Pressed for time
2. Pressure to perform
3. Professional conflicts
4. Collegial difficulties

Private problems:

5. Unpaid bills
6. The paper-boy did not deliver the paper
7. One of the children refused to eat
8. The cat ruined the sofa, etc.

You can see from the list that one little annoying thing does not cause tension, it is the accumulation of many small frustrations that causes the stress.

Other causes that lead to chronic stress are:

- Fear of the future
- The fear of losing a job
- Overwork
- To much responsibility, or responsibility in itself
- Competition
- Working with people you do not like
- Constant change
- Common insecurities

Exercise:

Write down the causes of the stress you suffered in the last thirty days. Consider that stress was caused by many little things and that the way out of stress was also through little things. Paying attention to the everyday little things will help you to build up and retain life long vitality.

Many people believe that they do not have enough time to play a sport. At the same time they feel even worse, because they feel that they have not enough time for themselves.

But time spend on solutions is the best way to avoid stress. You will preserve the feeling of being in control and you will be able to make important necessary decisions.

Stress and the Dangers of Stress

Positive stress, like the joy when we reach a goal, master a skill, get a promotion, complete a deal, increases our performance, adds pleasure and enjoyment to life and work. It also strengthens our immune system.

Distress always leads to a feeling of fight and flight. Our reactions are partly outside of our control because they originate in our reptilian brain (primitive brain), which takes over in life threatening situations. It is the reason that we, after a stressful situation, say: "I absolutely do not remember saying that." Or, "I do not understand how I could do such a thing."

If you have found yourself in a similar situation, you could until now do nothing to change the situation, because the strong distress signals of your reptilian brain had taken complete control of your thinking and doing.

Whenever you get a sudden feeling to run away or to become furious at someone, be aware that this is an inner message of the fight and flight reaction. Look for the cause and move out of the way!

Once stress hormones are produced they have to be broken down, so that they do not poison the body. It is therefore important to find an emotional and physical outlet. The most helpful are sport, climbing stairs and deep breathing exercises.

Emotionally, it is even more important that you either see a situation in a very different light, or that you see the people, who thoroughly irritate you, in a comical way, so that they lose the adverse power they have over you.

You must, on the other hand, be able to forgive people. You do not have to love those people or become their friend; just do not allow negative or destructive feelings bring you down. Learn to forgive or excuse people. You could write a letter and burn it. You could also decide to actually talk to them and tell them that you forgive them; that may be the best way.

And forgive yourself for all the foolish and negative things you have done to others, so that you can be free of guilt. You can do that in the same way as mentioned above.

If you look at it psychologically, then confession and forgiveness as practiced in the community of the Church can give tremendous release and have therefore a positive influence on stress release. But you could get similar results by talking to friends, relatives or other people you trust.

Statistics show that women live longer, because they have an easier time discussing their feelings and problems. Men often die earlier, while they would rather swallow their problems and kill themselves one step at the time with the motto: "Men don't cry and show their feelings."

I personally feel that it is more *macho* to show your feelings than to kill yourself a little bit every day by being "Cool."

Not only emotional, but also outside influences like heat or cold and a poorly ventilated room, which lacks oxygen, can cause stress and have a negative effect on your health. Feelings of oppression, claustrophobia, combined with headaches and lack of concentration, tension and muscle spasms can be the result of being cooped up too long in a confined area.

There used to be trainers in negotiation, who advised their clients to speed up their negotiations by holding their discussions in a confined, overheated, oxygen starved room.

Observing the Symptoms

Weakness, tiredness, exhaustion, lack of concentration, poor observation and a feeling that everything is frustrating and annoying, reactions of fright and flight (aggression, anger, fear, a wish to hide,) are all indications of distress and may endanger your health. Anger, aggression and irritation often show the fight reaction. In the flight reaction, the person usually avoids certain people, isolates themselves; cuts themselves off; avoids making decisions, etc.

Basically, stress can and should not be avoided. Healthy stress is as constructive in our life as distress is destructive. We all must learn to cope intelligently and sensibly in stressful situations. We must never forget that every situation in life is neutral. Until we evaluate the matter, and consciously or unconsciously give it a good or bad account, a situation is value neutral.

Stress reactions, which produce adrenaline and other accompanying components, are created to give people, for instance after an auto incident or in another dangerous situation, the energy and ability to react as quickly as possible to a demanding dilemma. All energy and strength are concentrated on sheer survival. The reptilian brain, which is needed exclusively for survival, takes control of our actions in crisis situations.

Our body and mind usually return to their normal calm quickly after a typical crisis situation. Once we overcome shock situations or other traumatic developments, without damage to our health, we return quickly to our normal condition. This is considered Type-A-Stress.

Type-B-Stress, on the other hand, is the result of undefined angst, constant fear, worry, doubt, poor self-esteem and self-confidence, a feeling of being at the mercy of others, of being helpless, manipulated or restricted. It stems from elements without a definite cause; therefore they cannot be avoided and are thus forever present. This continuous intrusion by distress destroys our health, because the factors that are part of this type of stress are not restricted by time and cannot be overcome in a period of regeneration.

I have witnessed unbelievably positive changes during my work with patients, who suffered from stress and manager burnout. I forced them to switch off in a positive manner with riding horseback in the woods, fishing, having a barbecue, enjoying nature, playing team sports, or enjoying companionship among friends. I have helped those people to switch off by living in the now and by turning their worries, doubt and fear aside. Although the first three days of regeneration were often unbearable for managers with burnout, most of them were not at all eager to go back when the first week was over. Technical and social skills are taught in the second week of training, so that the patients, when they return to their normal lives, will be more aware and have an easier time coping in their private and professional relationships. Distress no longer threatens their health.

For a typical manager, who finds himself in an everyday treadmill, and is already suffering from serious stress and illness, the possibility of shutting off and regeneration is hard to believe. This man often has the feeling that he has absolutely no time for himself. He has the impression that it is impossible to shut off and return to normal. But, just as the damage caused by stress is from the accumulation of many small things, so can the use of many small positive elements lead to something good; health to be precise. Stress is not the only cause of burnout; it is an accumulation of too many, hard to cope with, small irritations. In this manner, through the accumulation of many positive, useful and sensible components, we return to desired and lasting vitality.

In case, dear reader, you belong to that group of people, who have no time for regeneration, please think about the following: If you don't take the time for regeneration, relaxation and striking some kind of balance, your body will take the necessary time to at least survive. When this happens (heart attack, stroke stomach or intestinal ulcers, etc.), you will have no influence on the time, place and duration your body will demand. Your body will take what it needs, whether you want to give it or not.

Do not let it get so far that a physical collapse is imminent. The best way to avoid illness is preventive health, and I will give you enough ideas and techniques to practice so that you can enjoy perfect health and well being.

The ability to act sensibly

If you want to change the way you deal with stress in the future, you must learn to define a stressful situation.

Exercise:

For this reason I ask you to remember every stressful situation of this last month. Perhaps there were situations in which you suffered from cramps, headaches, indisposition, stomach or intestinal ulcers. Define clearly which situations lead to stress.

You cannot learn to deal more effectively with stress until you have defined a distressful situation clearly

For the second part of this exercise, you must write down how you can react in a more sensible manner to these situations in the future.

Self-doubt as Stress-factor

It is a lasting stress-factor, if you do not believe in yourself, your skills, and your future success; this can be disastrous for your health. It is, for this reason, very important to realize that you are a terrific person and to concentrate on your unlimited potential.

Exercise:

Make a list of everything you have done in your life that was a success. Go back to when you were a child, list all the small and big accomplishments of which you are proud or could be proud. Write down your talents and positive character traits. Be aware that you were already quite successful, overcame hurdles and difficulties, passed tests or perhaps were a star in sports.

If you believed that you would fail, you might often react by getting cramps; suffer from tension, poor circulation or breathing difficulties. As a result you lacked sufficient energy. Therefore, you must now become aware that there are no such things as failure, defeat or error.

Every person acts at every point in their life according to their knowledge and possibilities; otherwise they would do nothing at all. If you always try to do or give the best you can, you can never blame yourself for not giving the very best, no matter what the results are. Nobody can do more than give their very best, or give more than the can give.

If you produce a certain result, it is not a success or a failure, it is a result, whether you wanted that specific outcome or not. Only your evaluation makes this situation positive or negative. If things did not go the way you wanted them to go, do not consider them failures, mistakes or defeats, but see them as lessons toward your further development. Experience is the foundation for success and for moving ahead in every area of our life. If you do something that does not work, you have produced a result that teaches you how it does not work. You have moved forward and become wiser. Now you know one more way in which you will not reach the desired result.

Edison said, after failing 25,000 times in his search developing a battery, "I will succeed soon." When they asked him, "Why?" He answered, "I am running out of possibilities for failure." If you run out of possibilities for failure and keep on trying, you will from necessity produce success. When asked the question, whether he did not consider himself a failure after 25,000 defeats, Edison answered, "Why a failure, I have learned 25,000 ways how not to make a battery." He possessed prudence and valuable wisdom.

Experience leads to success. See every outcome as a lesson, as a step on the ladder of success, so you can build your life according to your wishes.

Exercise:

To develop unequaled self-esteem and self-confidence, you must first create a picture in your mind of the person you want to be, with the corresponding intellectual conditioning.

The easiest way to accomplish this is by sitting down calmly and seeing yourself on your ninetieth birthday. Many people are giving speeches in your honor. They are surrounding and praising you for your accomplishments, for who you were and who you have become, for what you did, what you have and who your friends are. Now write the speech you would like to hear when you are ninety, with all your credentials and qualifications. This is a good way to determine quickly who you want to be at the end of your life and what your true goals are. You can set your goals in stages, so that you can prepare and produce the desired results.

Needless Stress

At the bottom of chronic stress lies the ambitions that are too great, false evaluations and rules made by other people, which resulted in failures or disappointments. They cause the aforementioned catastrophic problems. You should have big dreams, visions and goals, as big as possible, but your performance and plans, your time division and the setting of goals should be realistic and feasible. Otherwise you will produce failures, withholding you from observing your schedule, thereby damaging your self-esteem. Setting a half hour to force a deal with a difficult customer, who usually needs three days to feel comfortable with a decision, can lead to unneeded pressure and stress. Remain realistic, but set your mind on the highest achievable goals.

Stress as Healer and Stress as Destroyer

We recognize that there are two types of stress. Stress type A is the stress we experience in a crisis. It releases hormones and gives us the energy to cope with life threatening problems. Stress type B results from undefined or less palpable predicaments, like vague apprehension, worry, doubt, fear of the future, a feeling of overwork and helplessness, anger and hatred. This type of chronic stress cannot be removed, while the causes and solutions are unknown. Therefore it does long term harm. Be aware that a single cause can usually be overcome, but the coming together of many single factors causes exhaustion.

A panic reaction is a clear sign of excessive demands and strain that has exhausted a person's energy, so that they can no longer react positively to a stressful situation. This "explosion of release" can lead to total confusion and lack of control, even to undesired reactions.

- Long-term stress factors could become a cause of illness.

- Stress leads to an accumulation and therefore an elevated level of adrenaline, nor-adrenaline, cortisone and other hormones.

- Extreme levels of the above mentioned hormones lead to several illnesses and reactions, if they are present over an extended period.

- Tears may appear in the arteries when the blood pressure is too high. This can lead to an elevated level of cortisone and a diminished blood flow, with the possibility of a stroke or a heart attack.

- Adrenaline and nor-adrenaline take care of fat removal, which could deposit itself in the arteries. This, again, is an onslaught on the body caused by stress.

Changes in hormone levels, resulting from stress, can diminish the body's immune capacity, which could lead to other illnesses, even to cancer. We could say, the longer a stress situation lasts, the more dangerous it becomes.

Do not Just React

The reduction of stress, or the attempt to change negative stress into positive energy, simply means that we have a positive response to demands, crisis and obligations, as opposed to just a reaction. In therapy, when we speak in a positive sense, we say that a patient responds to medicine. If we say that a patient reacts to medicine, it is usually meant in a negative way; the patient suffers from complications, for instance with an allergic reaction.

Do not just react to life, but respond. Accept what happens and make the most of it. Change your outlook, do not look at problems as difficulties but as challenges and opportunities, so that you can change and grow, learn and show your hidden talents. The way we look at things determines how we see a challenge, do we see a catastrophe and react with panic, or can we see a challenge as an opportunity to grow and develop.

Focus on success and a wonderful future give us strength and energy. If we focus on failure, possible problems and defeat, stress can make us weak and incompetent.

When it is dark behind and in front of you, look inward, look at your possibilities and hidden resources, and use them to lighten your future path.

If you demand of yourself to look for answers and solutions and try to find them within, you will quickly decide that you have far more resources than you believed. See a crisis as an opportunity that offers many possibilities, which you should not hesitate to exploit.

Women usually become older than men, while men learn from roll-play and their upbringing to bottle things up. They have a tendency to swallow their worry, doubt, anger and fear. This leads often to the same type of explosion as a water kettle with a too tight valve. Women talk easier about their problems, their anger, about things that happened, and get rid of their pent-up energy. Political prisoners and soldiers, who were able to talk about their horrible experiences, recovered faster from physical and emotional calamities than those who could not. The ones who could talk lived longer and healthier lives.

Team play is, for this reason, an important foundation for health and success. Develop a social network, so that you always have enough friends, acquaintances, co-workers and family members to catch you when the bottom threatens to fall out from under you. Friends with whom you can laugh and friends with whom you can cry will have a beneficial influence on your health. Therefore be a team player, be part of a team for balance and release.

I am not talking about whining and self-pity, or about psychoanalyzing your life to death. Just talk openly about what is bothering you and look together for solutions and ways to deal with what is wrong; then let it go. This will offer release and help you.

The ability to ask others for help is an important facet of health and success. Nobody can climb the ladder of success by them self. "Upwards together" should be your motto. There are no "self-made millionaires," because many people were part of the team and contributed to this man's accomplishment. People, who are afraid to offer or ask others for help will never become successful and reach their full potential.

You are not afraid to consult a physician and ask his or her help if you break your arm or have acute appendicitis. But people, who suffer from an emotional or mental breakdown, have a crisis or suffer from other problems, are often unwilling to ask for help. But it should be just as natural to ask for emotional aid as it is to ask for physical help.

Get together with your team and use the wisdom, skills and talents of all the members by brainstorming their ideas; in this way you can exploit everyone's talents in the best interest of all concerned.

Deadly Slogans

There is hardly anything worse for your body, than to stay in the office or torment yourself with clients, when you are sick or perhaps even have a fever. Many try to keep going with false determination, despite warning signals and acute symptoms of the body. They are determined to keep going and ruin the possibility to heal. The result is that you do not get completely better and keep suffering from lack of energy and chronic malaise.

Setting goals produces energy, illness results from lack of energy. Goals help you to relax, rest, restore and switch gears. The main cause of serious health problems or chronic illness is that independent business-men and professionals in sales and management believe that the company can't do without them. They refuse to delegate the work because they are convinced that nobody can do the work as well as they do.

Remember, in the future, this piece of Asiatic wisdom: if you want to know how important you are, put both your arms in a pail of water, draw them back out and watch for the spaces you left behind. That is how important we are in the evolution of the universe.

You probably know that I, in accordance with the philosophy of IBMS™, assess every human being differently. Nevertheless, this state-ment illuminates that we see ourselves, at least in several areas of our lives, as too important.

In my work with patients, I have concluded that many people find themselves in ill health, because they considered themselves irreplace-able. They are worn out, because the weight became a continuous load and turned into an overload. This inevitably affected their health.

Delegation is an indispensable tool for managers and the self-em-ployed. Only by delegating the work that you may find difficult or that can be done by others, just as well, do you give yourself enough room for the more important work that you must do yourself.

You would, after all, not think of cleaning your employees' desks, sweep the stairs or wash the dishes in the lunchroom. Just so, you should not do the work that can easily be done by others. To be a great manager means to be able to manage your life, privately as well as professionally.

This means conserving your energy and includes managing your time and health.

To be a leader, you must have a sense of responsibility, especially where you yourself are concerned. When you are weak, helpless and ill, you can neither help others nor fulfill your task according to your potential.

During my work in my clinic in Canada I had concluded, while dealing with top-managers from all over the world, that every one of them considered themselves indispensable to their company. They oversaw the most absurd details themselves, for instance, the ordering of paper, sometimes they even did the ordering.

Never allow yourself to say; I can hang on one more week, or in three months I will have my vacation. (Some even take their work along.) These people consider themselves indispensable. They actually believe that, in their absence, everything will fall apart. Avoid the thought that you are irreplaceable. Even if you can't leave completely, do find time for regeneration, relaxation, hobbies and time to spend with your family. Please, believe me! Listen to your body, because illness is always a cry for help. If you refuse to pay attention, your body will assert itself more intensively. There is no illness without a cause, no symptoms without a shortage of energy. Keep this saying in your mind.

Please consider objectively how dangerous it is to keep pushing yourself with slogans while your body is crying out, and you yourself are suffering from overwork and discontent. Suddenly and unexpectedly, without your ability to make preparations, you are torn from your work by an acute illness, stomach or intestinal ulcers, inflammation of the nerves, or even a heart attack or a stroke.

There will be no time for preparations, no time to work in new people and get some necessary items out of the way. You will be torn away from your work with many things left undone.

You can determine neither the time nor the duration of your collapse. This could really cause the failure of your business or your career. And this could happen because you were not willing to take the time, when needed, for regeneration, relaxation, compensation, hobbies, family, friends and the enjoyment of life. If you had acted wisely, you could have picked the time and duration yourself.

You can be certain that the body will take a rest when needed—whether you are willing to give it or not. It is therefore smarter to plan times for regeneration and use them. Listen when your body cries for help, don't ignore the signals, but react intelligently.

We have the medical potential to live fit and vital for 160 years (Cambridge University). If you want to live this long, you must think and take measures for your healthy development right now. Not when it is too late and you are forced by ill health and bodily limitations.

It depends on you; your fate is in every area of your life in your own hands. This includes the most important sector, your health. Every year you loose before 160 years of age, you have lost because of poor breathing, poor nutrition, poor exercise or lack of it and also by a false emotional or mental attitude. It is not too late to start over.

The Danger of One-sidedness

Life is characterized by diversity. To conceive the ability and achieve and sustain optimum results we need comparable diversity in our life. We can create this by bringing balance in our life.

You cannot just live for your job, not for your private life, not for your children, not even recklessly for yourself. You must strike a balance between hobbies, family, work, regeneration and pleasure, which helps to give your life an integrated, successful and maximum quality. A one-sided burden—no mater in what area of your life—always leads to wear and tear, stress, tension, deterioration, monotony, apathy, frustration and depression.

Make sure that you do not just take care of your own retirement, but also of the retirements of your employees. Take care, there are challenges and interesting possibilities. Only in this way will you and your fellow workers remain flexible, active and curious; you will all, moreover, enjoy your work with new challenges, progress and answers. Mental and physical exercises are a requirement for vitality and contentment.

Needless Worries

You have no influence at all on the development of the world economy, on the collapse of large companies or banks, and even less on tomorrow's weather. It is, therefore, completely absurd to fear, stew or worry over things you can't do a thing about.

Do not waste your energy on fear. Concentrate on the best way to improve your personal and professional situation. Do not concentrate on what others are doing or on the enterprises of people, who may be your competition or in the same line of business.

You are unique in the universe and can therefore produce unique results. Focus only on results and performance, while keeping your goals clearly in front of your eyes.

Burnout

Constant strain from doubt in yourself and your abilities leads to the so-called burnout-syndrome. Burnout leads to a feeling of being burned up, empty, weak and helpless. Burnout often results when people with low self-esteem, low self-confidence and a negative image of themselves try to overcome their conceived deficit, weaknesses or shortcomings. Those people spend more time at work, because they believe that they can overcome quality with quantity. This is never the case.

Another cause for burnout is when the person doesn't have sufficient self-esteem, self-confidence and discipline they can't live according to their own values, rules and principles. Instead, they follow the views of others. When you try to accomplish goals that aren't your own, there won't be any feelings of accomplishment, even when the goal is reached. Since there is no sense of contentment, you are left with a feeling of emptiness and burnout.

Only when you set your own goals and work on the realizations of your own dreams will you have a feeling of accomplishment. It will give you strength and increase your self-confidence and self-esteem since you will get a generous return for the work and effort you put in.

Doing work that makes no sense, either because it has nothing to do with your goals or is against your ethical and moral values, can leave you feeling empty and completely exhausted, even when you successfully finish it. Nobody who leads a life full of compromise can be happy or stay healthy.

It is the same with people who feel forced to stay in a catastrophic marriage. They stay because they fear other people's gossip, because there are children involved or because of financial reasons. Those people are destroyed by compromise. Whenever you do something you absolutely do not want to do, you risk your health. Long-term demanding compromises kill people in the truest sense of the word. These compromises are, in my opinion, the main causes of serious illness, even cancer.

Our body speaks in a symbolic language. For instance, women who put up with relationship problems over a long period of time are inclined to suffer from illnesses of the lower part of the body. Women who have many problems with their children or who cannot give birth often get breast cancer when the conflicts last a long time. People, who are in situations that they can literally not digest, suffer frequently from stomach and intestinal problems or from gallstones.

You cause your own tension and stress because it is not what happens in your life that causes the stress, but your reaction to what happens. It is therefore important that you program your behavior. Only then can you be sure of not becoming overwhelmed by difficult situations. Prepare yourself so that you are programmed and ready to act correctly when you are facing a negative situation. Simply picture your desired behavior in your mind and act accordingly.

How to Create a Strong Immune System

You can resist illness and stress only when you are in top shape and work toward the realization of your dreams. The path to optimal health—mentally, physically, emotionally and spiritually—includes the following:

- Regular and sensible exercise
- Good nutrition

- Restful sleep
- Freedom from addictions

Real health can only come through consistency, not with quick fixes like Slim *in Seven Days*, or *Ten Days to Financial Success*, or similar dangerous nonsense. Our attitude and our philosophy of life are the blueprint for our health. We have to decide on a path that enables us to realize our dreams.

The foundation for success is accepting our weaknesses and doing what we think is right for ourselves and our happiness. Too many people ignore the signals their body sends. They get more and more accustomed to the limitations and restrictions they accept as part of life.

I am no advocate for a 100% vegetarian diet or any other one-sided approach to life. I know very well, as a researcher in health issues, that a healthy person can drink a cup of coffee each day or a glass of wine now and then. But when we continually eat unhealthy, lay around watching TV, drink alcohol daily or have too many cups of coffee, it all has a negative effect.

I would like to point out that every form of extremism is fundamentally wrong. Extremists are hysterical people who suffer from mental problems. Extremism is not a natural phenomenon; it is abnormal and undesirable behavior. Life, and the quality of life, is made up of many combined but separate factors. Life is not black or white; it is not even gray; rather it consists of as many as ten million different shades of colors that we can use to shape more beautiful lives.

Regular Sensible Exercise

By the age of twenty-eight, our bodies start to break down. We can do nothing to stop or slow down this process of aging without putting in more effort. Many people who suffered a heart attack, joint or back pain could have avoided this by being more active. If you are in poor condition you have to struggle and work harder.

Muscles atrophy when they are not used. The blood circulation is diminished and muscles will waste even more through lack of oxygen. When you're inactive, you have less chance to heal, when you are hurt or ill, and the time needed for restoration becomes considerably longer. You become more susceptible to infections, feel weak and are chronically fatigued. Degenerative illnesses will follow.

Physical activity is the most effective way to reduce anger, strain and stress. If you have not been physically active for a long time, start small and build up slowly. Twenty minutes of exercise a day is sufficient, thirty minutes a day is good, and sixty minutes is excellent.

Good Nutrition

Another essential point is nutrition. Your nutrition represents the building blocks for the renewal of your cells. 98% of our cells are renewed within the time-span of eleven months and a full 100% within two years. Our body forms those cells with building materials found in what we eat. If you offer your body inferior material (bad nutrition) for the building of the cells then your body can only make inferior cells. The health of your individual cells determines the health of your complete body.

Eat only when you're hungry and stop eating when you're satisfied, not stuffed. Don't clean your plate just to be polite. Always eat "living" food such as fruit and vegetables, and only as long as you are hungry. Instead of eating at designated times, allow your body to find its own rhythm, independent of the hunger of others or times set by convention. Never starve yourself, especially to lose weight. Hunger emits stress hormones and discomfort, and long-term diets can lead to chronic stress with catastrophic results. Hunger and diets can lead to a deficiency of iron, vitamin C, calcium and electrolytes. But, eating too much food or junk food is just as bad.

Be sure to supply your body with a balanced amount of vitamins and minerals through healthy choices like fruit juices, fruit and vegetables. Drink plain water whenever you're thirsty rather than soda, coffee, energy drinks, and so forth. Avoid mineral water because the minerals cannot be absorbed and digested by the body and it can tax your energy supply, while carbonated drinks have a corroding effect on the kidneys.

Restful Sleep

Sleep is important for restoration, relaxation, health and the ability to work efficiently. Certain elements our body needs to live and survive are only produced during sleep; one of them is serotonin, a substance of the utmost importance for our existence. Low levels of serotonin can lead to insomnia, migraines, depression, and weight gain.

Some people drink a glass of wine before bed because they feel it helps them get a good night sleeps. However, alcohol disrupts the brain's regular sleep patterns and the rhythm of sleep, which is absolutely necessary for our health. Sleeping tablets lose their efficiency after about two weeks and sleep problems are usually worse than before. If you suffer from poor sleep, you should change your way of life and improve your diet so that you can sleep well without sleeping pills or alcohol.

If we don't sleep well, we increase our stress. Try to break this deadly cycle by falling asleep naturally and solving your problems rather than simply worrying about them.

If you find you have trouble falling asleep, listen to soothing music and sounds of nature, try some meditation and use my IBMS™ program as it can help you reprogram your mind for healthy sleep. Even when you can't sleep well, you should stay in bed with your eyes closed so your body has the opportunity to relax and restore.

Freedom from Addiction

Freedom from addiction is not just important for our health but also for our self-esteem and self-image. Even reducing simpler addictions, like coffee or energy drinks, restores our ability to deal better with stress. Caffeine destroys several minerals, calcium among them. They may give you a quick shot of energy then plunge you deeper than before into fatigue. Instead, try herbal teas or hot lemonade.

Using alcohol, nicotine and pills to solve our problems can be detrimental to our health or even deadly. Denial of addiction is the addict's main problem, making recovery impossible. Smokers insist that they could easily quit but just don't want to. Alcoholics say they don't drink regularly, or all that much; just now and then. They're only fooling themselves. If you don't believe you have a problem, even if friends and loved ones have mentioned that you do, you can't and won't work on solving the problem and your health will decline.

Exercise:

Keep track of your drinking (alcohol, coffee, energy drinks), smoking, and/ or eating. Check to see how much you consume every day; then add it all up at the end of the week. Write it down so it will really grab your attention.

You can only get rid of an addiction by changing your self-image. If you had a good self-image you wouldn't pollute your body with nicotine, alcohol, sugar and fats in the extreme. This means that you can no longer see yourself as somebody who smokes, is overweight, drinks alcohol or swallows pills. You have to see yourself as an independent, happy, healthy person. There are several ways to achieve this. You can consciously change your self-image by using the principles of pain and joy, or with the IBMS™ technique of conscious mental programming and conditioning.

Ask yourself whether the way you live reflects the image of the way your life could be, or should be. Do not go to extremes; aim for balance.

Good living isn't all or nothing, it's being in balance. If a big meal, sweets, or another pleasure add something positive to your life, enjoy it, but only in moderation. Keep in mind that the body needs time to recover from the pollutants that are put into it.

If you practice regular and sensible exercise, good nutrition, restful sleep, and abandoning addictions, you should have a healthy life. Don't overdo any one of those; rather live in balance. It makes all the difference.

Tomorrow Give 100%

Set your alarm for half an hour or one hour earlier than you do now. Waking up earlier will give you the time to ease into your day rather than rushing around filled with stress. When you do get up tomorrow clap your hands three times and shout: "Yes!" Take a deep breath then let it out. Stretch and reach up high, standing on your toes. Then go to the bathroom, look yourself in the eyes and say, "This is my day and I will use it well." It may sound silly, but give it a try. You'll find that when you start each day in this way you'll feel more energetic and positive, and be able to work on solving problems instead of constantly worrying. You will work at 100% capacity, instead of just a tiny fraction that you're used to.

Start your day with a healthy breakfast of fruit juice, fresh fruit, or a fruit salad. Give your body the necessary energy to start.

Support your body mentally, emotionally and physically and build self-esteem and self-confidence regularly with positive, goal directed self-communication. Say to yourself, before you tackle any problem, "I can do it! I can fix that." Even if people try to put you down or dissuade you from trying things, keep positive and know that negative people are simply unhappy with their own lives in some way.

The best way to avoid stress is to develop the knowledge that you are in control of your body and mind.

Humor versus Stress
Someone who relishes being alive and enjoys their work stimulates their mind positively and reaches an anabolic state. Stress, on the other hand, produces a catabolic state; it produces destructive, immune suppressing, hormones.

A good example of the effectiveness of humor is a story of the re-cuperation of Norman Cousins. In his book "Anatomy of an Illness" the then very ill actor, who suffered from cancer, writes how he literally laughed himself healthy by watching comedies.

Use humor for your own benefit and that of others. It will strengthen your own immune system and theirs. A friendly smile generates warmth, openness and confers energy. Negative humor (sarcasm) destroys team play and effectiveness. It leads to disharmony, competition and isolation.

Humor should never be at the cost of others. It's important that you can laugh about yourself and make yourself the butt of a joke. Humor reduces stress for all concerned, especially in tense situations. Don't take life too seriously.

Communication, combined with laughter, helps us to relax and solve problems. Here are a couple of true stories about the power of laughter: A nine-year old girl in a psychiatric hospital in New York had not actively participated in anything for one-and-a half years. One day, in just twelve minutes, she laughed out loud and joined in the group with the help of a professional clown. After two hours, she was behaving like a normal child. In the same hospital a depressed 72-year-old man threatened to kill himself by refusing to eat. Thanks to the help of the same clown the man was discharged and pronounced healthy within two weeks.

Think about the people who make you feel good because they make you laugh. Those people can see the irony in problems and in life itself, and they can certainly laugh at themselves. Consider how you can bring more joy into your life. Surround yourself with witty, positive people. Ask yourself what you can change in your life and how you can add some humor. Learn to look at life with more joy and optimism and try to live that way.

An Overall View of Basic Elements

Your behavior is determined by your self-esteem and by the way you see yourself. Therefore, you must let go of negative experiences in your life because they will influence your self-esteem and, in turn, negatively influence your future.

Thanks to experience, you are a new person every day. You are no longer the person you were 15 years ago when you made your past mistakes and experienced those failures. You can learn from your past and become a better person and let go of those negative situations and people with be at ease around you.

Too many people give up because they keep looking at the past and can't see that life can be different. They figure if they messed up before, they'll mess up again. If they were hurt or cheated or were failures in the past, that's how things will always be. But it doesn't have to be that way. Problems and challenges can help take you to a higher level in life. See problems as an opportunity to grow and tackle those old problems in a different way. Walking away from problems or pretending they don't exist only increases the tension and can lead to chronic stress.

Consider yourself the writer of your life, not just the actor. You can rewrite the script of your life and be the director. You no longer have to be a puppet at the mercy of someone else's wishes. Don't dance to somebody else's tune!

In Closing

Let me wrap things up. In order to live a life as healthy, stress free, and successful as possible you must:

- Let go of the past and do not fear the future. Only live for today.

- Determine your own future, goals and behavior.

- Follow sensible time management. You can't do everything, yet don't allow yourself to be distracted.

- Pursue active stress management with restful sleep, good nutrition, exercise, and positive internal dialogue.

- Focus on solutions, not on problems. Many people see life as an obstacle course, yet they are their own greatest obstacles.

- Never let other people stand in your way. You are the only one who can stop them.

- Always remain flexible and creative, and always live in the present. Avoid chronic stress by avoiding living in the past and the future.

- Only three percent of our fears become reality. And even a smaller percentage are actually catastrophic.

- Avoid people who drain your energy.

- Shatter loneliness with a smile. Be interested and caring in your relationships with others.

- Health is not just one thing or another; it's a combination of many factors that encompass your mental, physical, emotional and spiritual self.

- Take calculated risks. They offer you the opportunity to use your talents more effectively than before.

- Avoid being pressed for time, plan realistically. Don't let others put you under time pressures.

- Don't rely on others, on fate or luck, to be healthy and happy. Take full responsibility and control of your life.

Conclusion and summary

You now have all the knowledge and tools and training you need to live and enjoy the life of a Champion! If you apply what you learned in this book, you will not be in danger anymore to create or allow unnecessary stress, depression or anxiety in your life. Now you know that you alone are responsible about the way you make your decisions, the way you act and therefore what kind of life experience you create for yourself in your own life! You understand now that you are responsible and in control of the stress and emotional experiences in your life and that no other person or circumstance can have any influence over how you feel and act. You learned that Depression and Anxiety are self created emotional states and how you can prevent or overcome them fast and effectively by simply being your true self and by using the knowledge and tools you have now to control every part of your life.

You now know and understand that you are born to be a champion and how you can be and live like that champion you truly are. You are now in control over your life and destiny and nothing can stop you now from living your life to the fullest. Always remember you have a very simple taste:

"Simply the best of everything!"

Please write me and let tell me about your experiences or questions: instinctbasedmedicine@gmail.com or contact me via the following websites:

www.drleonardcoldwell.com

www.instinctbasedmedicine.com

and watch my videos on:

http://www.youtube.com/user/HealingNaturePress

listen to my radio show archives:

http://www.blogtalkradio.com/search/dr.-leonard-coldwell/archives and read my Blog: http://thedrcoldwellreport.blogspot.com/

You were born to be: Happy, Healthy, Successful and to live a life of the Champion you truly are!

Your coach, friend and believer in the champion in you
Your greatest Fan

Dr Leonard Coldwell

www.instinctbasedmedicine.com
www.drleonardcoldwell.com
www.theonlyanswertocancer.com

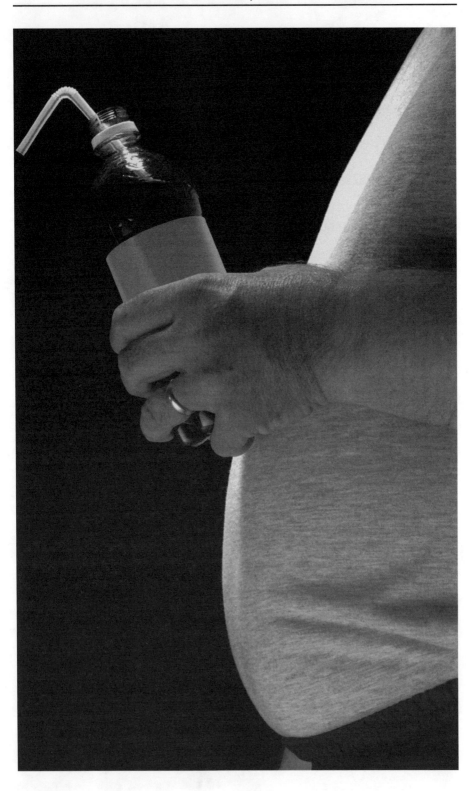

THE DIETARY CAUSES
OF STRESS

The main cause of physical stress is our diet, and on the top of the list are sugar, aspartame and artificial sweeteners.

Refined sugar has the same addictive and neuro-chemical as well as bio-electrical properties as heroin. It is one of the main causes for ADD and ADHD in children and even adults. It leads very often to insomnia and restlessness. I am sure that sugar and aspartame and related artificial sweeteners are having a major impact on autism.

Personally I have seen in many patients, with burn out syndrome and stress related disorders, that if they stop taking sugar, artificial sweeteners, high fructose corn syrup and all other chemicals that are used as sweeteners and take instead the 100% all organic, natural and safe product from www.justlikesugarinc.com available at WholeFoods and other good food resource places, that within a very short amount of time, often just days, ALL the symptoms of restlessness, nervousness, anxiety, depression, addictiveness, stress and lack of concentration simply disappear, if it is caused by diet related causes.

Dr Thomas Hohn MD NMD in Germany, conducted a private study for me in his clinics with his own patients and found that Alzheimers,

Multiple Sclerosis, Lupus and some Cancer patients and most of all patients with Restless Leg syndrome or undefended muscular spasms showed a very fast positive change after they had been taken off the sugars and sweeteners and had been put on the product of www.justlikesugarinc.com. Since these studies have been ongoing for only a couple of month, we have no final conclusion but one thing that a lot of patients report that their gums were getting healthier and, in some patients, even gum disease disappeared after they stated using Just Like Sugar.

We are just at the beginning in uncovering the health benefits of Just Like Sugar and are working on the implementation of a major study done by Dr. Thomas Hohn MD NMD.

Hyperactivity, restlessness, nervous ticks, insomnia and many other stress related symptoms can be caused and massively enhanced by sugar and artificial sweeterners of all kinds. Most shocking to me is that even the natural sweetener Stevia—is not always save because of the way its produced, it can even be highly toxic. Thank God that we have a final solution now for sweetenting, baking and use in all kinds of food: Just Like Sugar from www.justlikesugarinc.com and available at Whole-Foods.

My good friend, Dr. Betty Martini, says the following about Aspertame and Splenda. Visit her websites for more information.

Aspartame is a multipotential carcinogen
A Chinese proverb tells us to "Call things by their proper names." The sweetener producers assure us that the chemical aspartame aka: NutraSweet, Spoonful, Equal, E951, Canderel, NutraTaste, etc. is just an additive. To call aspartame what it is: It's an addictive excitoneurotoxic, genetically engineered, carcinogenic drug. It damages the cellular powerhouses, the mitochondria, debilitating cell function. It interacts with other drugs and vaccines. It often triggers polychemical sensitivity syndrome. It greatly intensifies toxic reactions to other chemicals. The body remembers aspartame and ones who have overcome the addiction often experience amplified toxic reactions if they should ingest it again.

The aspartame molecule consists of 3 components, two of which are amino acids that are beneficial nutrients when combined with other amino acids in our foods. However, if isolated, aspartic acid, 40% of aspartame, and phenylalanine, 50%, are highly toxic. Some individuals have the condition Phenylketonuria, and have intense toxic reactions to excess phenylalanine. At birth doctors heel-stick infants to analyze their blood to detect this condition. In such cases an excess of this amino acid can be fatal. Excess phenylalanine floods the brain and lowers the seizure threshold and depletes serotonin, the hormone you produce when you've eaten enough. As a result you crave carbohydrates and gain weight. Lowered serotonin triggers psychiatric and behavioral problems. The National Yogurt Association has petitioned the FDA to allow aspartame in yogurt unlabeled. Any dairy products used today must be organic.

The third part of aspartame, 10%, is a methyl-ester which immediately converts to methyl alcohol—deadly wood alcohol, (methanol). An ounce of this poison can blind or kill an adult. The methyl alcohol next converts to embalming fluid—formaldehyde, then into formic acid—fire ant venom. The whole aspartame molecule breaks down to diketopiperazine, a brain tumor agent.

The bouquet of a half dozen virulent poisons in aspartame is cumulative, and eventually eradicates good health in the same manner as regularly ingesting micro doses of arsenic or plutonium will certainly destroy you. In 1995 the FDA listed 92 symptoms of aspartame poisoning from over 10,000 volunteered consumer complaints. The list included 4 types of seizures, blindness, headaches, sexual dysfunction and death. Most were neurological complaints, since the chemical is neurotoxic. The results are diverse and dispersed all over the body. Some of us remember when there were no constant bombardments on TV of sexual potency restorers; Viagra et al. Aspartame destroys a man's ability and takes away a woman's desire, robbing marriage of a sacred delight. We have thousands of letters from victims who have been delivered from the devastations of this deadly concoction.

If people saw how aspartame is made they wouldn't use it. Bill Deagle, M.D. said: "Most people when asked how Aspartame is made do not have the first step of understanding. While an E.R. doctor and primary care physician in Augusta, GA in 1987 and 1988, I was told a number of interesting facts about the adjacent Aspartame factory. Bacteria with genes inserted generate a sludge which is centrifuged to remove the aspartame and many hundreds of contaminant organic and amino acids are present. We were told not to report illness or worker's compensation issues for fear of being fired by the hospital, now the Augusta Regional Medical Center. Many of their employees presented with psychiatric, neuropathy conditions, chronic fatigue and organic cases of loss of cognitive function. This powder from the dried sludge was then transported for packaging in factories elsewhere in the US, before sale as Equal and now the myriad of names of this neurotoxin."

It was known from the beginning that aspartame is a carcinogen and absolutely against the law. FDA's own toxicologist, Dr. Adrian Gross, told Congress at least one of Searle's studies "has established beyond any reasonable doubt that aspartame is capable of inducing brain tumors in experimental animals and that this predisposition of it is of extremely high significance. ... In view of these indications that the cancer causing potential of aspartame is a matter that had been established way beyond any reasonable doubt, one can ask: What is the reason for the apparent refusal by the FDA to invoke for this food additive the so-called Delaney Amendment to the Food, Drug and Cosmetic Act?"

The Delaney Amendment makes it illegal to allow any residues of cancer causing chemicals in foods. In his concluding testimony Gross asked, "Given the cancer causing potential of aspartame how would the FDA justify its position that it views a certain amount of aspartame as constituting an allowable daily intake or 'safe' level of it? Is that position in effect not equivalent to setting a 'tolerance' for this food additive and thus a violation of that law? And if the FDA itself elects to violate the law, who is left to protect the health of the public?" Congressional Record SID835:131 (August 1, 1985) In original studies aspartame triggered not only brain tumors but mammary, uterine, ovarian, testicular, pancreatic and thyroid tumors.

In 1996, Ralph Walton, M.D., did research with scientific peer reviews and showed that 92% of independent studies showed the problems aspartame cause. Then in 2005 and 2007 Dr. Morando Soffritti,

Ramazzini Institute in Italy, published two monumental studies.

In 2005 he completed three years of impeccable research using 1,800 Sprague-Dawley rats (100-150/per sex/per group). To simulate varying human intake, aspartame was added to the standard rat diet in quantities of 5000, 2500, 100, 500, 20, 4, and 0 milligrams per kilogram of body weight. Treatment of the animals began when they were 8 weeks old, and continued until spontaneous death. The results were dynamic: APM causes a statistically significant, dose-related increase of lymphomas/leukemias and malignant tumors of the renal pelvis in females and malignant tumors of peripheral nerves in males. These results demonstrate for the first time that APM is a carcinogenic agent, capable of inducing malignancies at various dose levels, including those lower than the current acceptable daily intake (ADI) for humans (50 mg/kg of body weight in the US, 40 mg/kg of body weight in the EU).

Doctor Soffritti's second ERF study in 2007 was conducted on 400 Sprague-Dawley rats in much smaller doses to simulate daily human intake. It was added to their diet in quantities of 100, 20, and zero mg/Kg of body weight. Treatment of the animals began on the 12th day of fetal life until natural death. The results of the second study show an increased incidence of lymphomas/leukemias in female rats with respect to the first study. Moreover, the study shows that when lifespan exposure to APM begins during fetal life, the age at which lymphomas/leukemias develop in females is anticipated. For the first time, a statistically significant increase in mammary cancers in females was also observed in the second study. The results of this transplacental carcinogenicity bioassay not only confirm, but also reinforce the first experimental demonstration of APMs multipotential carcinogenicity.

On April 23, 2007, Dr. Soffritti received the Irving J. Selikoff Award for his outstanding contributions to the identification of environmental and industrial carcinogens and his promotion of independent scientific research. It has only been received twice before in history.

Dr. James Bowen points out that "aspartame is a known destroyer of DNA. The mitochondrial DNA (MtDNA) is especially damaged, yielding the present epidemic of diseases aspartame consuming mothers pass on to future generations. Aspartame also directly damages the mitochondria, thus having a 'double whammy' effect on mitochondrial function! The summation of these many known severe toxicities and its immune, genetic, mitochondrial, and metabolic damages, show that aspartame will not only cause many diseases, which the FDA and CDC have already noted but it has pathways of approach to interact adversely with every conceivable pharmaceutical."

According to the second Ramazzini Study if a pregnant women uses aspartame and the baby survives since aspartame triggers birth defects and mental retardation the child can grow up and have cancer.

The European Food Safety Authority with people on its committee connected to the aspartame business attempted to rebut the Ramazzini Studies and blamed the rat deaths on "respiratory disease." They know full well respiratory disease is the dying process. Professionals had a big laugh over that. Every burglar has an alibi!

Dr. Morando Soffritti said: "In examining the raw data of our study, the EFSA (2006) observed a high incidence of chronic pulmonary inflammation in males and females in both treated groups and in the control group. Based on this observation, it was concluded that "the increased incidence of lymphomas/leukemias reported in treated rats was unrelated to aspartame, given the high background incidence of chronic inflammatory changes in the lungs . . ." In my opinion, this conclusion is bizarre for the following reasons:

First, the EFSA (2006) overlooked the fact that the study was conducted until the natural death of the rodents. It is well known that infectious pathologies are part of the natural dying process in both rodents and humans.

Second, if the statistically significant increased incidence of lymphomas/leukemias observed were indeed caused by an infected colony, one would expect to observe an increased incidence of lymphomas/leukemias not only in females but also in males. The EFSA (2006) did not comment on this discrepancy in their logic.

Finally Dr. Herman Koeter of EFSA fessed up and admitted that commercial pressure controlled them with these words in his article *EU's Food Agency Battles Attempts to Hijack Science:* "Science and politics make poor bedfellows. Just ask Herman Koeter, deputy executive director at the European Food Safety Authority (EFSA) which has felt the push and pull of national politics ever since the agency began operating four years ago."

Koeter described the various political pressures EFSA faces as it strives to maintain a firm line between its independent scientific research and the mire of EU politics. Hot decisions that had political repercussions included... *A Review of a Controversial Aspartame Study.*

"Pressure comes from the European Commission, national legislators, regulatory agencies and industry to tone down or beef up results. Sometimes the pressure comes in the form of a push for a firm opinion on controversial subjects, when science is unable to yield a clear answer," Koeter said. Now Dr. Koeter is no longer with EFSA but at least before he left he told the world the truth.

Attorney James Turner, author of "The Chemical Feast: The Nader Report on Food Protection at the FDA," was the consumer attorney who with neuroscientist Dr. John Olney, legally fought the approval of aspartame from 1973 until 1985. He has reviewed with disappointment the European Food Safety Authority panel's original and amended conclusions on the second Ramazzini Study.

Mr. Turner states:

> It is impossible to say that Aspartame is not a carcinogen. This conclusion of the 1980 FDA Public Board of Inquiry remains true today. FDA's own scientist Dr. Adrian Gross, who worked on the FDA investigative team that revealed dozens of legal volition in the Aspartame's studies conducted by Searle Drug Company, acknowledged that aspartame violated the Delaney Amendment because of this.
>
> The approval of aspartame was the most contested in FDA history. The sweetener was not approved on scientific grounds but through strong political and financial pressure and through the political chicanery of Donald Rumsfeld who ran the company making aspartame. The European Food Safety

Authority argues that the high incidence of cancerous tumors that occurred in the Ramazzini studies are caused by something other than aspartame. However there were high incidences of cancerous tumors in studies provided to support aspartame's FDA approval.

There was also a significant increase in human cancerous tumors like those in animals in the first year of aspartame's use in diet sodas. The record is too damning for any informed individual to risk their own health by consuming aspartame. Aspartame should never have been approved and actions to ban it started soon after approval as victims suffered from seizures, MS, blindness, cancer and death. The FDA listed 92 reactions attributed to this poison.

When I testified before Congress in 1987, I stated that 'just because a substance reaches the market it should not be treated as sacrosanct. It must be recognized that over time a substance that we know harms people will continue to harm people. If the standard of food safety is that a substance that only harms some people, but not all people is going to be allowed on the market, then special policies should be adopted to protect those at risk.'This was never done.

Since approval, victims of aspartame continue to develop neurodegenerative disease, suffer diabetes, drug interactions, obesity, heart disease and loss of vision. Never has the public been warned that it triggers birth defects, a catastrophe the eminent Dr. Louis Elsas warned Congress about. In fact the average consumer of aspartame is not aware that the European Food Safety Authority says that an acceptable daily intake (ADI) of aspartame is 40 milligrams/kilogram of body weight about the amount in a six pact of diet soda for a 10 year old boy. Nor do they know how to tell if that amount is being exceeded by intake of the more than 5000 food and drug products currently sweetened with aspartame.

Enough from EFSA! The entire aspartame fiasco is documented. The only responsible thing to do is ban it. And if they refuse to ban it, then it should carry heavy warnings including a statement of the ADI and the amount of aspartame in every product. The Ramazzini Study has confirmed twice what the FDA knew from the beginning. To loose upon an entire unwarned continent a chemical that destroys the fetus, triggers mental illness and cancer, and sickens millions without a word of warning is corrupt and depraved. EFSA is responsible to prevent such depredations not simply protect the greedy pockets of poison producers.

Mr. Turner tells the Story of Aspartame Approval in
Sweet Misery: A Poisoned World.
Here is that clip: http://www.soundandfury.tv/pages/rumsfeld.html
Russell Blaylock, M.D. Neurosurgeon: Author: *Excitotoxins: the Taste That Kills* and *Natural Strategies for Cancer Patients* commenting on both Ramazzini studies, said: "My review of the first Ramazzini Study concluded that the study was one of the best designed, comprehensive and conclusive studies done to date on the multipotential carcinogenic danger of aspartame. This second study is even more conclusive, in that it shows a dose-dependent statistically significant increase in lymphomas/leukemia in both male and female rats exposed to aspartame. These two cancers are the fastest growing cancers in people under age 30.

Also, of major concern is their finding of statistically significant increases in breast cancer in animals exposed to aspartame. With newer studies clearly indicating that toxic exposures during fetal development can dramatically increase the cancer risk of the offspring, this study takes on a very important meaning to all pregnant women consuming aspartame products. Likewise, small children are at considerable risk of the later development of these highly fatal cancers. It should be appreciated that the doses used in these studies fall within the range of doses seen in everyday users of aspartame. This study, along with the first study, should convince any reasonable scientific mind, as well as the public, that this product should be removed from the market.http://www.russellblaylockmd.com

Everything on aspartame is a matter of public record and the reports listed on web sites such as www.mpwhi.com, www.dorway.com, www.wnho.net and www.holisticmed.com/aspartame Dr. Maria Alemany, who did the Trocho Study showing that the formaldehyde converted from the free methyl alcohol embalms living tissue told me when I consulted him in Barcelona: "Betty, aspartame will kill 200 million."

Many times this poison is hidden in things that say artificial and natural flavors so you have to avoid processed foods. For 18 years I've taken the case histories of the sick and dying and it's hard when you hear a young girl with a head full of aspartame brain tumors cry: "I want to live, I want to live, I want to live."

Aspartame causes everything from MS, lupus, blindness and seizures to sudden cardiac death. Do not use it—your life depends on it. There have been three congressional hearings and efforts to ban it ever since it was marketed due to the political chicanery of Donald Rumsfeld who was CEO of Searle to get it approved. The FDA had revoked the petition for approval. However, if you don't buy it they can't sell it! Also do not use Splenda, a chlorocarbon poison. "Just Like Sugar" is a safe sweetener usually sold in Whole Foods. It's just chicory, orange peel, Vitamin C and Calcium.

"Deliver those who are being taken away to death; and those staggering to the slaughter, O may you hold them back. In case you should say: 'Look! We did not know of this,' will not he himself that is making an estimate of hearts discern it, and he himself that is observing your soul know and certainly pay back to earthling man according to his activity" (Proverbs 24: 11, 12).

The Lethal Science of Splenda:
http://www.wnho.net/splenda_chlorocarbon.htm

Studies have shown that sucralose can:
- Cause the thymus to shrink by as much as 40% (the thymus is your immune powerhouse—it produces T cells)

- Cause enlargement of the liver and kidneys
- Reduce growth rate as much as 20%
- Cause enlargement of the large bowel area
- Reduce the amount of good bacteria in the intestines by 50%
- Increase the pH level in the intestines (a high risk factor for colon cancer)
- Contribute to weight gain
- Cause aborted pregnancy low fetal body weight
- Reduce red blood cell count

Particular warning to diabetics: Researchers found that diabetic patients using sucralose showed a statistically significant increase in glycosylated hemoglobin, a marker that is used to assess glycemic control in diabetic patients. According to the FDA, "increases in glycosolation in hemoglobin imply lessening of control of diabetes."

For the most complete and profound information on these issues visit my friend Dr. Betty Martini's websites:

www.mpwhi.com

www.dorway.com

www.wnho.net

Just Like Sugar® 100% Natural, Without the Negative of Sugar

Mission Possible International is a global volunteer force in the US and 40 nations warning the world of aspartame.

We are constantly asked for a healthy sweetener and here it is!

I would like to introduce all of you to a wonderful all 100% natural FDA GRAS approved sweetener made from only the purest of ingredients. It is called Just Like Sugar®. This sweetener mimics the attributes of regular cane or beet sugar in every way without any of the negatives from sugar or artificial sweeteners on the market today.

I personally use Just Like Sugar® each and every day. I cannot tell the difference in taste between cane sugar and Just Like Sugar® in beverages, food and baked goods.

Just Like Sugar® is a wonderful natural alternative for those health conscious people, who choose a calorie-restricted diet. Just Like Sugar® is a great natural option for children and adult's a like suffering from diabetes or on restricted diet programs where standard sugars are not allowed.

Just Like Sugar® enhanced composition is a source of Natural Dietary Fiber obtained from Chicory Root, Calcium and Vitamin C, which should be essential ingredients in everyone's daily diet. Just Like Sugar® comprises a perfect blend of crystalline Chicory Root Dietary Fiber, Calcium, Vitamin C and the sweetness come from the peel of the Orange.

The health benefits of Just Like Sugar® are unlike any other sugar substitutes now available. Since it is 96% Dietary Fiber and clinical research has proven a diet high in Dietary Fiber greatly reduces the risk of colon and other digestive cancers, the use of Just Like Sugar® will greatly reduce those risks. The synergic action from the Dietary Fiber, Calcium and Vitamin C greatly increase the Magnesium absorption in the body. Chicory Root has been used worldwide for over 72 years to control blood sugar levels. Using this product will help stabilize the body's blood sugar levels for both Diabetics and non Diabetics.

Among the many other health benefits when using Just Like Sugar® on a daily basis, there are three that I think are very important:

- The more you eat the more weight you lose and many people have said their skin gets soft and your wrinkles disappear.

- The Nutrition Facts per a one hundred gram serving Size found: 0 Calories, 0 Sugar, 0 Fat, 0 Cholesterol, 0 Sodium, 0 Carbohydrates and 0 Protein.

- It does not contain any Soy, Yeast, animal derivatives. It is Gluten Free, Wheat Free, Dairy Free, Vegan Safe, there are on preservatives; it is not fermentable and will not promote tooth decay.

A copy of the Nutrition Facts report can be found at:
http://www.justlikesugarinc.com
under the heading Product Information.

My esteemed colleague Dr. Russell Blaylock, M.D. had an Excito-toxicity Analysis preformed on Just Like Sugar® by a FDA approved testing laboratory in September of 2005. A copy of the Excitotoxicity Analysis report can be found at http://www.justlikesugarinc.com under the heading Product Information. The test results proved there is No "MSG," No L-Glutamic Acid, No D-Glutamic Acid, and No Aspartic Acid in Just Like Sugar® as found in artificial sweeteners. This Sweetener is completely safe!

I strongly urge all of my readers to start using Just Like Sugar® immediately for your health, the health of your children and grand children. It is available in three formulations: Table Top, Baking and Brown. The product can be purchased from Just Like Sugar, Inc. and such fine stores as Whole Foods Markets, Henry's Farmers Markets, Sun Harvest Markets and thousands of other quality health food stores Nationwide. The product can also be found worldwide. A list of worldwide distributors is available on their web site:
http://www.justlikesugarinc.com

We do not have any financial interest or advantage by promoting this product!

LIVING A LONG LIFE IN EXCELLENT PHYSICAL AND MENTAL HEALTH

What is the use of all your success, if you are ill or die early? We all know examples of people who go through life as if they were chased by an unseen force. They run anxiously through life, from one job to the next, maybe even one relationship to the next. They have no time for themselves, their family, their friends or hobbies. By the age of 35 or 45 they may be highly respected, have accumulated great wealth and enjoy social and professional recognition, but very soon afterward they have a heart attack or stroke, or suffer from some other limitations.

If we observe those negative examples we realize that it's completely nonsense that we should try to overcome every job with force, perseverance and self-discipline, thereby completely neglecting our personal needs and ourselves.

Many people work without ever enjoying the results of their labor. Scientific research shows that 20% of all people suffer serious health problems resulting from work because they could not deal with professional stress; 7% died of the illness labeled as "stress."

The same research showed that another 7% did just the opposite.

They are successful, healthy, vital and fit. They enjoy excellent relation-ships, their family functions very well; they have good friends, pleasant hobbies and enjoy a wonderful quality of life.

What is the difference between the positive 7% and the negative 7%? In my opinion, the results of the research points to the principles found in the IBMS™ program; which is about...

Observing the Internal Signals

Learn to become aware of the signals of your body, the many aches and pains, because they are warning signs from your subconscious that something in your emotional and physical behavior is out of sync. They make you sick or destroy you. Learn not to ignore those signals, but to use them. They will help you to identify and eliminate the causes.

There are several ways in dealing with a conflict situation. You can look for a quick way out and swallow some pills, you can deceive your-self, you can dissuade yourself from looking for a cause, or you can read some books that offer a quick fix. They may tell you to take a vitamin cure or do some exercises, so that you will look good. But none of these will make you healthy or help your mind and body, and none of them will produce lasting results.

The only acceptable way is the one that corresponds with your own wishes, needs and dreams, and with all the elements that are part of your personality. You need long-term goals and an effective strategy.

Modeling Your Success

Modeling our pattern of behavior, our belief system and thought patterns, is a natural way of learning to live. We are trained by imitating emotional and physical behavior. People acquire their belief system, values, and inner convictions from their parents, grandparents, teachers, ministers and friends. This includes their gestures, physical and emotional behavior, as well as their approach to health. They either teach us to satisfy our needs and enjoy times for regeneration or they may teach us to live our lives with superstitions and ignorance. All this behavior is taught, they are acquired patterns of behavior.

If a parent smokes; the chances that a child will also smoke is about 65% to 70%. If one of the parents is an alcoholic, there is a 50% chance that their child will become an alcoholic, and if both parents are alcoholics the probability becomes 75%. We will often live a life as fit, or unfit, as our parents. They either take regular care of their health, or they completely neglect their physical needs.

We must learn new patterns of behavior and learn to live with these positive changes.

I have become successful in my work by studying and modeling my life after those who are healthy, vital, and successful—people who have succeeded in creating solid relationships and maintained these over a long period of time—people who were very successful in every area of life and who were brimming with health and vitality.

You too must learn to understand the patterns of behavior, belief systems and thought patterns of successful colleagues, friends and others around you and pattern your own life accordingly. You will save yourself many disappointments and time because you can simply follow the successful steps of other, learning how they deal with stress and take care of their health, and you will find it easier to reach your goals.

Basic Elements for a Wonderful Quality Of Life

Self-confidence is an essential part of optimal health. The more you accept yourself, the more gratified you are, and the more likely you will do positive things for your body, mind and spirit.

Self-confidence starts with viewing problems as challenges. You must use them as opportunities so that you can grow and develop, and avoid pushing them aside and destroying your health.

We must force ourselves to persevere, to make our own decisions and set our own goals so that we can fulfill our dreams. This is one of the most important decisions we can make in our lives. If we are willing to pay the price of success and are not willing to succumb, we will succeed in reaching our goal, no matter what happens. Even F.D.R., who was in a wheelchair, realized his dream to become president of the United States.

We must take charge of our lives by setting long-term and short-term goals. We must accept that life will hand us many challenges and that we will have to face a lot of interferences on our way to a wonderful life. We must learn to see ourselves as waves in the ocean, not the victims of waves.

The Danger of Emotional Conflicts

Neuro-chemical changes will take place in our body if we are exposed to real danger, such as an automobile accident. Those chemical changes protect us by giving us more energy and they may also prepare the body for the possible loss of blood, pain, etc. All this energy is focused on overcoming the momentary physical crisis as well as possible. When the crisis has passed, all our bodily values will return to normal.

It is nevertheless very dangerous to dwell on fears and conflicts that are not yet real. It weakens our body, mind and energy without being able to change our emotional outlook. Our bodies will keep running overtime in a dis-stress situation and suffer damage. If this artificial dis-stress situation is repeated, we introduce permanent and negative changes.

The crisis does not end and the body will never return to its normal condition. Migraines, backaches and even a heart attack can be the result. The 7% of the people who are in excellent health do not suffer less stress than you do, rather they have learned to cope with stress and know how to deal with the stressful situations in their life.

An unhealthy life that lacks a clear value system, a life in which a person merely tries to survive by paying their bills and living from day to day instead of building a financial independence they can enjoy, is a life that is miserable, pre-programmed, and without a healthy self-image.

We must learn to take life a little easier. We all have experienced that a situation, which looked threatening one day, looked totally different after a good night's sleep. We can hardly believe our worries of the day before.

A good relationship with our partner is just as important as excellent nutrition, regular sleep, physical and emotional fitness and a regular medical check-up. We must learn to take care of our health, nurse an illness and not go back to work until we are completely healthy.

There is no advantage in trying to function with a weak body and insufficient energy. We enjoy few benefits if we lose time by repeated relapse.

Family and Friends - The Foundation of Health and Success

A solid strong support system gives us energy, security, strength, vitality and success. Loneliness and isolation often lead to feelings of helplessness, which then leads to illness. It is extremely important to remember your family, friends and supporters that helped you along the way to your success. To be lonely and successful is a contradiction in terms.

In my therapeutic work, I met many patients who at first appearance seemed successful, happy and content; in fact, I thought they had it all! However, I soon discovered that the higher they climbed on the professional ladder, the lonelier they became even though they had material wealth and professional success. The problem was that they had lost their support system along the way. Their family, friends and children all left them along the way and they ended up alone, unhappy, dissatisfied and sick.

Loneliness generally leads to bitterness, which in turn leads to a lowered immune system. Bitterness arises as we become aware that we have not lived up to our potential as a human being and that the things that are really important in life have eluded us. Without family and close friends there is an emptiness to life no matter what the level of success. This feeling leads to self-pity and a negative attitude which depletes our energy, thus lowering our immune system with the result that we suffer a health breakdown.

I can honestly say that the people that I met that were the truly exceptional and successful people, in every case, were as attentive to their personal team (family, friends, etc.), as they were to their professional team. In addition, they were filled with energy and vitality, and their immune system was very healthy, thanks to the emotional support they received. Having a team and being a member of a good team are the best therapy against depression and frustration. Playing on a "team" enhances our desire to work and has a positive influence on our energy and health.

Yale University concluded in a research study that each person in our life influences at least 250 people who, in turn, influence another 250 people. Even if we reduce their number to 200, it still means that every person directly and indirectly touches 40,000 people (200 times 200). With this in mind, we should remember to behave as if we are influencing 40,000 people and that it is extremely important to our own success to treat everyone as if they were the most important person in your life.

If you have a personal and professional social network, it will catch you if you fall financially, emotionally or physically. Having people to help, bounce ideas off or work with saves strength, effort, and energy. In fact, comparable studies performed at several universities derived the following similar conclusion—only eight percent of the things that cause our fears and worries can be consciously influenced by our own thoughts and actions. As a result, since we cannot control ninety-two percent of our anxieties and fears, it is futile and a waste of time and energy to worry about the things you have no control over like the economy, world politics, the weather, etc. Instead, concentrate on the eighty percent that you can do something about and forget the rest.

Your relationship with your spouse or your life partner affects approximately eighty percent of your health and success. If you are very successful professionally, but your personal life is a disaster, your energy will be adversely affected and eventually your professional life will suffer as you feel more and more burdened with failures and setbacks in your personal life. The result is that you continue living feeling apathetic, indifferent, lethargic, and frustrated, all of which manifest into corresponding medical problems.

Success depends on team play. It is much easier to eliminate feelings of loneliness and helplessness with someone we love and who loves us. It is easier to cope with feelings of frustration, indifference and anger if you can share them with somebody! To experience lasting success and health, it is crucial to have a well-balanced and contented personal life, which is why your personal life should always be the highest priority when you set your goals.

To create great relationships you need to be yourself. Don't play a role just to satisfy others. Show the world who you really are. Then you have only people in your life that like, love and accept you the way you really are and you don't have to constantly produce stress by denying yourself to be the true you.

Dealing Well With Fear

We must learn to recognize fear for what it is: a warning signal to protect us. Fear can protect us in life threatening danger. We must learn to accept fear as a friend and helper. We must learn to control our fears and not let fears control us.

If you are faced with fear, first examine whether your fear is real. Is this real worry and is it justified? If so, why do you need protection? Should you be concerned for your safety?

If you have identified this fear and you feel it is justified, concentrate on finding an effective solution for the problem as soon as possible. Spend twenty percent on the identification of your fear and eighty percent on the development of strategies for coping with the situation.

The stressful situation and the threat to your mind will only disappear when you remove the dangerous situation. Many ancient teachings say that you must enter into the heart of your fear before you can conquer it.

But you must also learn to take calculated risks, because no life comes with a safety guarantee. To succeed at anything in life and find satisfaction you must always be willing to take some calculated risks.

Accept the challenges of life so that you can develop your mind. Continued growth and development are the greatest stress relievers. Your self-confidence, self-esteem and self-image will increase as a result, which will help you to deal better with critical life situations.

The Foundation for Top Performance

Strong self-esteem and self-confidence are also important aspects of a good quality of life. The way we see ourselves and our self-image, the way we view who we are and what we can achieve, determines our behavior in every area of life. Our self-awareness is the product of our experiences, the result of our day-to-day behavior.

The opportunities presented to us are formed by the way others see us. Just as we see the success in the lives of other people that inspire and help us to believe that we can also attain such prosperity, we build a self-image that corresponds with our ability to achieve. For instance, if we see a colleague cope calmly and efficiently with a hectic and demanding daily schedule, it opens us up to the possibility of reacting and behaving in the same unruffled manner.

Our self-confidence and belief in our ability to achieve is also influenced by the encouragement and confidence of others. People who believe in us and encourage us, who recognize our abilities, and who value our intelligence, will strengthen our self-confidence.

Other important elements in the building of a healthy self-image are physical reactions. When we hurt, are worn out and have no energy left, we become convinced that we cannot do our work. We may believe that we can't trust ourselves because we cannot trust our bodies. Our emotional and physical development can, therefore, have a negative influence on the results we produce.

Your Future

Learn to see the future as an architect, capable of building whatever you wish, not as victim who is at the mercy of life. With self-confidence your health will grow, and when you are in good health your strength and courage will increase, and as a result you will have a better self-image. The way you feel about your job also plays an integral part in the state of your health.

Exercise:

1. What exactly do you want to do and achieve in your profession?

Are you in a job you love? Do you need or want to go back to school? Do you want a higher position?

2. How does your current health fit in with how you want to be in the future? How do you want to look and feel? What can you do to make that happen?

3. What does professional success mean to you? When will you know you've achieved it? What will you have in your life and how will you feel?

4. How can you reach your professional goals? Is there someone who can help you? Do you have a plan worked out? Is there a time frame in which you'd like to accomplish this?

5. Make a list of things you need to do and people you need to talk to in order to achieve the professional success you desire. Take steps each day to follow your list.

Learned Limitations

Negative programming starts in our earliest childhood. Expressions like, "Don't do such things," "That's not right," "You will never be able to do that," are impressed into our minds at a young age. Parents, teachers, clergy, and other adults often impress their own fears and limitations on us.

To become aware of the learned behavior that limits your life—the programming that diminishes your potential to succeed—answer the following questions as accurately and as completely as you can. If you later remember something you forgot, please add it to your journal.

Exercise:

1. What are the limitations you were taught about love, money, a dream job or even health?

2. How did your parents, teachers, and others hurt your self-image and discourage you from making full use of your possibilities and talents?

3. Which dreams have slipped through your fingers because you were taught that they were foolish, difficult, or you simply weren't talented enough to make it happen?

4. If you followed your instincts and emotions, which talents, skills and possibilities would you now possess?

5. If you were absolutely certain that whatever dream you followed wouldn't fail, what would you do? What would your ideal self be like?

You can't really know a person by the way they behave and by the achievements you see at this point of time. We know a person by their wishes, dreams and goals, by their needs and by the person they would like to be with all their heart

Now, you must now develop a plan of action for every dream; a step by step plan for the realization of every goal you wrote down. Don't place limits on yourself, but don't go overboard either. Like everything in life, seek a healthy balance. Rather than letting your rational thinking determine your needs, wishes, goals and dreams, let your emotions and intuition decide what you can or can't do.

Living without Fear

As the saying goes, there is nothing to fear but fear itself. When we learn to cope with fear we will find that we can influence every area of our life, no matter the circumstances. It is not "what" happens in our life, but "how" we react to what happens that determines our future.

The more often we see a crisis situation as an assignment, and the quicker we work toward a solution, the stronger our self-image will become as we deal skillfully with the situation. If we do not recognize a stress situation, we must cope with the crisis while we are unprepared and will often lack the needed energy to do so.

By facing a crisis situation, goal and solution-oriented, we prepare the resources in our subconscious, so that we act skillfully in difficult life situations. We will be conditioned to act without shrinking back or with self-pity.

The lives of other people are not easier than ours, no matter what we like to believe. They have simply learned to cope more effectively when they face difficulties. Although we cannot always influence difficult situations in life, we *can* decide what to do and where we want to be. We can decide how we want to use our skills and talents and which self-image we want to create of ourselves.

Exercise:

1. What are your worst fears and anxieties?

2. Why do these make you afraid?

3. What is the worst think that could happen if your fears came true?

4. How could you handle or prepare for these worst-case scenarios?

To remove a fear you must study the situation thoroughly and act solution-oriented. As soon as we learn to accept the crises in our lives as challenges and turn them into opportunities for growth, our lives will change.

Exercise:

1. What successes have you achieved in the past? (No matter how small.)

2. What positive results did enjoy because of these successes?

Someone who loses hope in a crisis situation loses focus and no longer sees a way of escape, they are lost. Medical research shows that people who receive a diagnosis of a serious or chronic illness will experience a sharp decline of their immune system. If they lose all hope they often die quickly. By this example we can see that successful results depend on a person's outlook on life.

Exercise:

1. List all those situations in which you feel stressed, nervous, overburdened, overworked or tense.

2. Choose a few examples from your list and write down how you could improve your reaction to them in the future.

3. Think about one of the examples you listed above and act out your desired reaction as though it were really happening. To program this desired reaction into your subconscious you must run this "script" at least twenty-one times through your mind so you will automatically see and live this pattern of behavior. You don't have to do this all at once. You can run your new script three times a day for a week, but eventually you will create a positive program and your mind will no longer react with stress when you face the difficult situation.

Take a good look at people who conquer crisis situations. If possible, talk to them and find out how those people think and react, what their thought processes are and why they act the way they do. Try to install their thought process in your own mind. Form as many positive references as you can.

Don't forget to take a look at your own past. You have overcome difficulties before in your life.

Exercise:

1. Write down the crisis and problems you have faced and the difficulties you have overcome.

2. How did you do it?

3. What were you thinking then that you could apply to future problems you may face?

Your Personal Responsibility

Willingness is the secret of success. You must decide and prepare to accept the responsibility by giving the time and paying the price necessary to achieve the desired success.

I am the last person to tell you that life is fair and good. That is certainly not so. Life is neutral; it is neither for nor against you. You will run into just as many positive as negative situations.

Your destiny is the result of your mental and physical behavior. We can say that our future will yield the fruit of the mental and physical behavior of yesterday and today; our life is nothing but the reflection of all our thoughts and actions. If you do not allow a willingness to fail enter your mind, if you do not even consider this possibility, you will be guaranteed success. It's up to you, who you want to be, what you want to achieve and what you will allow in your life.

Accept responsibility and control over every area of your life, whether it is an assignment or a decision. Escape leads to stress. Because the task is never accomplished, you keep yourself in a stress-situation, which may have disastrous results.

If you do not like your current line of work, you may die from it.

Exercise:

1. Define clearly why you like or dislike your work

2. What are the fruits of your labor?

3. What does your work mean to you?

4. How could it be better?

5. If you don't like your job, how could you prepare yourself for a better one?

Emotional and Physical Fitness

Body and spirit work together through a cybernetic cohesion—what affects one touches the other. It is therefore not possible to work on emotional health and neglect the physical. You must therefore install, as you have learned in this program, an excellent emotional fitness program that includes physical health, fitness and energy.

This includes nutrition that consists of 70% liquid-rich foods and 30% dry foods, regular aerobic exercise, and other exercises that increase instead of use up your oxygen content.

We must also learn correct breathing, sit up straight and move as needed instead of staying in a seated position for hours on end. We must pay attention to the warning signals of our body; the aches, pains, limitations, etc. We must remove the source before we suffer lasting damage.

Decide intelligently who you want to be, what you want to achieve and then do it.

Exercise:

1. Make a list of your current or potential talents and skills

2. How can you use or start to use them more effectively?

If you prevent your mind from dwelling on your past and look for solutions and act accordingly, then the past cannot influence your future. Do not let mistakes or failures of the past influence your life any longer and don't allow those failures creep into your future.

Depending On Others

We are social animals, and feel comfortable, only when we are surrounded by other people. We all depend on friends, acquaintances and relatives to be part of our lives—people who cry with us when we are in pain and laugh with us when we are happy or successful.

There will be times when you feel anger at your own life or the lives of others; there will be times of self-pity and self-hatred, but put a limit on those time periods. Determine the time you allow yourself to grieve when you suffer a blow. This could be minutes or hours, or, with more serious situations, a few days or even a week, but then you must settle on a point in time that you will return to being active and stop nursing your grief. You must return to the present and think of your positive future so that negative emotions do not become part of a pattern or let you lose control.

Also, never believe that you are merely the victim of life's circumstances, because in reality you are the creator. Running away from problems causes stress; solving problems removes them.

Exercise:

1. Which tasks and problems do you regularly avoid?

2. How can you change this poor behavior step-by-step?

Another essential element of energy, health, vitality, harmony and happiness is the confirmation of self. You must develop a positive bonus system in which you reward yourself for reaching certain goals. The goals do not need to be large. Decide how you want to reward yourself when you have achieved a certain result.

Exercise:

1. Make a list of different rewards you can give to yourself after reaching certain goals. Be sure that they fit in with your budget and within the frame of the problem or situation you overcame or solved. For instance, you wouldn't reward yourself with a trip to Paris simply because you balanced your budget this month.

2. Reward yourself frequently, but only when it is justified.

Prepare Yourself for Life

If you are devoid of resources when you are in a crisis situation, you will panic. You must learn to prepare and program yourself, as I instructed before, so that you can react as well as possible in an eventual stressful situation.   Preparation does not mean that you should be afraid. Preparation means that you look for ways and means, so that you will be able to react in any situation that may arise.

To feel helpless is one of the worst emotional situations because helplessness has an extremely negative effect on your health and on your performance. Studies have shown that patients who feel helpless die earlier. People, who feel that they are in charge, even if their control is limited, have a better life expectation and a stronger immune system. In fact, medical specialists have found that those patients who could administer their own medicine and decide on their own lifestyle, were living longer than so-called dependent patients; those who lived in hospitals and were virtually helpless.

We must all learn, as quickly as possible, to instill a feeling of control in our subconscious, in our thought process, and in our behavior. We must install a pattern of behavior that takes it for granted and accepts it as absolutely normal that we are in charge. To run away, ignore or avoid problems sets in motion the beginnings of catastrophe.

Failures teach us to act and modify our behavior. We will unavoidably produce better and more effective results than before. When we learn from mistakes and act accordingly, our experience will direct us to the desired results.

If you know that a relationship is no longer working and you are only hanging on out of convenience, because of finances, not wanting to be alone, or whatever reason, then this relationship becomes destructive. After you have done everything possible to make the relationship work for both parties and accept that there is no hope, you must look immediately for a solution to end the partnership.

Guilt can cause incredible stress, and guilty feelings seldom disappear by themselves. People who have them can suffer their whole life as a result. People condition themselves by searching their subconscious for errors and failures and are no longer able to function. Their self-esteem is diminished and they are no longer able to look for solutions; they keep searching for excuses for their failures.

If you suffer from guilt, you must learn to face people with an apology or do something to pay your debt. You can also talk with them and come to an understanding. If this is impossible, look for another way to release your guilt.

Exercise:

1. In what areas do you feel guilty? Whom did you hurt and why?

2. Is there a way for you to redeem yourself and release the guilt as quickly as possible? Or is there no real reason why you *should* feel guilty?

Taking the First Step

If we are facing a large job and are focusing on the completed final result without subdividing the project into smaller parts, we often feel overwhelmed, or we suffer from anxiety, because we are afraid that we are not up to the task.

But if we divide the job in front of us into smaller parts that we can handle, we will experience small successes that will strengthen our self-confidence. As a result, we will do our work better and accomplish more. We will also finish the job faster than we thought possible. By dividing the job into smaller parts, that are easier to accomplish, we will feel assured that we can handle the whole job.

The first step is often the most difficult one. Once we start working on a job, the rest often becomes easy.

Asking for help, or looking for team solutions, when we face a conflict or must solve a serious problem is also important. Brainstorming, or sharing ideas, often helps us to move ahead. Using research material, changing our behavior, and working with a team often helps us to feel more confident. Members of the team will also feel better because they can contribute to our life; we will get a better understanding and move ahead together and fast than if we did it all ourselves. This does not only work for a work team, but it is also important and helpful when it involves our family.

A Feeling of Helplessness

Our quality of life is frequently burdened by feeling of helplessness. Those emotions can easily be removed though if you give yourself a feeling of control, thereby creating a sense of inner calm and security.

You can find a solution in the following way:

Exercise:

1. What do you feel helpless about and why?

2. What can you do to change your feelings to that of control rather than helplessness?

3. Make a step-by step plan of action and follow it.

Stress is like being in the ocean. You can either drown or you can have lots of fun. It depends on your decisions and preparation.

Your Value-Systems

If you want to live a life free of stress, it is important that you understand what your personal values really are. You can establish your own goal-oriented life by accentuating those values through further development and by enriching your life with regular successful experiences.

If you know exactly what you want, you will suffer far less stress because you won't be uncertain about your desires. It will be easier to make decisions because you know exactly what you want, and, as a result, you can make sensible, goal-oriented decisions that fit within the scheme of your life.

To do this, you must learn to build, develop, and expand your leadership qualities by creating pictures and scenes in your mind of your talents, skills and values, which you can then transform into reality. By doing this you can reach your full potential. And, when you live by your own value-system, you in turn give everyone else the opportunity to live by their own rules and values, giving them a feeling of significance.

Humor

We should not overlook one of the most important elements in stress-reduction: Humor! Nothing can break down stress and tension like humor. It lightens the atmosphere and relaxes everyone around. Problems lose some of their magnitude, making it easier to cope.

We must always try to turn negative situations into positive. Look for an opportunity to turn a difficult situation into a funny one, or try to find something positive in a bad situation and see what you can do with it.

A German proverb says: "If you shout into a forest, the echo will sound as you spoke." Therefore, we should never approach anyone with aggression, because aggressive behavior breeds aggression. If we remain cool and composed, there is a much greater chance that the other person will also stay calm. We must learn and practice what we know all too well: Treat others as you would like to be treated.

It isn't necessary to prove yourself more powerful to those who are weaker or ignorant. You don't have to build yourself up in the eyes of someone who is sick or helpless, because you know who and what you are. You know you can be proud of your work and profession and it isn't nice to rub it in.

We know that what goes around comes around, so we must try to be kind, and spread harmony and humor when and where we can because it will fill our life with wonderful feelings.

The Right Balance

If we want a body that is free of illness, we must learn to strike a perfect balance between our private and our professional life. Because you are the only one who receives messages from your own subconscious, letting you know when you have done enough or had enough, you alone can strike the right balance between your work and your private life.

Regular exercise should be a part of your daily life. Stretching and relaxation are two of the best that will help you to be able to move around well into old age. Movement is an important part of stress reduction, as long as you don't over exert yourself. Please, don't become a slave to any fitness and training program. Find out which exercise movements are best for *you* and create a well balanced program that suits you.

Take care that you eat meals rich in nutrition and energy, especially when you are faced with work that demands large emotional and physical input. Don't mix carbohydrates and proteins in the same meal so you avoid wasting energy in the digestion process. Avoid foods that take a long time to digest, like meat, when you must complete a difficult assignment because you will suffer from lack of energy.

Clinical psychiatrists have concluded that negative, emotional, conditions and depression are reduced or even fully removed with plenty of exercise. Walking and exercise can "burn off" certain types of depression. Regular exercise increases the amount of oxygen in our body and negative feelings, like frustration and listlessness, which are often the result of a shortage of energy, can be avoided or disappear quickly.

Don't follow a diet, because no special diet is tailor-made for your body and needs. Simply learn to eat only when you're hungry, stop eating when you're satisfied, and don't ever eat hard to digest foods, when you're under stress.

Hunger heightens stress to a large degree. Therefore, it's wise to eat small amounts of food when you feel hungry rather than to walk around hungry and wait for the clock to tell you it's time to eat. Learn to listen to your body, not to the dinner bell.

Sensible, regenerating sleep is also important to reducing and avoiding stress. Small power naps of a half-hour or an hour are not sufficient because the sleep cycle of the body doesn't start until after ninety minutes.

Sleeping pills are often responsible, or at least partly responsible, for permanent damage caused by stress, because if you take sleeping pills your body cannot fully recuperate. You can also become dependent on pills or even develop a resistance, something you definitely want to avoid. Alcohol isn't any better in helping you to sleep since it has a negative effect on brain waves and disturbs sleep patterns, so you can't fully regenerate.

Use your bed only for sleep, never for work. Never read work material in bed, only read for enjoyment. Do not study in bed, do not work problems out in your mind and do not create stress by focusing your attention on work related activities that you do not want to forget. You will not be able to relax and, because the thoughts are in your mind, they will become part of your dreams.

It's a good idea to have a notebook and pencil on your night stand. If you get an idea you can quickly write your thoughts down and your mind will not dwell on the thought.

It also helps to approach sleep by making self-suggestions and programming your mind to have a restful sleep. You can say to yourself, "I will sleep well, have wonderful thoughts and dreams all through the night. In the morning I will wake up feeling fresh, healthy and full of vitality." If you go to sleep repeatedly like this, you will program your behavior for the desired sleep and regeneration.

Even when you feel wide awake and cannot sleep, lie down anyway because your body will relax and start the process of regeneration naturally.

We need to find a balance in all things in life. Through learned behavior from parents, friends, colleagues, and others around us, we may pick up bad habits. Often, we don't realize what we keep doing wrong because it has become a natural part of our behavior.

Exercise:

1. Make a list of your unwanted habits and keep adding to the list when you recognize other faults.

2. How does the unwanted behavior stand in your way of optimal health and success?

3. What is missing at this moment from your ideal self-image?

4. What do you hope to gain from excellent health and vitality?

5. What will be the disadvantages if you don't take care of your health?

6. Develop a plan of action so that you will reach and stay at your ideal vision of personal health.

Living Without Feelings of Guilt

You not only have the right, but also the responsibility to live your life as is best for you, and to shape it in a way that corresponds with your wishes, needs and dreams. By doing this, you can use and promote your own talents, skills and opportunities more easily than if you're following someone else's rules.

So often we are talked into feelings of guilt by people who want to use and exploit us. There is usually no real context for guilt. There is frequently no malicious intent when people harm us. (We are not speaking of criminal elements here.) The guilty feelings we live with were drummed into our head when we were very young; programmed into our minds in our earliest childhood.

You not only have the right, but the duty to do everything possible to be happy, satisfied, healthy and successful in every area of your life. Anyone who tries to stop you is doing this for his own profit. It makes no sense to stumble through life with emotional falsehoods that force you to live with excessive humility, self-abasement and other life drainers.

Naturally, we must not behave without consideration of others, but we must learn to stand by our convictions and live accordingly. We must never try to reach someone else's goals, only our own. We should never try to live by the values, morals and ethics of other people or groups, only our own.

Learn to enjoy yourself, and have fun, so that you can relax. Set time aside to enjoy yourself every day, every week, or every month. Fun and pleasure offer the best opportunities for regeneration, happiness and health.

Imagine that you are nine years old again. At that age you were most interested in life; it was a time of your greatest curiosity. There was a willingness to discover your skills and talents, and a time to delve into new hobbies. Ask yourself what your hobbies were in those days, what you liked to do when you were nine. Scrutinize those needs and desires, because they may also bring you enjoyment and fulfillment today.

I have already admitted that I am a champion of team-spirit and team-play, so I want to point out here that it's important to have fun with others. Of course, there are times when we want to be alone and we should fulfill those needs too.

Don't accept the same line of thinking that many other people have who believe they can only shed the daily stress of life and work on vacations. We know from research and therapy, that many people suffer heart attacks because they don't recognize other ways to be free of tension.

If the requirements from work or from other areas of your life become too demanding, then your subconscious may react with shutting you off, frequently with illness. When it gets to this point, you can no longer influence a situation in a positive way. You are drawn away from participation in the threatening and ominous environment and forced to recuperate.

Exercise:

Read this exercise through before practicing.

Lean back in a comfortable chair or lay down on your bed. Close your eyes and imagine that you have reached the end of your life. Pretend you're 96 years old, or even older; as old as you hope to be.

Now, look back on your life and think about the accomplishments you wished you had achieved and the adventures you would have liked to experience. What joyful goals would you have liked to have reached?

Stay with these scenes for a bit then get out your journal and make a list of the dreams and accomplishments you wish you had achieved. Do what you can every day to make them happen.

The Importance of Personal Creativity

If you want to realize your talents and enjoy the life you deserve, you must develop the willingness to give your creativity a chance. Don't let "rational" thinking, or outside pressures by other people suppress or even stifle your creative activities.

To give your creativity a chance, you must be open to a new way of thinking and explore new ideas. You shouldn't just block new ideas, but should test them. You must evaluate new ideas and decide whether they would be right for you, whether they make sense, and whether you want to make use of them and make them a part of your own life.

You must learn to live in the now and let yourself be guided by your intuition, thoughts and feelings.

To give creativity a chance in your life you must let go of the past. Only when you are willing to try what is new and experiment with new information, will your dormant skills have a chance to work toward positive creative results.

When you dwell on difficult situations in your life you are often unable to develop solutions. But if you have planned ahead, and find that you are caught up in a difficult situation, you can use your resources to develop effective strategies and patterns of behavior. Preparing for possible problems is a lot different than worrying and fretting over them. When you create a plan of action, "just in case," and you face a certain problem or situation, you'll be prepared. On the other hand, simply wasting time by worrying solves nothing.

Having the awareness to live in the here and now as a happy, content, healthy and successful individual is the determining factor to living a healthy and successful life, unburdened by stress, in the future.

We must be aware that we cannot change the past, no matter how much we would like to. And no matter how long we agonize about what happened we can't influence today what happened long ago. What's done is done. We can choose to learn from it and let it go, or perpetually live in the past. The only point in time you can influence is today. What decisions will you make? What thoughts will you think? Will they propel you forward or keep you stuck in yesterday?

Just as you can't live in the past, you can't live in the future. So many people fall into the trap of "some day." This means that those people live their lives continuously in the future and are never truly living. They're the people who say, "After I leave school, after I get married, when the kids are grown, after my divorce, after I retire…" and suddenly they are old and realize with agony that they have really lived only ten percent of their lives. These same people will say, "I had so many plans and I wanted to do so much, but now it's too late." Frustration, self-pity, devastation, illness and sometimes even suicide are often the result.

Learn to live in the here and now. Let go of the past and preprogram the future in your mind and work on your goals and development. This is the only way you can develop creative solutions and effectively use the resources and possibilities that are at your disposal right now.

Also, the more creativity you allow in your life, the greater the resources and opportunities at your disposal in crisis situations will be.

Never let the past limit your life, enjoy the moment!

Breathing

In the Western part of the world we have learned to breathe incompletely. The oxygen we inhale reaches only the upper part of our lungs. Most people inhale just enough air to keep them from suffocating. Because the supply of oxygen plays an important part in the amount of energy we have, we must be aware that we cannot do our work when we don't breathe properly.

Consider the importance of our oxygen supply. We can live six weeks without nourishment and six days without water, but we can't live even six minutes without oxygen. The body gives the brain the message, "I'm suffocating!" The brain will produce stress hormones when it receives this message, and a chain of disastrous consequences will take place, leading to death.

Excellent breathing is important for our energy supply as well as for stress reduction and prevention. Research in several psychiatric clinics has shown that people who breathe deeply and calmly no longer suffer from fear, even though they have suffered from morbid fear before.

Every relaxation and regeneration system, such as yoga and meditation, use the power of breathing. We must learn to inhale deeply into the center of our body when we are under stress so that we don't only breathe with the upper part of our chest.

Exercise:

1. Sit or stand with good posture.

2. Breathe slowly through your nose for a count of 10.

3. As you inhale, first fill the lower part of your lungs (as if you are breathing into your stomach) then the middle part, then the upper part.

4. Hold your breath for 5-10 seconds.

5. Exhale slowly. Relax your abdomen and chest.

Practice this exercise for five minutes twice a day and you'll notice a big difference in your mood, thinking, and energy levels.

Nutrition

In my book, *Finally! Goodbye to Illness for ever,* I mention that we should avoid adding more stress to our lives with poor nutrition and foods that holds little liquid. Our diets should consist of 70% water containing foods—fruits and vegetables—and 30% of denser foods like proteins and starches. We should also approach our nutrition in a positive and energy-enriching way by separating carbohydrates and proteins. You should not eat protein and carbohydrates in the same meal.

Starting your morning with fresh fruit is one of the best ways to feel energetic and have better mental focus. At lunch time you can choose to have your carbohydrates or protein with vegetables and/or fruit.

We're all familiar with how tired we feel after a heavy meal, and how difficult it is to work. I encourage you to start a program of good nutrition with the help of your family physician.

You can get the products that I use to improve and protect my health from www.intacthealth.com or www.awesomesupplements.com and see the free information on www.instinctbasedmedicine.com and www.dr.leonardcoldwell.com

Sports and Exercise

Our body and mind do not get into perfect shape with heavy weight lifting and hours of exercise. Relevant research has shown that a brisk half hour walk in the fresh air every day is enough to keep us in excellent shape. Alternately, you can do a thirty minute aerobic workout—stair climbing, elliptical machine, treadmill, dance, etc. and still reap all of the benefits of increased oxygen.

Once you get into the habit of exercising, you will quickly realize that it has a very positive influence on your energy levels, mood, memory, and even the detoxification of your body.

Exercise is also one of the easiest and cheapest ways to reduce stress symptoms.

Regeneration

Without a balance between work and rest, and between strain and relaxation, your energy will not be sufficient to withstand the pressure of day to day life. Don't believe that you can outwit your body with a false feeling of comfort or with strenuous workouts. Everybody needs time for recovery, not just once a year, but every week and every day. The need for recovery is different for every individual, and you should find out what's best for you. But one thing is sure; a person who doesn't take the time to recover will fall apart in the long run.

I won't get into any specifics or give advice on how you should spend your time relaxing, since this is a personal thing. What I may find relaxing and the length of time I spend on it, may be far different than what you're wants and needs are. You need to do what's best for you, but do know that if you ignore the needs of your mind and body to take some time out to recuperate, you'll pay the price in the long run.

What I can offer you is a simple relaxation method that works for just about everyone. This doesn't take the place of pursuing hobbies or other enjoyable activities, but it's a nice way for you to unwind and refresh.

Exercise:

Read the directions all the way through before practicing.

1. Set aside 15 minutes for this exercise.

2. Sit or lie down and be sure you're comfortable.

3. Close your eyes and think about a place you'd like to be. This could be an island, a forest, a meadow or any place that makes you feel at peace. When you have this scene firmly in your mind in complete detail and you feel relaxed, move on to the next step.

4. Allow this feeling of contentment to softly course thorough your mind and body. Imagine it coursing through your toes, all the way to your fingertips, to your scalp, and everywhere in between.

5. Once you have yourself completely relaxed, you will now set a trigger so you can quickly reach this point of relaxation at any time in the future. For example, you could clasp your hands together or cross your middle and forefinger, you could even reach up and push the tip of your nose or tug lightly on your earlobe. The trigger you choose now will be the one you use every time in the future when you want to come back to this state of total peace and relaxation.

6. As we continue the exercise, imagine that you are filled with a radiant, shining light that grows stronger and brighter with each breath. The light increases in brightness and strength, spreading through you and surrounding you with a halo of brilliant light.

7. Imagine that you feel weightless, filled with positive energy and the strength of the universe. This energy flows through you, cleansing every cell in your body with positive energy, flushing away all that is negative.

8. Each time you breathe in; picture each cell of your body being filled with energy and strength.

9. After about 10 minutes you will experience a complete feeling of relaxation and regeneration. At this point you should set your trigger again—touch your nose, pull your earlobe, clasp your hands, whatever you have chosen as your trigger. From now on, whenever you perform your trigger touch it should bring you right back to this state of total relaxation and regeneration.

10. Open your eyes; do your trigger move and say, "When I do this, I will instantly come back to this state of complete relaxation."

With a little training you will be able to return to this state of total peace whenever you like. You will be able to regenerate completely in only a minute or two, as your entire body and mind recall the feelings of complete relaxation.

Never be content with less than 100% of happiness, success, vitality and health. Decide now that you will consciously accept all the possibilities, skills and talents you received at birth. With this book you will have the tools and directions needed to create a life full of enthusiasm and passion for yourself and your loved ones.

Remember you were born to be a champion, to win and to be happy healthy and successful!

EFFECTIVE
COMMUNICATION
INSIDE AND OUT

As I mentioned before, there's a saying that goes, "Whether you believe you can do something, or whether you believe you can't, you will always be right." This is because you stimulate certain areas of your brain and you will act accordingly. Therefore, it's incredibly important how you talk to yourself. When you tell yourself, "That's too difficult, I can't do that," you tell your subconscious you don't even want to tackle the task since it will result in failure. But, if you say to yourself, "I can do that! I'll give it all I have!" your brain will get a positive charge and will immediately create strategies to succeed.

With a strong conviction in your own abilities and creativity, you will develop self-confidence and create a solution-oriented foundation. You will strengthen your self-esteem with every small success, and this, again, will strengthen the basis for an improved quality of life.

If a job falls within the scope of your belief system, you will be able to do it! Nobody else can persuade or dissuade you.

Feelings

You have no doubt experienced the importance of your emotional attitude toward the success of a project. For instance, if you're irritated with someone or something, whether you are right or not, and go to work brimming with those angry feelings, you will not be very successful. If, on the other hand, you go to work feeling cheerful, perhaps after receiving some good news or after a pleasant conversation, you are in such a positive state of mind that everything runs smoothly.

How you feel also affects how you look. People who are depressed walk slowly, usually with their head down and shoulders slumped. Angry people tend to be very rigid and have a harsh frown on their face. When someone's in a good mood, they smile, look relaxed and move with ease.

Even if you aren't feeling in a good mood, you can actually put yourself in the right frame of mind, by mirroring the physical state of a happy person. Stand up straight, relax your body, and put a smile on your face.

In this way you're letting your subconscious know that you're in a good mood and your mind will soon follow the lead of your posture and facial expression. The simple act of "faking it" will stimulate the chemical in your brain, actually putting you in a positive mood.

Taking Control of Your Emotions

Feelings, also known as our emotional conditioning, are determined by two distinct factors: The use of physiology and internal interpretation.

Simple changes in your physical world lead to changes in your emotional world which lead to unbelievably positive results. You will be astounded with how simple effective solutions are when you make full use of your knowledge, skills, talents and strength.

During my work in research and education I have learned that solutions are always easy, unless you make them complicated out of ignorance, foolishness or greed, or by turning a simple solution into a difficult problem.

I want you to know that you already have all the skills to determine your own life and future. You have been given this perfect bio-computer, the human brain, and you can learn to use it to produce the type of life you desire.

The way you physically hold your body at any given moment sends impulses via your nerves to the brain. Your breathing, facial expressions, muscle tension, and gestures all tell your brain how you're feeling. In turn, your brain responds by activating neuro-chemical processes which dictate your mental and emotional behavior.

The chemicals in your brain, and those running through your body, are always responsible for your disposition. Since we can't influence our brain consciously or manually—excluding medicine and surgery—we must learn to use our body in such a way that we stimulate our brain in the most desirable way.

Exercise: Try this so you can get an idea of how powerful your brain really is.

Take on a posture of depression. Sit down in a chair, let your body and shoulders slump, look down with a sad look on your face, breathe shallowly and perhaps whine a bit. Pretty soon you won't be feeling so hot. If you remain in this posture for a few more minutes, you'll quickly feel depressed, miserable and frustrated, because the brain is sending this message based on your posture.

Now change your posture, switching to a strong and enthusiastic attitude. Sit straight, breathe deeply, smile and let out a laugh. You should find that you shook the depressed feelings off in a few seconds and now feel strong and bursting with enthusiasm.

Practice this exercise again and you will recognize the importance of the correct use of your body at any time. You will feel as you move and breathe.

The Second Element in Controlling Your Emotions

Besides the conscious use of physiology, there is a second internal aspect with which we can influence and control our emotions. I'm talking about the pictures you put in your mind, their strength and intensity, and of the words you choose to use and hear.

The way you communicate with yourself directs your successes and failures. Once you learn to control what you filter through your mind, you'll be able to use your God-given knowledge, skills and talents to produce the best possible results.

Exercise:

Read through the instructions before performing the exercise.

1. Think about a situation that still bothers you. Perhaps someone treated you badly and to this day you still have strong, negative feelings about the person or the episode that happened. Recall this event as if you were experiencing it all over again for the first time. See this angry, hysterical or unfair person exactly as you did at that time and be consciously aware of all the negative feelings you felt then, and feel even now, when you think about what happened.

2. Now, give that person in your mind huge ears, a giant red nose, give him large duck feet, shrink him in size and give him the voice of a cartoon character like Minnie Mouse or Popeye. Relive the situation in your mind with this person looking and talking like that. Give the person a silly nickname to go with the humorous scene in your mind.

3. Recall every detail of that episode, but with the person looking like this funny character. Soon you should notice that your feelings are now very different when you think about this person and/or the situation. You may need to perform the exercise several more times, but you will find that your feelings in relation to this person have completely changed. You can smile and perhaps even laugh, knowing that the person or memory no longer affects you like it did before.

4. If you repeat this exercise twenty times, those neuro-associations in

your nervous system will establish a new route, and the previous program with its negative feelings will eventually be erased.

Any time in the future, if this memory comes back to you, you should practice this exercise again and you will find that the picture weakens and finally disappears for good. No more will that negative episode haunt you.

This exercise shows the enormity of how our "inner pictures" influence our emotions, our reactions and our behavior.

Once you realize how simple it is to influence your emotions and behavior, you will see that you can develop a roadmap of success for your own life and even your relatives, colleagues, friends and acquaintances.

Anger

Nobody can make you angry. How you choose to act and react is completely up to you. Only you can make yourself angry by creating a situation for yourself and representing it in such a way that it makes you angry. You assess it and look at it from an angle that focuses your attention and causes distress stimulation.

If someone hands you a shoe, it's up to you whether or not you put it on. It's always your personal representation of a given situation that releases either negative or positive emotions. For instance, somebody can try to insult you, and you can let them get to you and react in a negative way, or you can simply let it go and say to yourself, "I could not care less about that person's opinion."

I realize this is often easier said than done, so I want to offer you a rather unconventional way for coping with situations that cause anger.

Exercise:

If somebody makes you very angry, and you really want to get mad, it's far better for you to get angry in your mind than to do so out loud because it will not have any negative repercussions.

Pretend the person who made you very angry was bending over, showing you their behind. In your mind take a running start and give him a sound kick in his derriere and enjoy your liberating blow! You will experience a redeeming release through this simple mental exercise so when you meet this person the next time, you will have little of the pent-up negative energy that might have caused a situation you would rather avoid.

A Point of View

If you talk with someone about a party you both attended, you often come to the conclusion that you have completely different opinions of the affair. You may be really enthusiastic, while the other person has a completely negative opinion. That's because it depends on your personal point of view of the situation. While one person concentrates on everything that is positive and beautiful, the other only sees people or situations they do not like.

Our emotions depend completely on where we direct our attention and on the images we build and experience in our mind. In turn, this determines how we react to a certain situation. Our behavior is dictated by our feelings and by the emotions we have at a certain point in time.

Because it is not possible to be objective in our own life, we are often plagued by doubt and fear, often because we have been trained to draw false conclusions from faulty information. We convince our mind with pictures and results that have nothing to do with reality!

So often we draw our mental experiences from bereavement, failure, overwhelming problems, from people who dominate us, and in turn we see ourselves as weak and helpless, small and insignificant. We feed our subconscious with mental images that have nothing to do with reality. But, because our subconscious sees those images as reality, we produce a feeling of inferiority and low self-esteem in ourselves.

If this emotionally charged situation is repeated several times we program a pattern of failure. Our subconscious believes that everything that happens repeatedly in the same manner is desired behavior and it will repeat the same program in similar situations.

You must become aware of the power those seemingly uncontrollable mental images have so that you can take control of your inner thoughts. As long as you believe that you cannot influence your mental pictures and thought patterns you will have to live with random reactions and fluctuating results.

When you finally recognize that you are the person who determines how you feel, act and produce the long-term successes in your life, a whole great new world of adventure and variety will open up. You can realize your dreams, no matter how impossible that seems at this moment.

Don't worry what other people think is right or wrong, because you are the only one who knows what happiness, health and contentment means to you. Feelings like happiness, harmony, peace and love are different for every person. Nobody but you can tell whether you feel successful or not, because you must create what is right for you. You know what makes you feel good and what is in harmony with your own rules and values.

Therefore, be aware of what enters your mind. Always pay full attention to your thoughts and keep your mind focused on your goals.

The Right Visualization

Our emotions are determined by the way the pictures in our mind are represented. The word "represent" indicates here that we see or rebuild in our mind something that happens, has happened, or could happen and we present it to ourselves "again."

Because we cannot see our lives objectively and because we are plagued by worry, fear and doubt, but also because we have been poorly trained with false information, we are all too often inclined to accept the negative rather than the positive. We let the pictures in our mind convince us of what might happen and this has nothing to do with what we really want.

Instead, we create mental images of loss, failure, denial, and overwhelming problems, images of people who dominate us and problems we cannot handle. In turn, we feel weak, helpless, small and insignificant. Those mental images create in our subconscious, information that has nothing to do with reality. Our subconscious sees those pictures as our present reality and creates feelings of inferiority, leading to low self-esteem and defeat.

You must recognize the importance of those seemingly uncontrollable mental images for the threat they are so that you can, from the start, avoid the real danger of future negative programming. You must recognize how important it is to let go of those thoughts and mental images that seemingly appear to come out of nowhere, so they will not take control of your life.

As long as you believe you cannot influence the images and random thoughts in your mind, you will live with accidental reactions and fluctuating results.

How We Can Understand Ourselves Better

Now you realize that you are responsible for the feelings you have at this moment, and that they depend on the thoughts and pictures you allow in your mind.

What's the use of having a pessimistic attitude so that you can later say, "See, I told you so!" What is the pleasure of being right when something bad happens? The worst preparation and waste of time is predicting a crisis, just so you can say: "I knew it all along."

Spend no more than ten percent of your strength identifying a problem and ninety percent on finding a solution and solving it. Because the brain cannot do two things at once, you must focus on understanding the most important task, so you can deal with that one first. If several problems need your attention immediately, sort them out in order of importance and start with the most important one.

We waste so much time telling ourselves, "I have to do this, oh that should also be done, and I shouldn't forget that," but thinking this way doesn't lead to solutions; only to stress and a hectic overloading of the brain.

End each day with an action plan for tomorrow. You should be fully aware of the next day's goals, what you want to tackle first and what else you should be doing after that. In this way you avoid poor sleep and bad dreams. By removing this exhausting train of thought, even if you don't write your tasks down on paper, pinpoint the main goals for tomorrow in your mind.

While working on this program you may say to yourself, "I've heard this before. Yes, it is very simple and completely logical. I already know this!" But how often have you actually put this information to use on a daily basis? This is a key to self-discipline and ultimate success.

With this program I'm not trying to offer you new or complicated techniques. What I want to do is teach you to understand yourself better, and how your brain and body function together. I want you to become at ease with your own natural tools and possibilities so that you will be able to summon all your strength, knowledge and skills as effectively as possible.

Only constant, sensible, goal-oriented and continuously updated behavior will attract success. Learn to use all the knowledge you have already acquired in life and at the same time practice the techniques you have learned in this program so that you can ultimately enjoy the highest quality of life.

Internal Signals

You already know that when you have a pain in some part of your body it's a signal letting you know that something isn't quite right. It's a warning signal sent from your subconscious, letting you know that we are doing something wrong.

There are several ways to deal with situations of conflict. You can look for a quick-fix and swallow a few pills. You can fool yourself and look for reasons things aren't so bad. Or you can read a book that offers quick and easy answers, like a vitamin cure or some other program.

Many so-called health programs are responsible for the complete destruction of many people's health because they promote a one-sided approach or element to take care of our health. Important information is neglected, relevant signals overlooked or put aside, and the necessary steps are never taken.

Spending a lot of time doing a certain sport or by regularly exercising will not make you healthy. Instead, it will lead to negative stress and the body will react when it feels threatened. For instance, the body can be overloaded by intense jogging because it produces too many stress hormones. By hiding behind a fitness program and overlooking the necessity of putting the same effort into our emotional fitness we often bring about a catastrophe.

The assumption that good nutrition can prevent illness is also basically wrong, because no single discipline can keep us totally healthy. Several factors play an integral part in our effort to become and stay healthy.

Someone, who pushes aside their needs and feelings unavoidably ruins their health. We all know that we must regularly replace the spark plugs and oil to keep our car running smoothly. Cars need regular maintenance. So, why don't we do the same for our bodies?

If we want to stay healthy, a necessary requirement for achieving success and attaining a good quality of life is to pay attention to the signals our subconscious sends out such as the stomachaches or headaches and other pains. We must explore the causes that made us sick and change our behavior.

Compromises

Every poor compromise you make in life leads to tension, anxiety and low self-esteem. When you go against your principles you experience a shortage of energy, possible illness, and emotional and physical stress.

Compromises are decisions you make but would prefer not to, but you feel forced to do it. Poor compromises often erase any chance of your life being better, more beautiful and effective. Instead, they give you mediocre satisfaction at best.

With a compromise you settle for less, giving a strong message to your subconscious that you are not really deserving of giving 100% to those things you truly want and care about achieving.

When these poor compromises accumulate, I've seen it lead to tragic health problems. In my work I came to the conclusion that compromises were the dominant negative causes of chronic illnesses. Say, for example, that a woman tries to maintain a marriage, even though her husband regularly abuses her, often coming home drunk, and openly humiliates her. This unbearable compromise destroys her health, and may result in cancer of the uterus.

Please examine your current life and choices, and decide to remove any recognizable compromises. Accept the necessary struggle and develop plans and strategies to remove your failures in this area, otherwise you will only live a life of disaster.

Here are some rules I follow in life, and you should too:

1. Never be open to blackmail.

2. Never be open to corruption.

3. Never ever under any circumstances make a compromise against yourself. Against the true you, your true self, what you are, stand for and believe in! Never!

Egotism

Egotism is good. Why? Because egotism is nothing but a component of self-preservation, and without it humanity would have died out long ago. I want to make it clear that I do not mean inconsiderate behavior; instead I want you to realize that the most important person in your life is you. You must either suffer the pain you bring to yourself or enjoy every victory you have won. The enjoyment will bring happiness and the suffering will be overcome.

People who aren't concerned with having a good quality of life don't deserve your attention or assistance. You will be happy, content and healthy only when you live in accordance with your own personality, with your needs and desires. Only then can you achieve success in every area of your life.

To realize the success you dream of, you must pay attention to your intuition, listen to your feelings and fulfill your needs. Do not chase the directions others give you because you will run the risk that, although perhaps successful, you may become unhappy, lonely or ill because you did not realize your own goals, but those of someone else.

A father, for example, can force his son to realize the dreams he did not realize himself, although the interests, talents and skills of the son point into a totally different direction. In this way we breed failures and losers, because we rob people of their own personality, their wishes and dreams, and we replace them with alien pursuits. These people live alienated from their own personality and will constantly be in emotional or physical stress.

But egotism plays another important roll. Once you realize and accept that you are the center of our own life, you will ultimately build up enough energy and strength to play a positive role in the lives of others. If you exhaust yourself, and if you become weak and ill, you will not be able to help and improve your own life, yet alone anyone else's life.

You cannot pull somebody from a swamp by jumping in; you need to stand on a solid foundation to pull him out of a mess. Become a self-sufficient person with good self-esteem and confidence, and be financially and emotionally independent. If you are emotionally and physically robust you can start to help other people.

The only true help is self-help; helping others to take responsibility, helping them to help themselves. If you really want to help your spouse, your daughter or son or friend to change their lives, help them to improve it.

Learn to take yourself seriously and grow into a mature, strong person so that you can have confidence in yourself and will be able to define and work on the realization of your feelings, needs and dreams.

Never forget; you were born to be successful!

Associations

You should be aware that unconscious thoughts or entirely unwanted associations between feelings and outside stimuli may cause stress and endanger your health. Although it's true that many neuro-associations do cause stress, we do not want to eliminate them. For instance, the brake lights from the car in front of us on the highway suddenly light up, our automatic programmed reaction is to hit the brakes, and it can be a lifesaver. The neuro-associations caused by the red light starts a physical reaction in our body.

But, mental pictures, emotionally charged memories and thoughts can also lead to immediate reactions. For instance, if you think about a person who had a strong negative influence on you, who treated you unfairly or maliciously, then those memories—the recall of mental pictures—can trigger feelings of fear, frustration, and anger.

Perhaps you had numerous bad experiences with a certain person whose behavior irritated you. Chances are, you have now unconsciously installed a program in your mind to react negatively to him or her either with annoyance, tension or trying to avoid the person altogether. Because this person throws a negative switch in your mind due to preprogramming, you prepare yourself for confrontation or rejection and no longer work on a solution.

If you've ever done something you really regretted, yet couldn't understand how or why you would behave in such a way, it is always the result of an automatic program that was triggered.

Such neuro-associations are dangerous if we do not become aware of them, because they can negatively influence your life again and again. Luckily, it's not too difficult to disconnect this programming by redefining your behavior pattern.

Yes, it is possible to change the way you act and react to situations, but many people tend to sabotage even their best efforts because they suffer from mixed neuro-associations. Even if they've programmed themselves for action and success, yet they also feel that success will lead to more pressure, greater responsibility, loss of spare time and friends, they will fail. Because those feelings of advantage and disadvantage are continuously present, this person destroys his own chances of success.

The same is true for relationships. Once a person has been seriously hurt in a past relationship, the neuro-association accumulates. To this person, another relationship equals pain and suffering. So, when a new relationship develops, this person becomes uneasy and starts to subconsciously sabotage the relationship due to fear of being hurt again.

If this person is you, find out which relationships you tend to undermine, how you hurt your own success, and in which situations you act, think and feel differently than you would have if you had given it more thought.

Useful Thinking

Sometimes you may be overwhelmed by the amount of work you have to do. When this happens, instead of feeling frustrated, getting more behind, and allowing the stress to build, simply tell yourself:

- I am a successful person; otherwise I would not be this busy.
- I'm grateful that others trust me with these projects.
- I prefer to do too much rather than not enough,
- I'm doing this so I can afford a better quality of life for my family and myself.
- I can even afford to take a vacation now and then.
- I would not be able to do so if I did not have this job.

Remember, you are the one who wanted this job and there was no doubt a very good reason you chose it.

Exercise:

Write down the following—

1. Why did I choose my job?
2. Why should I be pleased that I have this job?

You can influence your nervous system positively with this line of thought and condition it to reprogram your subconscious so that you will always be ready to deal with stressful situations. You must learn to produce new neuro-associations which will help you to feel good about yourself and your job, even in difficult situations.

If you consistently tell yourself, "I enjoy this work. I am happy that I have this job and that I'm so good at it. My profession is my calling." Soon you will become solution oriented, positive, have more energy, and can therefore work with less stress.

By focusing on solutions and other alternatives and by not focusing on anxiety, fear and possible failures, you produce self-esteem and self-confidence. And, because your brain now recognizes a solution-oriented way to deal with situations, you are programmed to handle them effectively.

Pay Attention to What You Let Enter Your Mind

Once you acknowledge that it is you and only you who determines how you feel and how you act and that you are responsible for the long term success in your life, a great new world will open up to you. You will recognize that can reach unbelievable heights and live all of your dreams. Every great inventor was at first ridiculed. Not until after their breakthroughs were they applauded.

Even though many people are afraid of change and therefore fight innovators, inventors, and people who rock the boat, do not let them change your mind. Many people are even unwilling to accept positive changes if they have become used to the negative things in their lives.

Don't worry about what others consider right or wrong for you because you are the only one who knows what makes you happy, content, healthy and successful. These are all emotional conditions, they are feelings, and how you obtain those feelings is up to you since they must coincide with your own rules and values.

I want to warn you against a serious danger standing between you and your success. They are the energy robbers—people with negative attitudes, who continuously question your success, ideas or possibilities, or try to divert you from action, and who drain you of your strength and vision.

Just as you must be aware of the thoughts you engage in, you must also pay attention to the people surrounding you and the influences that touch you.

Optimal and Effective External Communication

To produce a successful and stress free life you must have the ability to communicate, not just with yourself, but also with the world around you. If you want to communicate well with someone, you must first discover what type of person they are when it comes to communication style.

Visual people, who want to learn and process information, must receive visual images from their outside world. When they talk, you'll notice that they use "visual" words and sentences. They might say, "I can just *picture* that. I *see* it differently. It just *dawned* on me." This points to the fact that they use inner pictures for the representation of information and also to how they understand and process the material they receive.

People who are visual often speak with a nasal sound, because their breathing, which is often short and loud, takes place mostly in their upper chest, affecting the muscles of their shoulders and upper arms. When you want to explain something to them, you should try to express yourself in graphic descriptions, if you want them to understand it well. Show them photographs, pictures or drawings, and speak to them in a manner that they easily understand.

Say, for instance, "When you arrive at the blue door on the left," and make a gesture of opening a door so this visual person will sketch the picture in his mind. Let the person form a picture of what you want to convey in their mind. They will understand you better and be able to carry out your requests easily.

People who are auditory usually breathe deeper and their speech is deliberate and clear because they use the chest muscles. If you want to communicate well with them, you should express yourself in tones and pictures that speak to his auditory abilities. You'll know if a person learns best through hearing if they express themselves in an auditory manner such as, "That doesn't ring a bell. That sounds interesting. I hear what you're saying."

You should give these people the opportunity to repeat in their mind what you said. You can help them best by incorporating some of their own favorite words and expressions while you instruct and communicate with them.

The speeches of people who are kinesthetic are usually slow and sparse, their breathing is deep and their body is relaxed. Your communication should be more emotional. You can recognize a kinesthetic person by the relaxation of their lower body. They are often pale and communicate in a slow deliberated manner.

These people usually speak with the following expressions, "That feels okay to me. It just doesn't feel right. I know what you mean." People can, of course, use different ways of expressing themselves, but a kinesthetic person will use 90% of their innate kinetic system of representation—how they feel or perceive that others feel—so that they can produce results. Simply appeal to their emotional side and you'll be able to communicate with them most effectively.

Team Play

Nobody wants to be lonely and alone. Everybody wants to make friends, have a happy family and good acquaintances. We all need a team and want to be a team player. Therefore, you must recognize that you want to be a member of a team and willing to take the first step toward making friendships. You must have the courage to not only take the first step, but also take the second and the third if necessary. You don't relinquish anything if you approach others with true humanity and team spirit, rather it will enrich you and contribute to a healthy stress-free life.

Loneliness produces stress. The fear of being alone also causes extreme anxiety that can be avoided. Studies done at a California university have shown us that people who live in good social surroundings have fewer heart attacks than do people who live in large cities. When people leave the area where they feel socially at home, the rate of heart attacks reaches the same high level quickly.

The foundation of true team play is enjoyment. You must enjoy what you do and do it as well as you can, trying to fulfill the wishes and needs of others so that you can be proud of your accomplishments and results. Your self-esteem and self-image will increase if the activities you perform correspond with your skills and talents.

First, you must enjoy your own company before you can get along with others. You should be able to accept and respect yourself before you can accept and respect others, and be accepted and respected by them in turn. Remind yourself again and again that losers do not respect the accomplishments of others but prefer to diminish them. Winners always recognize the accomplishments of other people, know envy only in a positive way, and show their appreciation with encouragement and admiration.

Successful team play demands more. You must develop an understanding for the self-confidence of your co-workers. If you accept a colleague then, when you are ready to help them to achieve their goals and be more successful in their work and their life, they will return the favor.

The greatest strategies and solutions originate from the "we" approach because every player can enter their thoughts, strengths and talents, so that the final result is the greater achievement of the combined efforts of all participants.

I believe it's important that you understand the interests, dreams, goals, hobbies, fears, anxieties and opinions of your fellow workers. You can respond better if you understand each person's difficulties and failures, hopes and victories.

Someone who doesn't understand other people can't imagine why they act in a certain way. These people often react needlessly with aggression, anger or fear. Be aware that half of your professional success, your health, serenity and contentment is determined by your spouse or partner, your family, your friends, and by others who surround you.

No person can be content and work successfully when their private life is plagued by conflict, when misunderstandings affect their attitude, and negative thinking limits their concentration and energy.

Imagine that you had to abandon all the people who are currently in your private circle. How much poorer would your life be if the people who are now part of your life were no longer there?

People have a herding instinct; we need other people to be happy. We need recognition, a pat on the back, and a shoulder to cry on. What would all the money and success in the world mean if we had to live alone on a deserted island with nobody to share it with?

I've repeatedly seen that loneliness does more harm to a person than pain, illness, and even the knowledge of an imminent death. No matter what you achieve in life, it will lose its value if there are no people around you to share it with.

I would like to focus on another aspect of team play. Through my work and during my life I have learned to recognize that "To fulfill our wishes, we only need to help as many people as possible to attain what they desire."

If this sentence sounds extreme, you will quickly discover that behind this act of unselfishness stands the real fact that you can only be happy if those you care about are happy. You've probably heard the expression that shared happiness is double happiness, and you have surely experienced that if you share your sorrows with someone it will lose some of its impact on your life.

I'm not talking about, "I'll help you if you help me." If you enjoy doing things for others because it fulfills you and gives you validation and contentment, you will find that it will give you great pleasure to help others realize their dreams. Those people will become naturally devoted to you and wonder how they can help you enrich your life.

Learn to become a giver. Give graciously and you will find that you will receive more in return.

Fear of Failure

There are many fears that haunt people or stand in the way of success. There are great fears and minor anxieties that cause hesitation, produce stress and ultimately lead to illness. Research has shown that of the hundreds of fears people anticipate, no more than two percent become reality and influence their lives.

One of our worst fears is the fear of failure. This fear can paralyze a person and is the leading cause of most talents and dreams remaining unlived. These people never accepted their own greatness, never experienced their own wonderful personality, and never bring the miracle of their radiance into the lives of others.

The fear of exposure and the fear of being seen as incapable, prevents many people from making plans and acting on them. This fear can be so enormous that a person will not even take the smallest step in the direction of success out of fear that they may fail.

Trying is never failing. Not trying at all is the only true failure. Every action has a result. This result may be the one we wanted, or it may not be. It doesn't mean you've failed or made a mistake if you don't get the result you wanted, because you did the best you could.

If you have tried something, but the results weren't what you had in mind, it doesn't mean you have failed, as long as you recognize it as a learning process and a stage of development. You will learn to recognize the lessons in each of your undertakings that don't quite end up where you expected. Positive results are always the culmination of experience—both bad and good experience!

If you have learned something from what you consider to be a mistake, this mishap has already turned into a success and has helped to increase your self-confidence. You can take the next step by putting the recognition and knowledge to work and change your goals and start again. This time you will produce new and better results. The more results you produce, the closer you come to reaching your goal.

The formula for personal success is relatively simple: Take action, learn from the results, act again and persevere until the goal has been realized.

There are only two ways to fail: Giving up or not trying at all.

Humor

The best way to avoid or diminish stress is through humor. The ability to laugh at your own mistakes, or joke around when someone is under great pressure, or did something wrong, not only can make us popular; but it can help us and those around us by reducing the release of stress hormones.

It's been shown that seriously depressed patients start feeling better immediately when they adapt a friendly attitude, smile and laugh more, because they stimulate their nervous system in a positive way.

In *Anatomy of an Illness,* author Norman Cousins tells of how he cured himself from a deadly disease with humor.

Humor is an unbelievably important element in the quality of life.

How to Interrupt Behavior Patterns

A behavior pattern is a way in which we function. It's a program that results from repetitive physical or mental action that we have etched in our brain. To eliminate this installed pattern of behavior effectively and to replace it with a new and desired pattern, we must learn to interrupt the unwanted program each time it appears.

When the behavior or thought pops up, never allow it to play to the end, since the brain can't store unfinished information. When the unwanted behavior pattern or negative way of thinking is interrupted, the programming is weakened and ultimately obliterated.

Your next step is to replace the unwanted behavior immediately with the desired behavior. If we repeatedly interrupt the unwanted program and replace it with the new desired behavior, a new "program" will be installed. It doesn't matter whether the behavior pattern you want to change is emotional, mental or physical.

Your self-image, as well as your programmed behavior patterns, are directly dependent on the thought processes of your mind, and on the mental images you feed your brain. Everything you allow to be programmed in your mind by repetition will determine your self-confidence, your self-esteem, your ability to work and the results you will produce in your life.

The sooner you realize that your emotions, energy, health, and successes are no accident, but the result of continuous thoughts and behavior patterns, the sooner you will be in control of your life.

Getting Rid of The Past

Many negative experiences of our past will, by continuously repeating them in our mind, have a very negative emotional and physical influence on our well being. Think about something negative that happened in your childhood. Perhaps a teacher blamed you unfairly, yelled at you, or humiliated you in front of the whole class. Chances are, even today, so many years later, those pictures will produce the same feeling.

To really release yourself of the burden of the past you need to deprogram yourself and give those old feelings another meaning. This is relatively easy because the subconscious can't differentiate between what is really happening and what you are just imagining. Learn to erase or give new meaning to the negative mental trigger by, for instance, making it laughable or absurd. See yourself in the negative situation, just as it happened in the past, then change it. As we talked about before, make the scene humorous. Make the scene look like a silly cartoon and give the offender of your past a completely ridiculous voice and make them look very small. Soon you will be able to laugh or smile and the negative emotions will ultimately disappear if you use this deprogramming method regularly.

Another helpful method is to give the person of your past a different name that corresponds with the new image you've created for them. Whenever you have to deal with this memory, or even the person, in the future think about the new name you've given them, and they will lose the emotional power they have over you.

A third method for changing painful memories of the past is to allow the negative situation, just as it happened, run through your mind, and then quickly rewinding it. Now, run your "film" again, but this time run it with beautiful colors and rich sounds, and give it the ending you would have liked, or let yourself react in the way you wish you had reacted.

Our personal attitude toward situations—past, present and future— determines the stress levels in our life, and our success rate. If we have a positive solution-oriented and future oriented attitude toward life, and if we concentrate on finding effective solutions and actions while working continuously on the realization of our dreams and wishes, our lives will be far less stressful than when we have a negative attitude.

On the other hand, if we are distracted by worries, possible failures, and always fear the worst, our lives will become very stressful and we will program ourselves for a downfall.

Therefore, take control of your behavior—inside and out.

Controlling Your Behavior

Our behavior is significantly influenced by the internal communication we have with ourselves. This inner voice can be strong and assured, soft and insecure, sexy or even whiny.

The way we use our body also has a direct influence on our mood. For instance, if you let your shoulders droop, look down at your feet, and breathe shallowly; you will soon find yourself in a worse mood than before. As soon as you straighten up, breathe in deeply, smile and look straight ahead, you will immediately become aware of a positive change in your feelings.

To reduce stress in situations when you are under pressure it is absolutely necessary that you move your body in a strong, purposeful and energetic way. We will feel better as we move. This means that when we enter an emotional situation and act like we have a good attitude, strength and energy, we will send these signals to our nervous system and to our brain. In turn, we will actually begin to truly feel positive.

Pretending ultimately leads to the desired result. If we use positive internal communication and act "as if we are in control," we will have absolute command over our behavior every time we so desire.

Therefore, if you want to change your behavior in certain situations and be more effective than ever, you must simply take charge of your internal dialog and the way you use your body.

THE TRUE SECRET OF STRESS FREE LIVING

One of the best discoveries I've found in life is that we can only be happy, content, healthy and live stress free if we learn to accept ourselves and be ourselves. We need to live according to our own wishes, needs, and dreams, not somebody else's.

We are constantly conditioned to believe that we can't or shouldn't be, as we feel in our heart that we should be. Statements like, "You can't do that" or, "You should do it this way" have trained us to suppress our own needs and personality, replacing them with foreign characteristics, forced on us by others.

When we no longer live according to our own instincts, emotions and inner signals, we become restless and frustrated, which causes incredible stress. And, while we feel uncomfortable with being something we aren't, we simply don't have the strength or tools necessary to be the person we truly are. Many times we're afraid to be the "real us" for fear of what others will think.

The truth is, we were all created differently; there is no real norm for right or wrong behavior. (We aren't talking about criminal behavior!) It is impossible to set a standard for the "right" wishes, needs and dreams. Every person has the right to live as they want. They have the right to make mistakes, to develop, mature and develop their own ways of changing their behavior.

The most important requirement for real contentment and an optimal quality of life is the recognition that you are as you were meant to be, and therefore you are alright. You are empowered with unique, wonderful talents, possibilities and skills and there is no one like you on earth. It's this uniqueness that makes a future full of possibilities, opportunities, challenges and successes possible for everyone.

You will you enjoy a life without compromises, tension and pressure, without self-deception and duplicity, until you learn to accept yourself the way you are and use your potential to work toward your own goals. You are the only person with whom you have to deal with for the rest of your life, so you must learn how to get along with yourself. Every person must understand, accept, respect and love themselves. After all, how can you accept other people the way they are, if you have not accepted yourself the way you are?

If you really want to know yourself and find out your personal goals, values and rules, I urge you to thoroughly do the work I offer you in this program. Only when you really know yourself and your needs, can you give your life a direction that corresponds with your personality and true goals.

Positive Thinking—Positive Acting

Positive thinking alone will not change your life, because positive thinking is only a requirement for positive acting; while negative thinking is the prelude to acting negatively.

Your life will not produce positive results with positive thinking alone. All your wonderful dreams, those exciting goals, and inspirational mantras will be of no help in overcoming conflicts in your life—unless you take action!

The expression: "Everything will turn out positive if you think positive," has been the downfall for many people because *only positive behavior produces positive results.*

Positive thinking is an intention to perform a needed task to the best of your ability. It is the requirement for inner security. However, nothing will change in your life unless you start taking that first positive step on your chosen path.

True positive thinking means knowing exactly the chosen goal, and including the calculated results, you want to produce, no matter the difficulties and obstacles that are in your way.

The Power of Change

As soon as you make some changes, no matter how small at first, you will notice something interesting taking place. Other people may react irritable, or even aggressive, if they are insecure, because they thoroughly dislike the unknown or unusual. Of course, those who are secure with themselves will be happy and congratulatory when they see you making progress.

However, you must be prepared for the strangest reactions to your changes, because some people may refuse to listen or may even be hostile. Perhaps you've already experienced this when you've lost some weight or you have gotten a better job or a raise. Some of your closest friends or relatives may act disinterested, rude or even jealous.

The more people understand your new way of thinking and behavior, the more support you will receive when there is a crisis or when you are insecure or in doubt. As you do make positive changes in your life, be sure to include everyone in on it. Let them know what your plans are, the new methods you're trying, and any new information you've gathered. This way, they can adjust themselves to these new changes that may take place in your life and will be more willing to help you. People like to feel needed and included in your life, even in some small capacity. As I've mentioned before, you must be a team player to become really successful. Do not work on your goals in the secrecy of your room, let others play a part.

Hesitate No More

I think by now you understand the importance of recognizing which

negative behavior patterns you have acquired, which you want to change, and a good idea on how to program these positive traits into your subconscious. No matter how eager we are to change at times though, there is very often one thing standing in the way: procrastination.

Procrastination and hesitation are nothing but typical patterns of learned behavior. There are people who delve into a task immediately, look for solutions, develop a plan of action and start on the task at hand. These people are not better than you or me, but they have learned to motivate themselves. They have conditioned themselves to take action so that it has become a natural way of behaving and is now part of their personality. When you realize that getting things done quickly and efficiently is simply learned behavior, it becomes easy to program yourself into solution-oriented thinking and acting.

Stress that could have been avoided results from procrastination. In other words, procrastination is thinking about work instead of doing it. How often have you put work aside that increased, adding more to it, putting it off for days, weeks or even months, only to find that all your headaches were for nothing, because once you started looking for an answer the problem was quickly solved? Or, once you started getting something done and sticking with it, you found that the task wasn't as time-consuming or as bad as you expected? Once you got those tasks completed you felt so relieved, but only after you ruined your quality of life and diminished your energy for quite some time.

Hesitation and procrastination are serious stress factors that can easily be overcome. When faced with a task, ask yourself, "Can I solve this problem? Is this something I need to do or should do?" If the answer is yes, begin immediately.

Setting Goals

Goals give our lives direction; goals represent the perimeters of our territory so we can move confidently toward our unseen future. The future can be something strange, threatening and unknown, something over which we have no control, until we recognize that we can influence the direction of our lives with concrete goals and positive action. Once we realize this fact, fear of the unknown and the fear of "fate" will disappear because we know we are in charge of our future.

It's extremely important that you define the goals you want to reach in every area of your life. Having clear goals helps you to stick to your own interests, and makes it easier to get back on track if you stray a bit.

Ask yourself if your current life reflects your true aspirations. Does it show your achievements, skills and talent? No matter whether you answer this question with a yes or a no, ask yourself whether you know where your life is heading. Go deep inside and find the answer. What do you really want to reach in your professional and personal life? Do you have goals worth fighting for?

We are only content when we are growing, when we mature and develop. Personal growth and development are the true meaning of life. You will be really happy and content when you have grown as a human being, when you have explored your talents, possibilities and skills. On the other hand, you will be quite dissatisfied when you're at a standstill.

But how can you be proud of your development and success when your life has no direction, when you recognize no victories, and when you have not moved one step ahead? This is why it's so important to have goals in life. Besides larger goals, be sure to set smaller goals as well, so you can enjoy each small success on your way to your final achievement.

It's easy to plan short term goals if you know where you finally want to arrive. It's like taking a road trip. You plan each stage of your trip and look back on a well traveled day, then drive some more.

Whatever your dreams or desires, they can come true with continual goal setting and action. There are no limits on your road to success unless you set those limits yourself. In the philosophy of success we like to say, "Reach for the clouds and when you have arrived, go for the stars!"

Be aware that you are not in the world to survive, but to live. Live your life and enjoy it. You can do this only when you give and live 100% and refuse to live with compromises and limitations. Reach for the sky and set many intermediate goals so that you can measure your progress and celebrate small successes in between.

There is no such thing as good luck or bad luck. Your future lies in your own hands; you make your luck, which is simply the meeting of work and possibility. There will be many opportunities coming your way, so be prepared to make use of the possibilities that life offers you. In the long run it depends on your actions, what you make of your life, and how you use your full potential.

Reasons

We always need good reasons to act and persevere, because sometimes our level of motivation is not strong enough. We need strong reasons to get up when life throws us down; to be successful we need to keep moving.

You need a good reason to continue on those days when everything goes wrong, your best friend lets you down and another one cheats you.

Exercise:

Because they are your very own reasons, your goals, your level of motivation, your willingness to act, I want you to define and write down, now, what motivates you. If everything goes wrong, when it rains on your parade, when your check bounces and the dog chews up your new shoes, what keeps you going?

Please write down, as well as you can, the real motivating reasons that encourage you to persevere in similar negative life situations. What motivates you to improve the quality of your life and lift it to the level you desire?

Do not sell yourself short, demand and expect the very best. There can be no more compromises, excuses, or even half tolerated results. Expect the very best for yourself and for your life and do everything possible to turn your life into the masterpiece it is meant to be. To be able to do this, you must find good reasons to encourage yourself to fight, to act and persevere.

Motivation

As I have mentioned before, if you want to act goal-oriented, you must set a goal, so that you can act goal-oriented. It sounds trite, but I will say it anyway: "Action without careful planning is irrational."

It is important that the energy we use agrees with our behavior, so that we can motivate ourselves and consider the odds of reaching our goal, because the intensity and perseverance while we do our work are, in the long run, determined by the sum of our reasons for reaching this goal.

To encourage ourselves to act and persevere, we must recognize and understand our winning strategies. There are people who can distance themselves from situations. Those people may say; "I do not want to be poor any more, I will no longer be sick." Those people motivate themselves to move away from negative situations.

Other people motivate themselves by looking for pleasant rewards. Those people will tell you that they would like to become wealthy or want to be healthy.

Once you recognize in which category you belong it becomes easier to motivate yourself.

I use the "Joy-Pain" principle, and I advice you to move in that direction. The method is simple, and when you apply it diligently it has a powerful effect, because your motivation depends entirely on your emotional adjustment.

Focus your mental vision on your desired goal, and imagine:

- what will this project cost you?
- what will be the price you will have to pay?
- what you will have to deny yourself?
- what will be the pain you have to suffer when you do not make this decision?

Then imagine the opposite:

- what will you gain?

- what are the advantages when you do the work?

- how much better and richer will your life be?

- how will the quality of your life, your self-esteem and success improve?

- will non-action cause hardship and action produce pleasure?

If you are still not acting, it will probably be because you have not suffered enough pain. Imagine in your mind the pain, then create a great joy, both as intense as you possibly can, and correlate them with non-action and action; you will recognize that you have no choice but to act. You will find that this method will be a strong force; it will help you to reach out and achieve your goal.

Strategies

You have now decided to act, and are strongly motivated to tackle your imagined goal. The next important step will be to make the right plan; what is the best strategy on your path to success?

It makes no sense to do something and expect it to go well by itself. Perhaps what you would like to do right now is the correct thing, but maybe it is not the right time, or it may just be wrong to take the first step right now.

This means that you must first consider which approach will be the best. If a task can be done with just one simple action, the question still remains whether there are other ways, and then it is up to you to compare the pros and cons and decide on the best way to do so. If this way turns out unsuccessful, it was still not wrong, you did get results and by making some changes you can modify your approach as needed.

With greater assignments there are often "Several ways to get to Rome." It is absolutely necessary to plan carefully, so that you can act goal-oriented. Organize the chosen task into small steps you can control. This is not only important for the work, but also involves the allotted time, so that you can proceed with your plan and reach your final goal.

In this way you avoid pressure and stress, you can be content when you finish a step and become more motivated to take the next one. By dividing your task in small steps you will feel, moreover, more confident that you will be able to do the job. The first step is frequently the most difficult one, and once you master a job, the rest will go smoothly.

When you have decided to tackle a job, do not be tempted to put your work off until later.

Act swiftly, and if you have to put things off, renew your goal, so that your well planned strategy will not fall by the wayside.

Believe in your own creativity! If your intuition told you that you can reach a certain goal, your mind will develop the path to succeed.

This does not mean that you cannot follow the example of successful people, people who have already arrived at their chosen destination. This pattern of thinking, behavior and action of successful people I call molding. It is the pattern of selection in nature.

Perseverance

I have mentioned already several times that it is important that you persevere on your way to a goal, and not give up half way. I am not thinking of hanging on for dear life, because that only causes more stress and illness.

What I do mean is that once you have considered a goal attainable and worth fighting for, then this goal is worth your perseverance, even when you run in to seemingly insurmountable stumbling-blocks or must deal with envious and negative people, who try to defeat you.

Make my already often mentioned opinion your own: An obstacle standing in your way is not a problem; it's a challenge to help you grow!

You are on your way to success with great self-confidence, and by overcoming obstacles your confidence grows, because it increases with real life experience, including the compliments you receive in your work.

In conclusion I would like to say:

1. Concentrate only on success. Follow your intuition, and follow the positive image you have made of yourself. This does not mean that you should ignore your weaknesses, You should define your weaknesses and remove them. This means that you should think positive and solution-oriented about your actions and results, so that you program a strong self-image.

2. Learn to see failures as challenges, as opportunities and possibilities to grow, mature and develop. See failures as learning material in your further positive development.

3. Follow the example of those people, who live as you would like to live and who behave as you want to behave. Your subconscious will give you the information, so that your actions and behavior will produce the results you literally "have in mind." The subconscious is prepared to pass on your inner messages, as long as they are not absurd.

4. Surround yourself with positive people, because those in your immediate surroundings portray a lasting program for your subconscious. I am not speaking of the dreamers, who float through life, but of those people, who concentrate on solutions, search for answers and who are working actively on creating a successful life. Stay away from people who question everything, who condemn everything with a negative prognosis, who stop you from acting and discourage the realization of your dreams, wishes and goals. Surround yourself with people who make you feel good and who help you to be yourself; they will contribute to your enjoyment in being the person you really are.

5. Never fear the future, because we know from experience that from the hundreds of fears only a few will become true, and even those

will become true in much weaker form than we anticipated. We usually have very little influence on future developments. Prepare yourself for eventual crisis and dangers, then let go. Unless a difficult situation becomes acute, it should have no importance in your life.

6. Look forward to your future with pleasure, because with this book you have learned to take control over your life and determine your own destiny.

Final Observation

Many outstanding scientists have proven that the impossible can become possible. Great inventors have been criticized and attacked, but they have something that sets them apart from other people, they have an inner dream, they carry a mental conception of their life, and from the results they can and want to produce.

At this point I would like you to create a picture of yourself, to fashion an image of your life and future that it is so fast and enormous that you are willing to do everything that is necessary, so that you can produce, build and obtain every success you desire.

I am absolutely convinced that we as human beings can produce with our mind, with inspiration and all other possibilities with which nature has endowed us, the ability to realize every dream we carry inside. I am convinced that there isn't a goal we can imagine that we cannot realize.

Our subconscious knows our possibilities exactly; it recognizes our skills and talents and therefore, after many years of research and experience, I dare to say: everybody, and I mean everybody, can reach the goal they creates in their mind; because once the wish is planted in the mind, the brain creates the possibility.

I am absolutely convinced that every human being can reach everything, really everything; they make up their mind to achieve. But do not forget that the foundation for success is the willingness to do everything that is needed to reach that desired success.

With the IBMS™ I developed, I put everything you need at your disposal, so that you can turn your life into the adventure and experience you always dreamed of, with all the success, harmony, contentment, health, happiness and peace you could desire.

When I developed my IBMS™-training system, I wanted, above all, that my system would be clear and easy to use and reproduce. My argument was to develop a system that led to great personal achievement and success in every area of life, so that every person would have the possibility to turn his or her life into a masterpiece.

Therefore, I want to point out one more time that you are the only person who can fill your life with success, harmony and happiness. Nobody but you can take away the worries, fear and sorrow; you alone can remove the conflicts in your life.

Only when you fully recognize that you are the only person in the world who can have a permanent influence in your life; your life will become truly your own. In this book I have given you, not just scientific data and facts, not just methods and strategies, but real life strategies to achieve anything you want in life.

If you develop the willingness to act in correspondence with your own personality, if you keep working on the realization of your wishes and dreams, if you do every day two or three things to improve your life, so that you come closer to your goals, your life will become the experience and adventure that it can be.

I have tried to introduce you to a philosophy, which helped me personally. By refusing to use expressions such as, "That does not work" "That is not possible" "That will never do," so that I could prove to you that everyone can reach all the dreams and wishes they would like to attain.

You have a wonderful, promising life ahead of you. The life of a leader or a colleague, who is accepted, and respected, valued as a member of a team. Take your life in your own hands and work with all your strength and possibilities, so that you can make out of your life the masterpiece it is meant to be.

Now start immediately!

WORKSHOP FOR
SETTING GOALS

Nobody can make effective, clear and quick decisions without distinct goals and values. Making decisions is, for many people, a cause of serious stress.

If you want to make quick, clear and effective decisions, decisions you can stand fully behind, you must first determine where a decision will lead you and at which goal you want to direct your energy.

You remove a serious stress-factor when you know exactly where your decisions will lead you.

It will be easier to make a decision, if you ask yourself before you make a decision: "Will this decision bring me closer or move me away from my goals?"

If you have set yourself a clear goal, it will be much easier to get back on track, when you have temporarily lost your way.

A person, who has not set any goals at all, will, of course, end nowhere. Their life will be without successful experiences, and they will miss the security of developing and moving ahead.

Because you will want to give your life a distinct direction in several areas as soon as possible, so that you will not waste time and energy by wandering around without a goal, I have prepared a workshop in goal-setting. Please follow this workshop as exactly and scrupulously as possible, because this goal-setting workshop will become the map for your future, an outline of your territory. Without a map you will flounder and lose your way.

Because you have this map for the future, you can look back and check why you made certain decisions and why you started a certain task and it will help you to return quickly to your chosen path.

While you write down your goals and plan your strategies, your subconscious will receive the messages and get the feeling of being in control. A feeling of helplessness, which is a serious stress-factor, can be diminished and even completely removed.

Our work-shop will start with a systematic conditioning of the brain in the desired direction; therefore I must ask you to follow my directions accurately, **do not skip any part or change the progression.**

Step 1: Approach this exercise when you have time to be alone. Simply go back to the time when you were still a child and you could enthusiastically write out a list of everything you wanted from Santa Claus. Put your mind in a mode of expectations. Feel confident that everything is possible.

Now make a list of all your personal wishes and dreams for the future. It does not matter whether your desires are realistic and whether you expect to realize them. Just imagine that you pop up in a fairy tale or fable and in the next few hours you can ask for anything you wish, no matter what.

It is, of course, not so easy to think this way, but you should try to take life a bit lighter from now on, with a bit more humor perhaps, like the child that is till hidden in you—somewhere.

Now write down everything you would like to enjoy, if you could have it all.

Step 2: You can now put the book aside for 24 hours if you like, because you have encouraged your subconscious to contemplate your dreams, wishes and goals.

Write down any new thoughts and ideas that will come to you every day and put them all down. You will even find empty pages at the end of this book for all the information you will gather during your work.

After a 24 hour break, or when you decide to continue, write down why you want to reach and realize every single goal.

You will see which fantasy is really a goal and which one is not, because if you cannot define why you want something, it is not a real goal.

Now write down again every goal you chose, and write down at the side why you want to achieve and realize this goal.

Step 3: Now, scrutinize each goal for its effectiveness and answer the following questions for every goal you wrote down:

1. Is this really my own goal?

2. (Many goals, for which we strive, have been programmed by our environment. Frequently we do not realize that a goal is not really our own.)

3. Is this goal morally acceptable and am I willing to live with the consequences?

4. Does this goal fit in with the scope of my other goals?

5. Can I motivate myself emotionally to work on the realization of this goal?

6. Will I fulfill my wishes when I work on the realization of this goal?

Please write down all those goals that you could answer with an unambiguous "yes."

Step 4: Now, scrutinize every goal again.

Please answer the following questions:

1. Will I be happier when I reach this goal?

2. Will I be healthier when I reach this goal?

3. Will I have more friends when I reach this goal?

4. Will I be more at peace when I reach this goal?

5. Will I feel better about myself or more secure when I reach this goal?

6. Will my relationships improve when I reach this goal?

7. Will I have more self-confidence when I reach this goal?

If you cannot say yes to at least one of those questions for one or more of your goals, strike them of your list.

8. Now write down the remaining goals and leave space for a two-figure number.

Write beside every goal in parentheses the number of months or years in which you want to realize this goal. One month, three months, four years, etc.

Step 5: Consider the following concepts:

1. Many goals should be large goals, so that they will encourage you. They are needed to push you forward in your development and to help you use and exploit your full potential.

2. Other goals should be of long duration, so that a short-term set-back or failure will not lead to frustration or cause you to give up.

3. Other goals must be small in scope or should be daily accomplishments, so that you will experience success regularly; this will keep you grounded. You will receive signals that you are coming a little closer every day to the fulfillment of your long-term goals.

4. Many goals should be without end; those goals will demand perpetual development or improvement. This will prevent stagnation in your life.

5. Some goals, such as education or a training-course, which demand a certain amount of time, must of course be taken in account ahead of time.

6. Your goals must be absolutely specific. A nice car or a beautiful house is not a goal; a distinct goal demands a specific definition, for instance: "I want a white, two floor house. It must be 2400 square feet and have six rooms, two full baths and one half-bath; it must have an extended basement with four rooms, the ceilings must be seven feet high. The lot must be two acres, with 400 feet adjacent to the woods and the street must have side-walks; the house must not be further than an hour's drive from an airport or a 20 minute drive from the center of a city, where I can buy everything I need.

For a goal to be effective, it is important that you program it into your mind as exact as possible. Only when you have defined it as exactly as you want it, will you be able to make a quick decision when you go house hunting. If you, moreover, write down what you absolutely do not want, it will be easier to make a decision.

Step 6: Now identify the four most important short-term goals and write them down in order of importance:

Step 7: Please write down the important values of those goals:
1. Identify the goal:

2. Write down all advantages you, or those around you, will enjoy if you reach this goal.

Now, to give yourself an extra push in the right direction, move to:

3. Write down what it will cost you, when you do not realize this goal. What will you have to give up and what will be the social, emotional, or physical pain if you do not reach this goal?

4. Write down all the obstacles and difficulties you will have to overcome in reaching your goal:

5. Now make a list of all the knowledge and skill you will need to realize this goal:

6. Now define the people, advisers, teachers and others you will need and in which organizations, social clubs you must participate to successfully reach this goal.

7. Write a plan of action, develop a strategy of the manner on how you want to reach this goal.

Set a date for the finish of your project.

8. It is important that you deal with the corresponding tasks immediately; you will find that you will become really motivated only while you are working on, or after you set your goals—never before.

9. Be specific in every area, because your mind is now being programmed. It will be prepared to set goals, develop plans and strategies, so that it can give you directions in all corresponding areas.

My physical goals

Write down everything you are or would like to be, what you do or would like to do; and everything that has to do with your body: weight, appearance, clothing, etc.

Now follow with your physical goals the same directions you used for your life-goals. Repeat your examination in the same manner as before.

My intellectual goals

Write down everything you want to do for yourself, what you want to reach or achieve: the books you want to read, the languages you want to learn, etc.

Follow again the now familiar questions and directions.

My spiritual goals

Define your spiritual goals: peace, harmony, emotional development, etc.

Follow the same directions.

My creative goals

Write down what you want to achieve, create, invent, develop, etc.

Follow again the same directions accurately.

My family goals

What are the goals you want to achieve for and together with your spouse?

Follow the same directions.

My career-goals

This should include everything you want to achieve in your profession.

Follow again the same directions.

My social goals

What would you like to achieve for your environment, your friends, your team, your co-workers, etc? What would you like to do more often, more intensively, what would you like to create?

Follow the same directions.

My financial goals

Write down what you want to achieve financially, and what you want to own. Do not just write down what you want to earn, but what you would like to possess: house, car antiques, property, etc.

Follow the same directions.

My goals for fun and games

We all have some foolish wishes and dreams or we have some crazy ideas, things we would like to do, but that do not quite fit in our normal way of thinking. Perhaps we would like to buy something strange but we have not bought it so far. Now write down all the foolish things you would like to do or buy.

My goals for immortality

Do not be afraid to write down those things that you would like to leave behind, that would leave traces of your existence. Things you may want to do that will outlive your earthly existence, perhaps something you invent or develop, a book you may want to write or something else you want to accomplish.

Follow again the same directions.

My goals for regeneration

Please write down exactly how you want to regenerate yourself, what do you want to do to keep your balance? This will include relaxation, breathing exercises, short breaks and long vacations.

Follow again the same directions.

My activities

Congratulations, you did it. You made a map for your future. From now on you know exactly the decisions you must make in every area of your life, so that you will come closer to your desires and goals. So that you can break through the wall of indirect passivity and are able to start immediately, I would like you to write down the most important goal in every separate area.

Now write down two things under every separate goal that you could do today or tomorrow, so that you can come—if only a little—closer to your goals:

Goal 1: My life goals

Goal 2: My physical goals

Goal 3: My intellectual goals

Goal 4: My spiritual goals

Goal 5: My creative goals

Goal 6: My family goals

Goal 7: My career goals

Goal 8: My social goals

Goal 9: My financial goals

Goal 10: My fun and game goals

Goal 11: My goals for immortality

Goal 12: My goals for regeneration

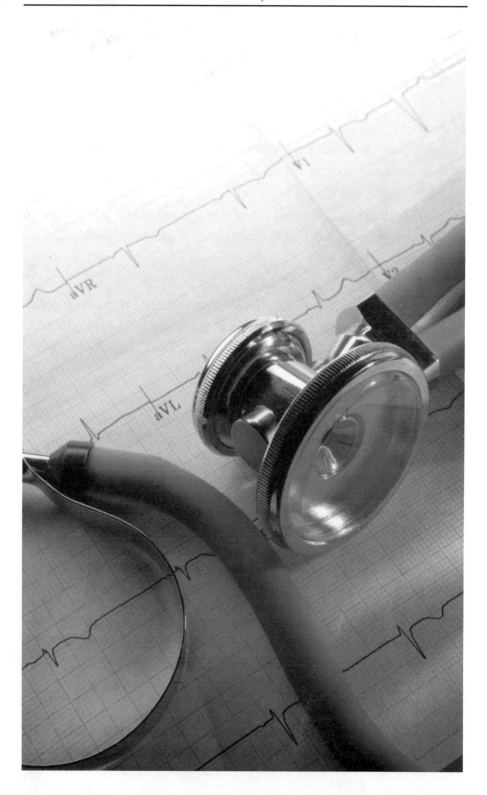

THE IBMS™ STRESS REDUCTION AUDIO SYSTEM

Frequently Asked Questions

What is an IBMS™ session?

A IBMS™ session is the culmination of 30 years of research and clinical practice which have identified ways to produce the perfect combination of music and open suggestions for individual interpretation that enhance brain function. The audio based program generates a mental visualization process, unique to the listener that facilitates a specific positive reaction to the sounds and words transmitted in a particular session. The process employs music purposefully composed to help synchronize the brain hemispheres and promotes the generation and growth of new *dendrites* (neuron connections). The music focuses the brain on specific brain frequencies in conjunction with specific verbal suggestions. This process stimulates the nervous system enabling the listener to be revitalized and energized in 20 minutes.

What are dendrites?

Dendrites (neuron connections) are the connections between the nerve cells in the brain. The more dendrites you create, the higher your brain capacity—or, rather, the more efficient your software. Dendrites are like putting faster, more advanced microchips in your computer so that the computer becomes more effective.

Why do I need IBMS™ sessions?

Everybody has stress, but if you regularly take time to regenerate, recharge and revitalize, you are likely to avoid most major health challenges. An IBMS™ session provides your brain/body with the regeneration necessary to help you feel happier, healthier, younger and energized.

What are the immediate benefits of experiencing a session?

After a session, most people feel a sense of calm with more energy and lucidity than before. They generally feel rested and better able to cope with and solve problems. Most report that they are better able to sleep at night. The more sessions people experience, the better their results become.

What does a session include?

A session consists of a 20 minute audio program: It starts with a 5-minute musical massage that induces relaxation and clears your mind.

This is followed by a 15 minute narrative with stimulating musical accompaniment that takes you on a mental vacation. The narrative employs messages that generate personalized mental images to create maximum benefit. After a session, most people feel as though they just had a restful night's sleep, leaving them energized, regenerated and revitalized!

Note: The techniques, sounds and music used in the audio session are based on modern science, clinical research, and therapeutic experience and have no religious or organizational affiliations.

Why is it crucial to listen to the sessions through stereo headphones or earphones (ear buds)?

The sessions are designed to deliver specific sounds to each ear in specific frequencies at specific times in order to achieve the highest neurological stimulation. It is imperative that the sessions be heard through stereo headphones or earphones (ear buds); otherwise, they have little effect.

What happens during a session?

Each session is derived from 30 years of scientific research and therapeutic experience. The music and suggestions are delivered with precise timing at a specific brain frequency in order to function at exactly the right moment to enable the brain to maximize its capabilities. The opening 5 minute "musical massage" induces you to physically relax and clear your mind. In this relaxed state, your brain becomes very alert and begins to function at optimal capacity. You are thus primed to process the subsequent 15-minute self-activation message and stimulate whatever conditioning you want to achieve; i.e., relaxing and regenerating, optimal breathing or taking control.

How many IBMS™ sessions should I experience for optimum benefit?

Imagine you are installing a new software program in your computer (brain). In order to operate the program, you must complete the installation. So it is with Dr. Coldwell System™. To complete installation it is crucial that you experience a session at least once every day for 21 days. If you skip a day, the process must be restarted. It takes 21 CONSECUTIVE days to generate and permanently install new dendrites (neuron connections). Remember, your brain is a sophisticated computer; it operates on your personal software. After 21 consecutive sessions, use your IBMS™ sessions according to your stress level.

What can a IBMS™ session do for me?

IBMS™ users report the following results:

- Increased energy
- Stops slumps/dips during the day
- Improved optimism
- Improved self-esteem
- More effective management of life problems
- Improved sleep patterns, awakening rested and alert
- Increased productivity
- Calmer nervous system
- Enhanced libido
- Increased coping skills
- Clarity
- Improved quality of life
- Reduced emotional pain and suffering
- Accelerated recovery from physical manifestations of stress
- Enhanced immune function.

How are IBMS™ sessions different from other stress reduction programs?

IBMS™ sessions are designed in such a way that all the suggestions follow a very specific sequence—an audio road map that unlocks the power of the brain by using the real language of the brain (individualized symbols). There is no outside manipulation of any kind in any of IBMS™ sessions. Manipulation creates dependency on someone or something outside your control. IBMS™ targets the root cause of emotional and mental stress. As you experience each session, your brain functions at its optimum learning level, building new dendrites (neuron connections) by absorbing new stimuli that you alone create to achieve your specific goals.

Through these sessions, you will be able to define and resolve the root cause of your individual stress-related challenges.

What is the fundamental difference between a massage, a facial or other physical relaxation therapies and an IBMS™ session?

Massages, facials and other forms of physical therapy are wonderful for muscle relaxation and better blood and oxygen flow. However, the benefits are short term (lasting only an hour or so) and do not address the root cause of mental and emotional stress.

How do IBMS™ audio stress reduction sessions differ from other audio programs?

*   Many audio tape sessions are created by authors who are often inexperienced, misdirected, naïve or lacking in specific scientific knowledge and education.

*   Much of the background music on many of the stress control audio programs is incorrectly used, often providing wrong messages or having no effect at all.

*   Many narrators' suggestions are uninformed, naïve and lack scientific foundation and thus can actually be harmful.

*   World Wellness Organization's research showed that all audio programs tested functioned only in the alpha state, which does not produce permanent results.

*   All other researched stress management programs relax a person for more than 7 minutes causing the brain to produce sleep hormones that can leave the person tired for the entire day, thus negating subsequent benefits.

NOTE: Dr. Thomas Hohn, M.D., noted stress therapist, has stated that no other tapes or audio systems available have achieved the results that IBMS™ consistently achieves with his patients. There is no comparison!

What is so "unique" about IBMS™ programs?

IBMS™ sessions target the root cause of emotional and mental stress.

The sessions transport you to the "relaxation zone," a state of profound relaxation that stimulates the brain to become acutely focused and alert. In this state, your brain has the ability to create hemisphere synchronization (when both sides of the brain function at the same time) building the new dendrites (neuron connections) necessary for permanent, positive changes. This is the perfect state for regeneration and self-programming.

What benefit do I get from being in "Relaxation Zone?"

You can most efficiently program all the mental, emotional and/or physical changes you desire. You will find you can define and eliminate the root cause (negative life circumstances or unhealthy behavior) of your mental and emotional stress. Furthermore the relaxation zone is an ideal state for decision making and developing individualized action plans. You are able to think with a previously unknown clarity, free from outside mental manipulation, which in turn allows you to take total control of your life through effective self-conditioning. Because IBMS™ is entirely a *self-help* system, you automatically learn through repetition to control your neurological conditioning in the most beneficial way.

How can these sessions make positive changes in my life?

In order to make a positive change in your life you must first commit to change. Then it is necessary to program your brain to produce the change.

Effective programming requires that you use the language of the brain to visualize the change through your own symbols and personal motivation in order to shape a lasting result. IBMS™ is the only system we know of that has decoded the language of the brain to allow you to achieve permanent positive results. IBMS™ is not a positive *thinking* system; it is a positive *action* system.

Will I feel energized after an IBMS™ session?

By entering the relaxation zone, you give your nervous system a break.

Your body and mind are able to recharge, which can provide you with the regeneration equivalent of hours of restful sleep. Thus you feel energized and ready to handle life's challenges; full of energy, self-confidence and determination.

Is IBMS™ like hypnotism or meditation?

IBMS™ sessions are the antithesis or opposite of manipulative (hypnosis) or passive (meditation) techniques. It is a self-actuated action program in which you are always in complete control. Each program is narrated in the first person ("I" form) so that you create uniquely personal pictures in your mind as you follow the narrator's "neutral symbol" suggestions.

Because you associate with your personal experiences, your brain ignores any symbols that hold no meaning for you. In this way, you control the outcome of your session, the true definition of a self-actuated action program.

What is the most important benefit of an IBMS™ session?

Self-reliance through self-control—An IBMS™ session provides the perfect *self-conditioning* state for stimulation of the brain to produce all the neuro-chemical and bioelectrical changes necessary for optimum health and regeneration. With this new energy and mental and emotional clarity, you can take charge of every aspect of your mental, emotional and physical health. This is possible because the dendrite building process allows you to add permanent, usable knowledge, skills, and techniques for your life development. The more you use the system, the more you benefit from the system.

What items do I need for an IBMS™ session?

You need a CD player with stereo headphones, a comfortable chair (recliner) or a bed, a quiet dark place (eye cover optional) with no sound (TV, phone, dogs, children, etc.), and a blanket to avoid chills. Do **NOT** use candles, incense or any aromatherapy products as artificial fragrances will distract and detract from the overall benefit of the session. You do not need any external stimulation whatsoever, and we strongly suggest that you have none in order to achieve optimum results.

What can I expect from the first session?

Typically, the first session is not as effective as those that follow because of normal skepticism, fear of the unknown, and the natural curiosity to analyze the music and narration, all of which are distracting. These distractions typically disappear after the 2nd or 3rd session. You will progressively feel better and more energized after each session as the effects of the sessions build upon one another.

What can I expect from subsequent sessions?

The second session is more effective than the first, but the third session is even better because your nervous system becomes used to the deep physical relaxation and mental clarity and instinctively craves more.

Around the fifth session (each person reacts differently), there is typically another breakthrough as you discover a relaxed sense of focus and ability to cope. Typically, by the sixth session or so, the brain begins installing positive neurological changes (i.e.: building dendrites), at which point you learn how to control your stress more effectively, feel more energized, and experience more joy. It is at this stage that self-acceptance and self confidence improve with each session. But the magic number is 21, at which point the software (dendrites) is usually permanently installed so that all subsequent sessions have immediate benefits as needed.

When and how often do I need a session?

Everybody can benefit from an IBMS™ session. Although the outcome varies for each individual, you especially need a session whenever you feel particularly stressed or run down. Remember that it is on-going stress without a break that can cause a health breakdown, so a session will provide the necessary break for the regeneration you need to maintain your health. How often you need a session depends entirely on your individual stress level. Stress is like dirt—it keeps piling up unless you wash it off or reduce it. In other words, you need to keep reducing stress on a frequent basis or it can lead to a health breakdown.

NOTE: It is impossible to overdose on IBMS™ sessions, and there are no known adverse side effects.

How long do the effects of a session last?

The effects of a session can last quite a while, but it depends entirely on your individual stress level. Since there is no limit to how many sessions you can have, you should simply have a regenerating session when you feel particularly tired, exhausted, depressed, hopeless or weak and need to regenerate.

CONCLUSION:

Because IBMS™ sessions have a positive impact on your brain's capacity to visualize and create, you soon learn to gain more control over every part of your life, which automatically leads to improvement in your self esteem and self-confidence. Elevated self-esteem and self-confidence contribute to improved mental and physical health.

I developed a specific CD action set "The Stress, Depression, Anxiety Pack consisting of 10 CDs plus a free bonus CD:

(see www.instinctbasedmedicine.com)

1. The 3 basic stress reduction sessions: Total Relaxation, Breathing Therapy, Self Healing

2. The champion 3 CD package: Take charge of your life, Bring out the Champion, Life Solutions

3. Trauma erase

4. Successful Relationships

5. Youthful, Beautiful YOU

6. Woods Retreat

Plus a bonus CD: Dr Coldwell live on: You are born to be a Champion

Disclaimer: This system is not intended to diagnose, treat, cure or prevent any disease. IBMS™ sessions are intended to be used by mentally fatigued, highly stressed, but otherwise mentally healthy people. This process is not designed to address clinical depression. This is an educational self help system and as such every outcome is the sole responsibility of the user. There is no external manipulation in any form. The audio programs are instructive, self-help training sessions. IBMS™ sessions cannot and should not be used as or construed to be a substitute for a physician's visits, diagnosis, treatment, advice or any other therapy-related issues. If you have any concerns about any mental or physical conditions, ask your physician before using this product. Dr. Coldwell and the producers and sellers of this system assume no responsibility for any negative side effect from the use of this system or products. All information, systems and products have been previously published in other languages. All original rights and international copyrights are with Naps University Verlag GmbH, Germany.

Legal Notice:

IBMS™ is a patented scientific concept, its trademark is legally protected, worldwide. People, who use IBMS™ without direct authority of Dr. Leonard Coldwell will be prosecuted to the full extend of the law.

EXAMPLES OF SELF-HEALING WITH IBMS™

So many people have healed themselves of a severe illness during the past years with the help of my **Instinct Based Medicine™ System IBMS™** that it is impossible for me to provide exact numbers. Among these cases of successful self-healing are many which occurred, because of the proper application of the self-learned training exercise technique described in my book *The Unlimited Power of the Subconscious*, published by Hugendubel. Other people have, on the other hand, used my cassette program for guidance and still others have received the techniques for self-help from my seminars. In addition, there were many men and women who came to my **Instinct Based Medicine™ System IBMS™** training centers in order to receive instruction from me or from one of my **IBMS™** trainers, who were trained by me personally. Among these people were several incurable cases of which doctors had already given up but, who had refused to give up on themselves.

At this point I would like to emphasize once more that neither I, nor any of my **IBMS™** trainers are healers. We are only an aid to your own success and to your health. It is you, who realizes the success that you desire.

However, please take note: the profession of an **IBMS™** trainer is registered and these individuals   are trained by me alone. They are only allowed to call themselves **IBMS™** trainers after they have received a certificate to that effect, which is signed by me personally. **IBMS™** is trademarked as a scientific concept worldwide and may only be carried out by myself and by persons who are licensed by me.

At this juncture, I will describe several self-healing cases that demonstrate how belief in an individual's infinite inner power, coupled with effective implementation of the **IBMS™** -techniques, lead to healing. This description should give you hope so that you never give up no matter how difficult the circumstances are. All of these patients were interviewed by the journalist Ulrich Grefe and published in many of his publications. These healing examples are published in my former books mainly in: *The Power of the Subconscious Mind* (Hugendubel Publishing). Some names have been changed.

Recovery from Gout and Obesity

Klaus suffered from stomach bleeding, intestinal ulcers, acute circulation problems, and severe gout. Every day, he went to the doctor to have a substantial amount of fluid extracted from his knee. His family doctor advised him to change his diet; otherwise he could expect the worst. Klaus was overweight, and ate as much in a day as others would consume in a week.

Klaus came to me upon the recommendation of a friend, who had suffered from a "fatal" illness and was now fully healed with the help of my tools and technology. It was a good reference, but I needed to determine whether Klaus was committed to doing whatever was necessary to restore his health. When Klaus confirmed that he would cooperate wholeheartedly, we talked about the advantages of a healthy diet. We also talked about overeating, junk food, and the disadvantages of a bad diet. This would prepare his subconscious to accept the fact that a change must take place.

I explained to Klaus that his eating habits were nothing else but acquired abnormal behavior. He could easily be deprogrammed or reprogrammed for health. Klaus agreed, after a lengthy conversation, to put a massive block in his subconscious.

As we began therapy, I asked Klaus to think about a situation in which he had eaten a little bit, and immediately felt extremely satisfied. After that, I asked Klaus to imagine eating fresh fruits and vegetables, while feeling happy and energetic. We anchored this experience in his mind, so that eating healthy, fluid-rich food gave him a feeling of incredible health, vitality and energy.

I also asked Klaus to envision his future with positive mental images. With his eyes closed, Klaus pictured himself looking in the mirror and seeing his new slim and healthy body. He experienced feelings of pride and excitement. We also practiced self-healing exercises in which Klaus programmed his subconscious and mentally activated his body to heal itself of gout.

We met two more times for therapy. After the third session, Klaus' chronic pain and discomfort from the gout had disappeared. He no longer needed to visit the doctor to have fluid extracted from his knee. Ultimately, Klaus lost over 100 lbs in 19 weeks, without being hungry. The old, destructive eating habits were gone for good and so was his gout.

Healing of Psoriasis

When Donna visited me, she looked exhausted and overwhelmed. She wore white gloves, and could barely move her arm or bend her elbow. She suffered from a horrible case of psoriasis on her elbows, hands and knees. An odor of decay emanated from her and puss oozed from her open sores. Donna had avoided public places, like restaurants, for the past 15 years because other people would lose their appetite and stop eating when they saw her hands or smelled the stench of her wounds.

When Donna took her gloves off, her hands looked pitiful. Her fingernails were rotting away and her hands were covered with puss and fresh blood. Donna's husband came with her and could not hold back his tears.

I discovered that Donna was hesitant to speak openly in the presence of her husband. For this reason, I politely asked him to leave the treatment room. When we were alone, I asked Donna if she had made any compromises in life. I was looking for something which might have poisoned her soul and made her life unbearable. Clinical tests showed that her liver was toxic and I suspected that her skin was ridding itself of toxins, stress and negative emotions.

With some hesitation, Donna blurted out the truth. Many years ago, her husband had an affair with her best girlfriend. Evidently, she found out during an argument with her girlfriend, when she triumphantly boasted about the affair. In response, Donna decided not to confront her husband about the affair. She asked her girlfriend not to tell him anything either, in order to save her otherwise good marriage.

A few weeks later, Donna's skin disorder surfaced. It gradually became worse, and after a few months the horrible infection affected her whole body. Her joints, hands and feet were severely affected by psoriasis.

When I told Donna that stress and toxic emotions were the cause of her illness, she agreed to let her husband come back into the session to talk about this situation.

When confronted, Donna's husband collapsed and broke down in tears. He was devastated by the affair and his inner guilt and condemnation caused him to suffer from stomach ulcers. As the session progressed, I left the room so that they could talk about the problems they had both suppressed and reconcile the situation.

Overall, Donna and her husband came to see me 15 times. I taught Donna to breathe healing light into the source of her mental wounds. She learned to forgive her husband as well as her girlfriend by programming her subconscious. Over time, I helped Donna eliminate the buildup of hatred in her soul and helped her reconcile her emotions. She gradually reached the point of complete healing and recovery. Looking back, it is a miracle that Donna recovered in six weeks. Her psoriasis completely disappeared and Donna never experienced a relapse.

Another Healing of Psoriasis

For 12 years, Janice suffered from psoriasis and puss oozing over her entire body. She was afraid to go out in public. Janice couldn't move without blood or puss coming out of her hands, elbows or knees.

Through detailed questioning, I learned that Janice's husband had forced her to eat snails at a restaurant. Janice didn't want to do it, but her husband insisted and even threatened to divorce her. In response, Janice gulped down the snails.

Three days later, Janice felt itching over her body. This condition became worse every time she ate, and eventually her body was covered with puss and scabs. Janice's joints and hands were affected the worst. She was hardly able to move because of the pain. The cause for this illness was a false neuro-association. Janice held on to feeling "those disgusting snails" (as she called them) inside her, which made her emotionally and physically sick.

I helped Janice recover by using a relaxation exercise. When Janice was completely relaxed, I helped her to destroy the false neuro-association by revisiting the day that she had been forced to eat the snails. I asked her to vomit up the snails in her mind, so that her sub-conscious would be given a symbol of liberation. After we had repeated this exercise several times and she began to feel relieved and liberated. Then we created a new neuro-association. I asked her to experience mentally, again and again, a conversation in which she told her husband that she would absolutely never eat snails again. Janice visualized herself pushing the plate away, while feeling great about her actions and standing by her decision.

Janice conducted this mental exercise several times. As she continually practiced and trained herself, the correct behavior appeared more real than the previous behavior in which she ate the "disgusting" snails. Within days, Janice's inflammation diminished and the psoriasis began to disappear. After eight weeks, Janice fully recovered and was never bothered by psoriasis again.

Healing of Breast Cancer

I clearly remember the first time that Elaine came to my office. She was in her mid-thirties and suffered from breast cancer. The doctors removed her right breast and treated her twice with chemotherapy. Elaine was in terrible shape. Her hair was falling out. She was frightened and emotionally devastated.

After a short consultation, I learned that Elaine suffered from depression and a gripping angst. Since her early childhood, she was not able to leave the house or sleep in the dark alone. Elaine's constant fears led to an inner resignation and a decreased will to live. As she became more and more depressed, her body began to self-destruct.

Elaine was on the brink of a nervous breakdown. In therapy, we started doing relaxation exercises, which helped her, calm down and internalize a peaceful mental state. Elaine quickly learned that our feelings and emotional outlook affect our perspective on life. The quality of our life depends on our perception and what we think about is what our future will hold.

If someone can't envision the future, then healing is impossible. Before anything else, a person must believe that a bright future and optimum health is conceivable. As all religious books of the world state over and over again, that faith (or the power of belief) is the greatest force in human existence. In the final analysis, everything depends on whether you believe in your own success and healing.

With simple techniques and exercises, as I have described in my book *The Unlimited Power of the Subconscious*, we eliminated Elaine's fears. Like a beautiful flower, she began to blossom. As therapy continued, Elaine visualized her life integrated with her career and husband, who lovingly and enthusiastically stood by her side. Within a few weeks, Elaine was vibrant and full of energy. Previously, the doctors had given a life expectancy of six months. Now, she had every reason to live with passion.

Two years later, Elaine returned to the center with a large knot protruding from the scars of her former operation. She was terribly frightened, but felt hopeful because of her success two years earlier. I referred Elaine to the chief of surgery in a nearby hospital, who discovered something astonishing. The first operation was terribly botched. The cancer had been cut in two and half of it remained in Elaine's body. As any physician can confirm, this woman would have had less than three months to live because she carried a severe malignant tumor, the size of a walnut, in her body. This is the worst thing that can happen to a patient. The chief of the hospital had never seen anything like this, nor thought it possible. Half of the tumor was left in Elaine's body, but the tumor had isolated itself and had been pushed upward by the body's attempt to expel it.

Once the tumor was surgically removed, there was no need for chemotherapy. Elaine was told that she would never again be able to have children, but she quickly became pregnant. For this reason, Elaine remained under my care during pregnancy. The doctors told her that her baby would be sick, and possibly suffer from birth defects. After nine months, Elaine gave birth to a healthy child. There were no complications or difficulties during the birth. Elaine's beautiful little girl is now five years old. She is full of life, energy, health and vitality. She does not get the flu or colds, unlike her older brother and her playmates. Elaine is happy and now realizes that there is no incurable disease.

Help for Breast Cancer

I'm always astonished when patients refuse to open up and identify the root cause of their illness. They seem comfortable with their condition and limitations. They don't seem to care that their illness has lessened the quality of their life.

In therapy, my patients are encouraged to adopt a new way of thinking, as they learn to identify the root cause of illness. This enables them to recognize the connection between energy-draining compromises, stressful emotions and the development of severe illnesses.

When I asked Greta, who suffered from advanced breast cancer, about the possible cause of her illness, she had no clue. Greta had a large open sore on her left breast, and was looking for an alternative to surgery.

Greta often talked about her mother and how fortunate she was to inherit furniture from her. The more Greta talked about the furniture, the more obvious it became that this old furniture continuously reminded her about horrible things in the past. Indirectly, she wanted to get rid of this old furniture and decorate her place in her own style

Once Greta realized these suppressed thoughts and emotions, her behavior changed visibly. She seemed relieved and her eyes became bright and lively.

Greta mentioned that she had a driver's license but had not driven a car in the past 13 years. I immediately recognized this disclosure as the next building block. I needed to know why she had suddenly stopped driving. I realized that her low self-esteem and self-confidence paralyzed her from driving and that she didn't have enough energy or strength to address this problem.

As therapy continued, Greta admitted that she had been married twice and suffered a miscarriage. Finally, the picture was coming together. We used the **IBMS™** technique to address her repressed emotions, as well as her feelings of fear guilt. After five days of therapy, the wound on her chest began to close and her ulcer visibly diminished. Eventually, Greta was completely healed and restored to her full health.

Greta is a textbook illustration of repressed emotions. She swallowed her feelings, (rather than dealing with them openly and honestly) and therefore could not identify the root cause of her illness.

An impending crisis is also common with **IBMS™** therapy. This happens when the patient becomes aware of problems that were previously suppressed. Confronted with these issues, the patient can't escape into his or her dream world. This often causes patients to become angry or frustrated with their **IBMS™**-therapist.

Finally, the client is self-aware and accepts full responsibility for their health and emotions. This is an astonishing and wonderful phenomenon. Often, the patient looks ten to fifteen years younger. Their eyes sparkle, and they appear to be more relaxed. Even if the patient remains physically weak, they are now mentally balanced and optimistic about the future. Their strength and energy are visibly restored. Afterwards, healing and recovery is accelerated at high speed. In more than 90% of all cases, astounding physiological changes occur. Even doctors are amazed at how fast cancers recede or diminish.

Healing of Spinal Muscular Atrophy *(severe form of Muscular Dystrophy)*

When Hans came to my office, he was in pitiful shape. He used to be an accomplished athlete and worked professionally as a building engineer. Now he was unable to climb stairs and could hardly move. Hans spent his days in a wheelchair or in bed, as he suffered from severe pain. The doctor diagnosed Hans with Spinal Muscular Atrophy.

Even though Hans was stricken with illness, I was impressed by his courage. He said, "As long as I can breathe, I will fight." Hans had heard that my techniques were effective, even in the most hopeless situations. He was determined to do whatever it took to recover and become healthy.

As we began to talk, I discovered that Hans wanted nothing less than optimum health. We began by stimulating his brain because the healing and regeneration process is initiated by the brain.

Doctors had given Hans a maximum life expectancy of 12 to 18 months. (These were opinions from experts of medical universities.) Although they offered no hope for healing or recovery, Hans courageously placed himself in my care for **IBMS™** self-healing and therapy.

I asked Hans to visualize himself at a fitness center, which was filled with symbols that facilitated healing. Because the subconscious works with symbols, Hans worked out step-by-step in his mind. He visualized himself using a variety of exercise equipment. With each mental workout, Hans strengthened every single muscle in his body. He programmed his conscious to see himself as healthy and strong. He visualized himself interacting with his children and wife as a healthy man. These mental exercises strongly motivated Hans, and enabled his subconscious to perform the powerful act of healing from this incurable illness. After four weeks, Hans was completely pain free. It was the first time in 12 years that he was pain free. His muscles substantially improved, which was also confirmed by a medical exam. After six weeks, Hans' success was clearly visible. His arms and legs, which hung previously lifeless in the joints, began to take their natural shape. After eight weeks, Hans could climb steps by himself. After eight months, he could do light physical work. Ultimately, Hans activated his self-healing power and created a new quality of life for himself.

Today, Hans is one of my best friends. Whenever I see him, he is happy and filled with zest for life. I share his story because it confirms that everyone possesses a God-given power to heal himself. Dear reader, you too can improve the quality of your life, even if you are severely ill, if you are willing to do whatever is necessary to restore your health.

Healing of a Spastic Nerve Condition

At our **IBMS™**-training center, I noticed a painter who moved his eyes quickly back and forth, without ever looking at someone directly. His eyelids were swollen and it appeared that he was under the influence of drugs.

His name was Leon. As I began to talk to him, I discovered that Leon had been taking painkillers for the past 15 years. The medicine affected his stomach and inner organs. Leon could hardly stand the pain, and saw a variety of doctors and specialists. One doctor gave him the option of severing the nerves in his face with surgery, so that he would no longer feel the pain. However, this surgery would paralyze half of his face, and there was no guarantee that the nerve endings wouldn't join with the other nerves, causing pain again.

I felt sorry for this industrious and talented man. I did an **IBMS™** exercise with Leon, and estimated that he could reduce his pain substantially after six months of intensive programming. To my surprise, it happened much sooner than that.

I was relocating to America and did not have enough time to concentrate on Leon. I asked my medical manager to take over using the **IBMS™** technical method. After the second session, Leon's pain, which he endured for 17 years, completely disappeared.

To our astonishment, Leon ran around in the center telling everyone (whether they wanted to hear it or not) how well he felt. Leon could not believe what had happened to him. He was now completely free of pain, and even his back pain completely disappeared.

Leon's recovery proves that you do not have to take expensive medication or undergo surgery to be liberated from illness. The power of your own mind will enable you to handle any obstacle that comes your way. It is always wise to set goals. If you don't accomplish your goals, it does not mean that they are unattainable. You must look for new ways and possibilities to make things happen. When it comes to your health, you must look for ways to eliminate or reduce your pain and suffering and restore your health. Never accept limitations, or settle for less than you can be. You don't have to live with pain or illness. Don't allow your mind to dwell on negative thoughts. Keep working on improving the quality of your life and don't allow your mind to accept limitations, pain or illness.

Success is a journey. If you are on your way toward achieving your goals, then you are successful. If you focus on your health, then you're on the way towards improving or restoring it. If you don't give up, you will find a way to improve the quality of your life. I am 100% certain of that.

Healing of Osteoporosis

Gertie was in her early fifties, but looked at least fifteen years older. She limped into my office, hunched over from pain. Gertie was in a terrible, catastrophic state, mentally as well as physically. Gertie had been married for 30 years to a well-known corporate executive. He was an alcoholic, and physically abused Gertie. He threatened to kill her, and she lived in constant fear for her life. Twice, he had thrown her down the stairs. If her husband would "lose it again" (as she called it) Gertie planned to escape by jumping through a window, into her car, which was ready to go with a full tank of gasoline. Gertie had osteoporosis in a very advanced state and her overall physical condition was that of a handicapped person. Her mental condition was catastrophic and her physical condition was not much better.

I tried to convince Gertie to leave her husband immediately. She refused to do so, but did agree to undergo **IBMS™** therapy. At first, we did several strengthening, regenerating, and relaxing exercises to stabilize her energy reserve and prevent a total collapse. After a few days, Gertie was ready for a new get-away plan. While her husband was on a two-day business trip, she called a moving company, temporarily moved in with friends, and later into her own apartment.

During this time, we continued to meet and also talked over the telephone, to prevent a mental or physical collapse. For a year, Gertie and I worked on stabilizing and building up her mental and physical condition. I also supported her during the difficult divorce procedure and visits to lawyers. After 18 months, Gertie wrote me a letter. She said that her physician discovered that her osteoporosis had disappeared, and her bone density and elasticity was comparable to that of a healthy person. I've kept this documentation for my records. Gertie's story illustrates that compromise (not standing up for yourself) can destroy your health and literally cripple your body. She was restored to full health by eliminating unhealthy compromises in her life and ending her relationship with her abusive husband. Gertie was also strengthened with relaxation exercises, which enabled her body to heal and restore itself.

Healing of Sexual Disturbances

Katrina, age 26, came to me at the advice of her husband, who had heard of my success in treating emotional problems. Katrina loved her husband very much, but didn't want to be intimate with him. Three years ago, she had given birth to their first child and lost interest in having a physical relationship with her husband. As soon as her husband touched her, she felt repulsed, and wanted nothing to do with him. Of course, her marriage was now in danger, and something had to be done.

In therapy, the first step was identifying the root cause of the problem. Katrina's negative feelings started with her child's birth. The baby was conceived out of wedlock. They married quickly and then the baby was born. As a strict Catholic, Katrina suffered from guilt. Her guilt subconsciously manifested itself by punishing herself and her husband. This guilt made her think that sexual intimacy was dirty and disgusting.

When Katrina started **IBMS™** therapy, she learned to accept her situation. She practiced relaxation exercises and mentally returned to the past to recall a positive sexual experience with her husband. Katrina associated herself with the loving, tender feelings that she felt for her husband. She remained in this condition of association for at least ten minutes.

The next morning, Katrina and her husband both called to thank me, independently of each other. They both had a wonderful night together. It took only one session to resolve this problem. It isn't difficult to resolve such conflicts. Most of the time, it only takes a little push to get people back on track with the behavior, feelings and actions they desire.

IBMS™ treatment is simple and easy, but never trust anyone who lacks the training, knowledge and experience that is necessary to produce results. When people come to therapy, they must be carefully trained and conditioned, so that the conflict is permanently resolved. Nothing is worse than a relapse after recovery.

Help for Multiple Sclerosis

Anna was diagnosed with multiple sclerosis. She was living in a dream world, which had nothing to do with reality. She swayed back and forth between reality and fantasy. Her subconscious began to fight the part of the brain that was in control over discerning reality from fantasy.

When someone has multiple sclerosis, their immune system regards the brain as a foreign object. Their body begins to attack certain nerve endings, which are damaged and destroyed in the process. Anna was already paralyzed on the right side of her body. Her balance was completely destroyed, after many years of excruciating pain. In therapy, I explained to Anna that she needed a miracle, and it had to come from within. This realization enabled Anna to change her thinking and behavior with unbelievable energy and strength. Gradually, she started to accept reality. She learned to make the best of situations, which she previously was unable to do.

After two months of **IBMS™** therapy, Anna reported that the following health problems were resolved:

- severe leg cramps & numbness
- inability to stretch her legs
- inability to pull her legs up close to her body without the use of her hands
- uncontrollable nervous leg twitches
- intense feelings of pins and needles in her legs, feet and hands
- sensitivity to changes in the weather
- acute sensitivity to pressure: like in the fairytale, *The Princess and the Pea*. (Every wrinkle in the bed sheets caused her pain and discomfort)
- bladder problems
- sensitive finger tips
- pain associated with hot and cold temperatures; and
- back pain.

Healing of Severe Depression

When Connie visited my office, she cried uncontrollably. Her boyfriend explained that Connie was unable to work and could not be left alone. For months, she had been on sick leave from work and her condition was becoming worse.

Connie worked at the university cafeteria. One of her co-workers was domineering, controlling and verbally abusive. Connie was on the verge of a nervous breakdown. She felt weak, helpless and did not believe that she was capable of doing anything successfully.

In **IBMS™** therapy, Connie built up her energy with relaxation, visualization and breathing exercises. Connie immediately felt stronger. She promised not to make any major decisions in the upcoming month. Connie was advised to take it easy, and only do things that she wanted to do. Rest and recuperation would enable her to overcome her depression.

After the third relaxation exercise, Connie felt like herself again. She felt motivated to return to work. I was pleased with Connie's attitude, but feared that she might relapse. It is absolutely necessary to initially create a reserve of energy. After the patient's energy level is stabilized, they are equipped to deal with the unpleasant situations as they unfold. They are able to cope with their own thoughts and behavior, and never again suffer an energy depletion or imbalance.

For the next ten sessions, Connie programmed herself mentally for success at work. She imagined herself at the cafeteria, acting calmly and confidently, especially with her domineering co-worker. Connie imagined herself in stressful situations and programmed feelings of confidence, power, and security into her mental pictures.

When Connie returned to work, she discovered that the programming worked perfectly. She had no interpersonal problems at all, even with the bossy co-worker. For the first time, work was fun and rewarding. Her depression had disappeared, and Connie felt like herself again.

Healing of Anxiety Resulting from Rape

Marlene was raped by her father when she was ten years old. As an adult, she was claustrophobic and feared closed spaces and staircases. Occasionally, Marlene checked into a mental hospital, but that made her condition worse. Adding insult to injury was that Marlene's rape was kept secret, and she lived together with her husband and parents under one roof. Whenever her father stepped into the room, she would sweat profusely and was unable to speak or think clearly. Marlene's anxiety led to physical problems that stumped doctors and healthcare professionals.

After an initial consultation, Marlene's feelings of helplessness turned into rage. Whenever her father was mentioned, Marlene would literally explode. She screamed about what a pig he was, and how dare he take advantage of her innocence and trust. Marlene's outbursts ended with tears, which brought her relief. Afterwards, she would talk freely about feelings that were previously repressed.

Marlene and I did an **IBMS™** programming exercise in which she attempted to forgive her father on a mental level. This was not easy for her, but after three exercises, Marlene was finally able to let go and forgive.

Fortunately, Marlene's rape was an isolated incident. The rape must have been an impulsive act, or perhaps her father was under the influence of alcohol or drugs. I suggested that Marlene confront her father, and talk openly about what had happened. When she did this, her father remembered almost nothing about the incident. He was aware that something had happened, but remembered only vaguely that he suffered a nervous breakdown and had gotten drunk at a bar.

After Marlene confronted her father, she was able to come to grips with the situation and finally, put this incident behind her. Marlene was liberated from her fear and paranoia.

During **IBMS™** therapy, I helped Marlene create an anchor which enabled her to summon feelings of euphoria and happiness whenever she needed them. Marlene imagined herself climbing stairs and entering small, closed-in spaces. I anchored these mental images with happy and euphoric feelings. Ultimately, Marlene established a new neuro-association in her mind, which enabled her to climb stairs and stay in tight, closed-in places without anxiety or apprehension.

Previously, Marlene had been in psychotherapy for more than 18 years. She had been treated for psychosomatic illness and also been hospitalized in the psychiatric ward. With the help of **IBMS™** therapy, Marlene was able to change her neuro associations, identify the root cause of her anxiety, forgive, and let go of the past. Her recovery took only five weeks, and Marlene's anxiety was gone for good.

The Non-Acceptance of a Hip Implant

Bert was an intelligent, well-educated man who wanted to commit suicide. He suffered from excruciating hip pain as a result of a childhood accident (which his parents ignored.) Bert received a hip implant, and the surgery was successful according to the doctors. When Bert was back on his feet, however, his hip constantly jumped out of the joint, which made walking nearly impossible.

Plagued with pain, Bert tried to repress or ignore the pain. This only made the problem worse. During a short session, I discovered that Bert hated himself because of his physical limitations. Emotionally and intellectually, he was not willing to accept his physical handicap.

Bert repeatedly mentioned being separated from his wife, but that he would take good care of her and their children. Bert repeated this statement so many times that I suspected something else was wrong. To challenge Bert, I praised him for being an excellent father, and how sensible it was that he had separated from his wife, after he recognized that his marriage was doomed from the beginning.

All of a sudden, Bert shouted, "That's not true at all! My wife separated from me. She did not know who she was dealing with, or who I really was. My life was going no where, and she couldn't bear my self-pity any longer!"

That was the turning point. Bert identified the root cause of his problem. His hip was out of joint because mind and body rejected it. He also needed to develop clear goals, future perspectives, value systems and rules. We dealt with these things through continuous mental programming. As Bert began to develop feelings of self-confidence and self-esteem, his perspective started to change.

After talking to his wife, Bert was hopeful that the relationship could be restored. He began to set new goals and develop a clear value system, so that he could accept himself again. He stopped feeling sorry for himself. After a short time, the tension and disjointed feeling in his hip was gone. Stress had caused the hip to jump out of its joints. The initial good work by the orthopedic surgeons could now be amplified and enforced. Bert was a new man, with a fresh outlook on life.

Concluding Remarks

Although many of my clients say Dr. Leonard Coldwell healed me, this is not correct. It was not I who healed them; they healed themselves. That I contributed to their healing is the development of trust in themselves and in their own self-healing powers through explanation, training and demonstration. I am the one who knows how it should be done and I can relay what everybody must do himself.

I am not able to heal you, you must heal yourself. The **IBMS™**-System is a tool for self-healing. I can show you how to use this tool and can put this tool into your hands, however, in the final analysis you must use this tool.

Of course, some of the people, whose amazing cases of self-healing have been described by me here, had occasional doubts, apparent relapses and fears during periods of stagnation in the healing process.

That is, of course, part of the maturation process in every human being. What brought these people finally to the point of healing was the unwillingness to give up the will to live; they were determined to become and remain healthy.

I call those people victorious, because they changed their inactivity, their doubts and their behavior and their false thinking patterns. I respect the way they took control of their lives. They changed their diet and did everything necessary to regain their health.

These people are the true victors because they conquered their illness. The harvest they reaped was a new quality of life and the knowledge that they will be able to handle any problem that confronts them. Those people now know how to come to terms with difficulties.

I would like to say once more, success gained with **IBMS™**-training is produced and maintained by the clients themselves. We are only teachers, trainers and confidants who help to resolve emotional problems and conflicts and who search jointly for solutions to these problems and conflicts. We help to develop clear plans and strategies and to carry these plans through. Sometimes we provide care for our **IBMS™** clients beyond the initial treatment and give advice for checkups and renewal appointments to reinforce new behavior patterns and techniques.

Sometimes, we also work together with the family members so that they will know exactly how they should conduct themselves toward their loved ones in order to help them overcome their limitations, conquer their illness and maintain their health.

We must all work together toward the realization of a total therapy in which physicians, consultants, natural healers, psychologists, psychiatrists and **IBMS™**-trainers, health researchers and all other persons, who concern themselves with the health of people, share their thoughts and ideas and develop an increasingly improved concept of total health. Only in this way can humanity benefit and we, as responsible health providers, have the obligation to ensure that in a few years the exploding costs in the health industry will be reduced and that the statistics, that show that 87% of all people are frequently ill, become obsolete.

It would be wonderful for me, if you would be one of these miracle cases, one of the victors, whose successes I can describe in my next book. Should you be ill, be prepared that you will not only hear about miracles in reference to other people, but that you can become the subject of a miracle story. The healing lies in your own hands and the tool, the possibilities and the potential you possess is already within you. I hope that you have learned from the above examples of self-healing.

There is always a way and you are the only person, who can really set your healing in motion; you alone are responsible for your life, your future and your health. If you have learned this, I will have accomplished a lot with this short venture into **IBMS™**-technology.

The above described healings are, of course, only a few of the many from my practice. I chose these stories to encourage other people, who may have similar problems, to take problems into their own hands and fight for a better quality of life.

I would be pleased to hear your comments and questions in respect to my book. I would also be interested in your personal experiences with my **IBMS™**-system. It could help others to make their own lives more successful and beautiful. If you are very successful in your profession, your health, or your relationships and could help other people to build up their courage and ability to persevere, or if you have overcome an illness which was considered incurable, then please write to:

Dr. Leonard Coldwell, 1150 Hungryneck Blvd., Suite C 379, Mount Pleasant, South Carolina 29464
or email: isntinctbasedmedicine@gmail.com and visit the websites
www.instinctbasedmedicine.com and www.drleonardcoldwell.com.
Your reports of success can encourage others.

GET YOUR LIFE IN BALANCE!

Every Health Challenge Mentally, Emotionally or Physically comes only from being out of balance.

The simple truth is that you can only be sick if you are not in sync with your true self. Your life gets out of balance when you live outside your comfort zone or if you do not live according to your true personality, what you stand for, really want, who you really are.

Illness comes when you don't embrace your inner values, talents and possibilities. Sickness comes only when you live in fear, worries and doubt, in hopelessness, a feeling of helplessness or unworthiness, with lack of self love, self confidence and hope. It means you are not living consistent with your true you, your true personality and character traits.

All sickness means you are violating natures (or Gods) laws. Because the way you were born or created was perfect in design and function. But starting in our early childhood, people around us and we ourselves started to "mess" our perfection up.

It sounds very simplified but it is true: If you live in keeping with your true self—love, respect and trust yourself—you will be healthy. The sicker you are the more you are distanced from your true personality and your life's mission of personal development and spiritual and emotional growth.

You cannot have Stress, Anxiety or Depression if you are in balance with who you really are and what you really stand for.

The challenge to you now is to find out what exactly that is. The information contained in this book that you just read can help you to find your individual answers and solutions as well as your inner goals, dreams and personal motivation for your entire life. The IBMS™ can help you to define your personal mission in life and can give you the knowledge, techniques and tools to be all you can be, achieve and have. Embracing the Champion in you and living a life without fear or emotional tension is only possible if you don't do what others expect from you or tell you or want you to do. The solution is this—no matter what it costs, you have to realize your own dreams and goals and never make a compromise against yourself and what you really are and stand for! Because, in my opinion, that is the only way to get seriously or chronically ill. If you deny yourself to be "you" in the whole meaning of the word for too long or if you are constantly compromising yourself you will get sick, unhappy and eventually you will die young!

You see, the path you take to get to your *Only Answer to Stress, Anxiety and Depression* will cause you to find your own way to be truly you! There is no way to have stress, anxiety or depression if you are yourself and live the way you feel is right. Just use common sense and your instinct to make your life the masterpiece it is suppose to be—and then there will be no health challenges. Grow and develop yourself all the time so that life does not have to make you act by giving you challenges.

And finally, I will give you my personal regime:
- Once a year do the full body and colon cleanse from
  www.mybepure.com
- Use only shower filters and under sink or whole house osmosis water filtration systems from www.intacthealth.com
- Take Quint Essence, Vitamin E and D from
  www.awesomesupplements.com
- Take the metal cleanse and silver hydrosol from
  www.helpingamericannow.com
- Once a year for at least three weeks eat foods only from
  www.greatwholefood.com

If you follow this regime, you will have a nearly zero risk of developing unnecessary health challenges or stress, anxiety or depression caused by toxins, acidosis or nutritional deficiencies.

Please visit the following Websites:

www.instinctbasedmedicine.com
www.drleonardcoldwell.com
www.theonlyanswertocancer.com
www.intacthealth.com
www.greatwholefood.com
www.justlikesugarinc.com
www.ktradionetwork.com
www.healthfreedomusa.org
www.mpwhi.com
www.paulnison.com
www.awesomesupplements.com
www.mybepure.com
www.helpinamericanow.com
www.womenfoodsexandpower.com
www.rense.com
www.RSBell.com

Dear friends please accept that you were born to win, to be a champion and to live a life in success, happiness and health—with the highest quality of life possible. If I can help you in any way to achieve your goals please write me at instinctbasedmedicine@gmail.com and I will answer your question. (The only exception is if you have EarthLink as your email or others that will try to make me reply to an authorization email—I will not!)

Life is good today! See you far over the top

—Your friend Dr. C (Dr. Leonard Coldwell)

Again, if you have any questions or suggestions please write to:

instinctbasedmedicine@gmail.com or go to

www.instinctbasedmedicine.com You may also visit

www.drleonardcoldwell.com

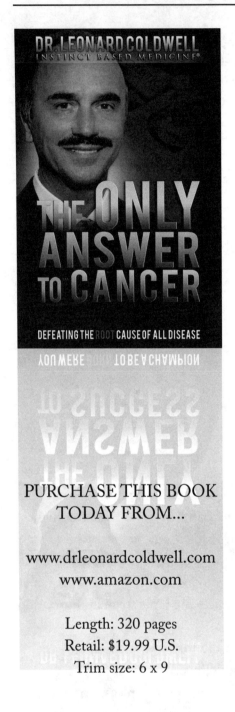

PURCHASE THIS BOOK
TODAY FROM...

www.drleonardcoldwell.com

www.amazon.com

Length: 320 pages
Retail: $19.99 U.S.
Trim size: 6 x 9

www.21cpublishers.com

All illness comes from lack of energy, and the greatest energy drainer is mental and emotional stress, which I believe to be the root cause of all illness. Stress is one of the major elements that can erode energy to such a large and permanent extent that the immune system loses all possibility of functioning at an optimum level. *The Only Answer to Cancer* is a book of hope, and Dr. Coldwell wants the reader to understand that there is always hope, no matter how bad Their health situation is right now. The journey to ultimate health can begin today!

In his lifetime, Dr. Leonard Coldwell has:

- seen over 35,000 patients

- had a 92.3% success rate with cancer and other illnesses

- had over 2.2 million seminar attendees that wrote to him, sending in their comments and life stories.

- He has had over 7 million readers of his newsletters and reports.

"I have seen many patients that Dr. Coldwell cured from cancer and other diseases like

Multiple Sclerosis and Lupus and Parkinson's and even muscular dystrophy and many more, and I am still in constant awe of Dr. Coldwell's talent and results."

—Dr. Thomas Hohn MD
NMD Licensed IBMS Therapist™

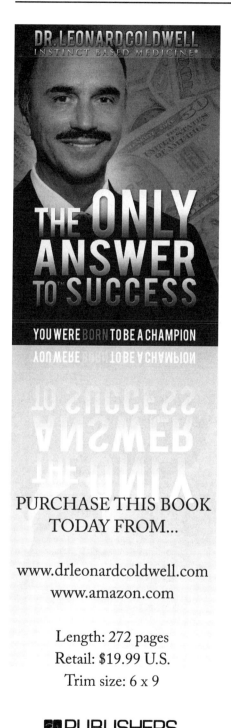

PURCHASE THIS BOOK
TODAY FROM...

www.drleonardcoldwell.com
www.amazon.com

Length: 272 pages
Retail: $19.99 U.S.
Trim size: 6 x 9

21 PUBLISHERS
READING YOU LOUD AND CLEAR

www.21cpublishers.com

With this book Dr. Coldwell offers you an opportunity to turn your life into the masterpiece it was meant to be.

Outstanding relationships with your colleagues, contentment, stability, a life filled with enthusiasm and passion, with inner harmony, happiness, vitality, health and strength; these will become a part of the your life when you apply Dr. Coldwells IBMS™ principles. Anyone can reach freedom and the feeling of being in charge of their own life, because freedom means to be free of manipulation, of outside influence and deception; everyone can be free of fear and free of the past.

"I won the Olympic Medal in Japan only because of the help, support and coaching of Dr Leonard Coldwell. "
    —Uwe Buchtmann – Olympic Medal winner

"Dr Coldwell trained, consulted and coached for the largest companies and most successful people around the world. His success is legendary. Dr Coldwell is a living legend and everybody that ever had the honor to experience Dr Coldwell on stage or in person knows that Dr Coldwell has changed his life for the better."
    —Professor D. Wilkening Chief Editor The MTC Journal.

About the Author

Leonard Coldwell is considered as one of the leading authorities of self-help education for cancer patients and is called by many authorities the world leading expert on cancer. Dr. Leonard Coldwell is the most endorsed holistic and alternative doctor. His cure rate for so called incurable diseases in Europe is legendary. After sixteen years as a General Practitioner in Europe, Dr. Coldwell left general practice to concentrate on his applied research in stress and stress related diseases, with particular emphasis on cancer and other "incurable" diseases.

He hosts the widely popular radio show The Dr. Coldwell Report. He and his co-host, Kelly Wallace, bring you eye-opening and health-saving shows on modern day issues that affect the world. He has some of the most sought after guests covering topics related to health, healing, and fighting for patients' rights. You can email Dr. Coldwell at... instinctbasedmedicine@gmail.com or contact him via the following website: www.drleonardcoldwell.com

The following are Dr. Coldwell's Historically used health protocols put together for you from www.awesomsupplements.com

7029	Dr Coldwell's Acid-Alkaline	7328	Melanoma Nutritional Health Support
7038	Acne	7329	Lymphoma Nutritional Health Support
7066	Dr Coldwell's Candida Remediation	7330	Sarcoma Nutritional Health Support
7083	Cellulite Control	7331	Leukemia Nutritional Health Support
7101	Wellness Maintenance	7332	Colon Carcinoma Nutritional Health
7110	Weight Loss	7333	Kidney or Bladder Carcinoma Support
7111	Athletic Endurance	7334	Liver Carcinoma Nutritional Support
7119	Arthritis/Rheumatism	7335	Lung Carcinoma Nutritional Support
7128	Liver Cleanse	7336	Pancreas Carcinoma Nutritional Support
7137	IBS/Crohn's/Colitis	7337	Brain Carcinoma Nutritional Support
7146	Parasite Elimination	7338	Breast Carcinoma Nutritional Support
7155	Yeast Management	7339	Prostate Carcinoma Health Support
7164	Herpes Wellness	7344	Multiple Sclerosis
7173	Inflammation	7355	Cysts
7182	Lupus	7362	Gout
7191	ALS (Lou Gehrig's Disease)	7366	Prostate Health
7199	Adrenal Exhaustion	7371	Eyesight/Macular Degenerative
7209	Acid Reflux	7407	Depression and Anxiety
7218	Autism Wellness	7434	Migraine Headache
7227	Metal Detoxification	7443	Menopause
7272	Neuropathy	7444	Libido
7281	Asthma Wellness	7452	Stress
7290	Mineral Deficiency	7454	ADD and ADHD Management
7308	Thyroid Wellness (Hypo)	7470	PMS Wellness
7326	Calcium Wellness	7471	Blood Pressure Wellness